A SMALL FORTUNE

A SMALL FORTUNE

A NOVEL BY
AUDREY BRAUN

PUBLISHED BY

Published by AmazonEncore
P.O. Box 400818
Las Vegas, NV 89140

ISBN-13: 9781935597650
ISBN-10: 1935597655

For A. R.

PART ONE

1

I don't know why I'm awake. I set the alarm before I fell asleep but it hasn't gone off. It's dark outside. The smell of fresh rain sifts beneath the mottled windows of our hundred-year-old Victorian. The clock reads 5:57 a.m.

My first thought is that I have to fix something, and fix it fast. My second thought is that I can relax. My husband Jonathon, the King of Organizational Protocol, has already seen to the details of our trip to Mexico—passports, tickets, arranging the cab. But he's also the one who's shut the alarm off and let me sleep in.

I shove the duvet from my legs. We need to leave for the airport in twenty minutes.

Oliver appears in the doorway. "Why are you still in your pajamas?"

"Where's your father?"

"I can't find my flip-flops."

"You can buy new ones when we get there," I say from the bathroom as I slip into my white linen pants, the first sign I'm about to trade in the Portland rain for a week of sultry, hot sun. Maybe the alarm *did* go off and I never heard it. I stayed up too late copyediting the latest volume in Dee Dee Dawson's Legends of Lust series. I've only had four hours of sleep, and most of that was spent dreaming of my red pen scratching in and out of *primal*, *sultry*, *hot*, and *moist*.

"I'm not walking around in new flip-flops!" Oliver yells from somewhere in the house. "The place between my toes will hurt!" That edge in his voice. I look forward to the day he sheds this surly sixteen-year-old who dislikes me more than he dislikes all the other things he dislikes in the world. I keep hoping for the return of Ollie, a boy who adored me.

I snatch up the last of my toiletries, and I'm midway down the stairs when drums pummel two floors up from the basement. I take a deep breath. Led Zeppelin, "Immigrant Song," if I'm not mistaken, which is one more thing Oliver dislikes about me. I listened to Zeppelin as a teenager, too, and one would think that's a good thing, to have this in common, but Oliver assures me I've never listened to Zeppelin the way *he* listens to Zeppelin, and drives the point home with an eye roll.

"Jonathon, where are you!" I yell, as if he can hear.

I pull out my cell. Oliver keeps his phone on vibrate in his back pocket and will feel it even if he can't hear it. *Get your ass up here*, I text. I've never sworn at him in a text before.

The drumming stops with the final crash of a cymbal.

I make it to the front hallway just as Jonathon appears at the front door with the tote bag from last summer filled with suntan oil and flip-flops and what must be mildewed towels from the coast, all of which we tossed into the garage months ago. He looks as if he's been awake for hours, all smiles and coordination. He's wearing a white T-shirt and jeans, his blond hair soft and uncombed around his face. I haven't seen this side of him in ages. His expression has been set on fatigue for so long I've forgotten how it's supposed to look. He appears younger. Happy. He hasn't shaved, and the stubble gives his mouth a brawny kind of sex appeal.

"Where have you been?" I ask. The double meaning isn't lost on me.

He smiles, digs the flip-flops out, and hands them to Oliver coming up the basement stairs. Then he kisses me on the lips—with intention—slow and soft. A kiss that says we're on vacation now and he couldn't be happier. A kiss I don't want to ruin by mentioning the alarm.

Oliver slips into the flip-flops, and the smell of mildew fills the foyer. The flip-flops are at least a size too small.

"You're not going to wear those on the plane, are you?" I ask, sounding more critical than I mean to.

Oliver rolls his eyes, plugs his iPod buds into his ears, lugs his backpack over his shoulder, and is the first to head out the door and into the cab.

✦ ✦ ✦

It's been years since we've taken a family vacation. One might assume being married to the president of a bank means my life is lined with cash and jewels and exotic vacations. But these days banks are failing, and Jonathon's is only a small local outfit to begin with. Pacific Savings and Trust, "The People's Bank" written in small letters beneath the name on billboards. I once made a joke about it being a subliminal reference to China, the nation with all the cash. Jonathon didn't think it was funny.

My mother's interest in playing the stock market and then her subsequent death is what brought Jonathon and me together eighteen years ago. I may be my mother's daughter in many ways, but investing in the market isn't one of them. The world of finance doesn't interest me in the slightest. What interests me is the fact that Jonathon, who never plays loose with the family budget, who likes to remind me we're in a recession every time I purchase a pair of shoes, has arranged this last-minute vacation, and it couldn't have come at a better time. He didn't say so, but I'm sure it has something to do with how on edge I've become. I've tried hiding it. I've tried writing it off as fatigue, work stress, PMS, any excuse I can think of, hoping it will disappear on its own. It hasn't. I work out twice as hard at the gym, but it's only a temporary fix for the stress buzzing beneath my skin. I've tried yoga, then meditation, but my mind journeys off to more anxious corners in a dark room full of sweaty people than it does when I sit alone in my kitchen with a cup of coffee and the glassy voices on NPR.

"We're due for a change, a vacation," Jonathon said over dinner just a week ago. "It's spring break. What do you think about Mexico?" More than anything I wonder if this trip is his attempt to give our marriage the jumpstart it so badly needs. I would have packed that night if he asked me to.

But the day has come so quickly that it feels as if we've been instantly transported from our kitchen chairs to a Mexican cab without seatbelts, speeding through the crowded, lumpy cobblestone streets of downtown Puerto Vallarta.

A glare ricochets off everything. Especially harsh on eyes from the Pacific Northwest. I try deciphering Spanish storefronts, but even without the glare I have no idea what anything means. I minored in German, which seems the opposite of Spanish—all somber quotes and fairy tales where eyes are plucked out, bellies cut open, a boy forced to live with scissors for hands. "*Verstehen Sie die Auswirkungen?* Do you understand the implications?" my professor liked to shout at the front of the room. "The poor child bloodied everyone he came close to."

That seems like a century ago.

Gutierrez Rizo, a sign reads, and I whisper it on my tongue.

An ancient-looking man waves a Polaroid camera on a corner next to a donkey in a sunhat. I start to point it out to Jonathon, but he's pecking on his BlackBerry in the front seat. I watch for several minutes. He doesn't look up. Not once. It's as if he's been to Puerto Vallarta before. He hasn't.

Oliver mopes behind aviator sunglasses in the backseat opposite me. I can hear the tinny music through the headphones in his ears. He'll be deaf by the time he's twenty. A good mother would make him turn the music down. He presses his forehead against the window.

"It's dirty here," he says.

"Look at the ocean," I say. "It's beautiful." How would my favorite author, Joella Lundstrum, describe it? Peacock blue. Undulating. A sensual invitation. I'm afraid that sounds more like something out of Dee Dee Dawson's Primal Pleasures series.

"Maggie says you can't even drink the water," Oliver says with that edge again. Maggie is his girlfriend of three months.

I find myself aching for the younger version of him, for the son I no longer have. A mix of longing and rage spread like a stain through my chest, and I suddenly burn for the days even before that, the days before marriage and motherhood when my work with literary novels felt serious and important, when the prose I combed through halted my breath, stunned me with clarity, articulated feelings for which I had no words. My days seemed grounded, purposeful, charged with forward momentum. The future was still unknown to me. Whom would I marry? Where would we live? When would I become a mother?

"Maggie doesn't have to drink the water," I say, stupidly. "And neither do you."

He rolls his eyes with a slow, scornful headshake.

I roll my eyes with a slow, scornful headshake. Sometimes mockery gets a small laugh. This time it doesn't.

Last night I slipped out of bed when I heard Oliver slam the door on Maggie's Honda. I looked down from the bedroom window to see him stomp up the walkway with fists at his sides. Maggie jumped out and caught his arm. Oliver turned and whispered angrily in her face. She rose up on her clunky boots and did the same. Then Oliver raised his hand to her cheek. Gently. It rested there as he leaned into her ear. Maggie lifted her arms around his neck and they kissed. It went on long enough to make me squirm. They stopped, and one, then the other, laughed.

"Celia. Come to bed." Jonathon's voice had been startling and strange in the dark.

I had slipped into bed, thinking we had a flight to catch in the morning. For the next week the three of us would squeeze into a two-bedroom condo, share all our meals, sit side by side at the beach, swim together, walk the promenade at sunset. What on earth would we talk about? If ever I needed to rest up for something, this was it.

But Jonathon's hand slid onto my breast. I started to turn away. "I love you," he whispered, and the shock of his tone held me beneath his cupped hand. How long had it been since he'd said it like he meant it? How long since I'd said it that way myself?

I'd turned toward him and touched his cheek, resisting the impulse to pull away. I lifted off my camisole and kissed him with more passion than I was used to mustering. He tasted like toothpaste. My own breath was probably sour after hours of working with clenched teeth. I kissed him like I meant it anyway. There was nothing wrong with me. This was what I repeated to myself, going through the motions—hands, tongues, lips. I tried picturing a scene from Legends of Lust. The heat, the undoing, the explosion wild enough to leave a room soaked and in shambles. I was a slender nymph who could not get enough. More, more, more. I wanted others to see us, to feel our lust. Yes, yes, yes.

It was no use. Our lovemaking, at best, is like well-rehearsed theater. A quick performance carried out with exactitude in the dark. At worst, it comes to a halt during intermission, the final act never to be seen. Jonathon has begun to suffer periodic episodes of impotence. I can't help but feel it's because of me.

Afterward, I sat on the toilet near tears, waiting to pee in the ghoulish orange glow of the nightlight, frustrated at a world that's done nothing to me. My husband is a decent man pushed to the brink by an industry he has no control over. My son, a teenager doing what teenagers do, which in a sense makes him perfectly normal. What reason do I have to be so upset? Why am I so often teetering on the verge of rage and tears?

The front door had opened and closed. Oliver's heavy foot-steps, like a stranger's, creaked the stairs. He's already taller than Jonathon, and thicker across the chest, but his face and coloring are identical to mine. Anyone can see he's my son. Same gray-blue eyes and dark wavy hair. Same narrow jawline. Same button-white teeth and that trademark dimple that came from my mother's side of the family. When Oliver was a baby and smiled for the first time, it was that dimple that helped me move beyond the strangeness of becoming a new mother and into more familiar territory. It made me miss my mother more than ever, but at the same time I felt her presence in the face of my beautiful boy. It was the most extraordinary gift Jonathon could have ever given me. I thought about this as I curled into the reading chair, opened my laptop, and began working quietly while Jonathon slept soundly across the room.

I draw in the stale cigarette smell of the cab, look at Oliver moping beside me, and let it go. The truth is, I don't really mind getting paid for the guilty pleasure of combing through racy romance novels. I'm grateful for the distraction, not to mention the paycheck. These books are recession-proof, barreling through like a million sexy warships keeping the publishing world afloat. And at the end of the day, Oliver's a good kid, a really good kid, on the honor roll every term since he began high school.

"I know it looks less than pristine here," I say. "But keep in mind you're coming from Portland. The whole world looks dirty compared to that."

Oliver sighs and checks his phone. He snaps it closed and throws me a sad little smile, that rare crack in the sullen armor that means he feels bad about something he's said or done to me, or feels bad about something that's been done to him. He's checking in like a boy on a playground, making sure his mother's still close. And that's the thing. I am. I always will be. All he has to do is ask.

"I'm going to squeeze fresh orange juice for breakfast in the morning," I say, patting his leg. "You'll love it. I'll make omelets. After that, take your pick. We can swim at the beach or the pool. I'm looking forward to a run on that beach."

"I hate swimming," Oliver says.

I roll my window down and dip my head out like a dog. I come back. "You might change your mind when the temperature hits eighty-five degrees."

"Doesn't the condo have air-conditioning?"

"Yes. But you won't be in it much so it doesn't really matter."

"Great. I'll go outside and get cancer instead."

I curl my hands into fists. I look between the seats at Jonathon up front pecking methodically on his BlackBerry.

"Are you working?" I ask.

"Crackberry," Oliver mumbles, his hands now drumsticks whacking his thighs.

Jonathon doesn't seem to hear, doesn't even notice when the driver slams his brakes and whips between a car and a motorcycle, clearing bare inches on either side.

"Jonathon?"

He hits Send and turns around and appears to take a second before recognizing me, as if his mind has been miles away and only now returned.

"What's wrong?" I ask.

He glances at his BlackBerry, holding it slightly away to read the screen without his glasses.

"What are you doing?" I snap. "You haven't even looked out the window."

"There's nothing to see, Dad," Oliver says, his forehead still glued to the glass, fingers now rapping the edge of the vinyl seat, causing it to vibrate beneath me.

How can Oliver even hear our conversation? I reach down and cover his hands with my own. "Please." He gives me a snarky eye roll, but his fingers still.

"Sorry, honey," Jonathon says. "A little work thing I had to take care of." He smiles his smile. The one meant to soothe me, but lately it has a way of making me feel worse. "The bank needed my approval on something," he says. "It's fine." He raises his face toward the glaring sunshine, horns blaring, pedestrians swarming. "We're here. We made it." He turns back in his seat.

I feel the usual hint of instability, as if I've just entered a familiar room only to find someone has rearranged all the furniture without telling me.

Several more blocks of whipping corners and the cabdriver says, "This is it!" He turns and stops abruptly, throwing me toward Oliver in the seat. Oliver glares with embarrassment, as if I'm making a fool of myself on purpose. The car stops on a hill outside a white two-story complex with terra cotta tiles on the roof. Coconut palms tower above the thick grass. I rise from the car and glance up. Large balconies jut out with clear views of the ocean. Most have small tables and chairs, and when I imagine having breakfast up there with the blue ocean spread out before me, I feel a warm affection for Jonathon.

"It's beautiful," I say, as Jonathon translates dollars into pesos. "Oopsy," he says, "that's not right." Oopsy? Since when does Jonathon say *oopsy*? Oliver helps the driver pull the luggage from the trunk. A green-and-yellow bird flies overhead and lands on the branch of a tree covered in pink fuzzy blossoms. The air has the distinct tropical smell I know from Florida and the Bahamas. A lush, moist green mixed with sand and salt, and as the breeze picks up there's the smell of smoke and meat and garlic on a grill.

It's far more arresting, more alluring and peaceful than the picture Jonathon showed me on the computer. It's easy to imagine a place like this transforming one's apocalyptic stress, to borrow a phrase from Joella Lundstrum. The ocean breeze picks up, and I'm taken by surprise when the caress of linen against my skin makes me think of sex. Not the kind where a touch leaves me feeling more alone, but the greedy kind I experienced during the affair I had with Seth Reilly. For years I boarded up the wonder of that affair into a hidden corner of my mind. For the sake of my marriage I repressed memories too painful and dangerous to re-lease. But as I begin to unwind, the memories escape—breathless chases up the stairs to his apartment above his bookstore; deep kisses inside the door; one by one, the shoes, scarf, jeans, blouse, bra, dropping across the floor; the final pull of panties down my freshly shaven legs. I can nearly feel myself standing there reading the spines on his bookshelves while he gazes at my naked body, his fingers twirling the tips of my long hair, his lips warming my cold, rain-soaked wrist. *Anna Karenina, Les Miserables, Moby Dick*, aphrodisiacs in my mouth and in my eyes.

"We're heading upstairs," Jonathon calls out. "Are you coming?"

The cab has already pulled away.

Jonathon slowly emerges into focus, fumbling with the luggage in his arms, a gentle wind lifting his fine, thinning hair.

"Yes," I say, taking a step toward him, and then another, as my linen clothes stir in the breeze.

2

The only thing I notice about the condo is the clean, white-tiled floors and the modern wicker furniture. I'm too busy rummaging for my swimsuit, leaving the rest of my clothes in a heap next to my luggage on the bedroom floor. I slip into the red bikini I bought for the trip, and over that, the silky, chocolate-colored cover-up. I pass Jonathon looking through cupboards in the kitchen, and Oliver in the living room inspecting wires on the television for video games.

I reach for the door and turn. "You sure you don't want to go for a swim, Ollie?" I cringe. Why did I call him that? He's hated it since he was twelve.

Oliver surprises me with a laugh.

"I know. I forgot," I say.

"It's no big deal," Oliver says with his dimpled smile, and my heart dissolves into a bowl of steam. *It's no big deal.* He may as well have said he loves me.

"I'll join you in a second," Jonathon says without looking up.

I close the door.

I'm in Mexico, clattering down a stone path in my flip-flops on the way to a pool. It's eighty-five degrees. Sunny. It feels good to lay out the facts in my mind. I'm starting to breathe clearly again after months of sucking air through what has felt like cotton-filled lungs.

Then I think of the BlackBerry and Jonathon's smile in the cab. The other day I happened to walk into the bedroom just as he was throwing his BlackBerry across the room, which is something I'd do but is so unlike Jonathon in every way that for a second I felt frightened. He pinched his temples and shook his head at the floor, and then he apparently realized I was standing there and quickly composed himself. "I'm sorry," he said. "The thing keeps losing calls. I'm president of a bank. It looks bad." He walked over and retrieved the BlackBerry from the floor. It had left a black mark on the glossy white floorboard. "These things cost a fortune. There's no excuse for them not to work."

I wonder if it really was the bank he was texting in the car or if it had something to do with one of his investments. Jonathon loves playing the market more than my mother did. I always know when he's "riding the Dow Jones," as I like to tease him, because little beads of sweat break out on his lip while his fingers creep like cautious spiders across the keyboard of his laptop. It occurs to me that he might be having an affair. I imagine scrolling through his messages while he showers. *Room 120. I cannot wait to be inside you. All the waiting and sneaking around is killing me.* Deep down I suspect I wouldn't find a single thing of interest, and for a moment I'm not sure which bothers me more.

The pool is a long, rectangular design of small lapis-colored tiles giving the water the artificial blue of toilet bowl cleaner, and yet it's undeniably gorgeous and inviting. An elderly, pear-shaped woman in a black-and-white polka-dot one-piece is reading a paperback through dark sunglasses that nearly cover her face. A palapa shades the rest of her. Several chairs down, a deeply tanned middle-aged man is sunning himself in a blue Speedo while reading a copy of *Le Monde* and sipping a can of Jumex through a straw. The sound of laughter, and then a man in the garden twenty yards away catches my eye. He's Mexican, early to mid-thirties, dark blue T-shirt, khaki shorts, and work boots. He's watering the potted plants and picking up the pink fuzzy blossoms, which continue to fall like snow. But he's also maneuvering in and out of the affections of a small blond dog. I guess the dog belongs to the woman the way she's smiling and shaking her head at the two of them. It's clearly a game, and the man simultaneously works and teases the dog with the swift movements of a matador. He's striking. A look of elegance is clear from a distance in the strong lines of his jaw and nose, and in his lean, muscular arms and chest.

He steps clear of the Chinese windmill palms and grins. "*Buenos días,*" he says to me, with an upward nod as if we already know one another. The dog licks his bare leg, and the man laughs and jumps back. "You cheat, Pepe," he says to the dog in perfect English. "I was distracted. But all right. One point for you."

"*Buenos días,*" I say, feeling silly and, strangely, a little high-spirited at once.

He glances up again with the same friendly grin.

The sun penetrates my skin. It sinks into my bones, relaxing me in a way I haven't felt in who knows how long. I choose a lounge chair off to myself with the most direct sun, plop my things down, and peel off my cover up. I lather my skin in SPF 30 cocoa butter, knowing instinctively that the matador is watching. I lounge back, open an old Joella Lundstrum novel, and lose myself in someone else's troubles.

I also fall asleep.

When I wake, everyone's gone and the breeze has picked up, scattering more pink blossoms in and around the pool. I check my watch. Nearly an hour has passed. My face feels warm and tight. I roll onto my stomach and adjust the crotch of my bottoms. My finger is still hooked inside when the gate opens and the matador nods hello.

I jerk my finger free and smile, conscious of the fact that we're alone. I fold my hands beneath my cheek and close my eyes. Why do I expect him to walk right up to me? I brace for the sound of his work boots on the concrete. When they never come, my eyes spring open to find him across the pool, his back to me as he winds the hose against the building. It's my first look from this angle, and my heart gives a single pound against my chest. He removes his gloves and drops them into a white bucket, which he bends over and picks up. This is such a cliché. Even as I steady my breath, it feels like something straight out of *Wicked and Wanting*, pool boys specializing in the pleasuring of women. It's just the memories of Seth making me feel this way. I should have never allowed myself to go there. I swallow, badly in need of a drink.

He strolls toward me with a small rake he now uses to gather dead leaves and tree debris beneath the red hibiscus no more than four feet away. "What are you reading?" he asks without turning.

Blood pumps into the tips of my fingers. My book lies on the ground next to me. "Joella Lundstrum?" I say as if I'm unsure.

He nods, still raking. "Lundstrum. She's big here in Mexico. I assume she's big everywhere."

He has virtually no accent.

"You've read her?"

He stops and leans on his rake, suddenly looking right at me. "My favorite is *Road to the Open Sea*."

I sit up. "Really? I liked that one, too, but if I had to choose a favorite I'd pick *The Feast*."

"Haven't read that one yet."

"Oh, you should!" I say in a voice too eager for conversation with a stranger. "I think it's her best work."

He meets my eyes and smiles. "Then I'll be sure to pick it up."

My hands begin to sweat. We're only talking about books, and yet it feels as if I'm laying myself bare.

"I'm Benicio," he says.

"Nice to meet you," I say, but I'm cut short by the gate opening.

Jonathon, legs as white as concrete. He has on the leather sandals I bought him for this trip, which in the store seemed perfect, but on his feet, and especially here at the pool, they've taken on an effeminate flair. Mandals, Oliver calls them.

A look exchanges between Jonathon and Benicio. Is it jealousy? That would be a first.

Jonathon isn't wearing a shirt, and his white belly protrudes slightly over the waist of his brown swim shorts. The fresh, happy look he sported when we left the house this morning has disappeared. He seems pensive, completely out of place. He belongs in a bank.

"Nice talking to you," the man says and ducks away from Jonathon's glare. In the last second he turns at the gate and smiles as if he knows I'm watching. I squeeze my sweaty hands into fists.

Then the gate clicks behind him and he's gone.

I stand and begin to gather my things. I feel Jonathon's eyes on me.

"What?" I say.

"I had no idea you looked like that beneath all those layers of clothes you wear back home."

I glance down at my oily body, already browning from the sun. All the time at the gym has carved my muscles into lean, taut flesh. I haven't worked so hard for the purpose of looking good, but there it is. I think of Benicio's eyes on me moments before.

"What took you so long?" I ask. "I've already had quite a bit of sun for the first day."

"I was just putting things away," he says.

"Strange how Oliver was nice when I was leaving," I say.

Jonathon laughs as he shuffles over in his stiff sandals and drops his towel and small beach bag on the chair next to mine. The corner of his BlackBerry pokes out. "Don't worry. It didn't last." He puts his hands on his hips and surveys the pool.

"He hates it here already, doesn't he?" I say. "He hasn't even seen anything yet, but I know he's made up his mind."

"He's sixteen, Cee. Have you forgotten what it's like to be sixteen?"

I recall my high school years and want to laugh. The self-doubt and loathing had been overwhelming. Worse than that was the longing, and not even knowing for what. "No," I say. "In fact, some days I think I'm still sixteen myself."

"Well, you still look it. That's for sure."

This sounds strangely lewd coming from my husband.

"My head is starting to hurt," I say. "I think I'll go inside and lie down."

A hard expression crosses his face. His eyes fix on something in the distance. An empty road up the hill, and just below that, two men talking and laughing against a white car in an adjacent driveway.

I turn back to Jonathon. He meets my eyes, and his expression quickly shapes up.

"Aren't you going to take a swim with me?" he asks.

I search his features for a trace of what I've just seen. Some days I feel as if I'm losing my mind.

"I promise to swim with you later," I say.

He kisses my forehead. "Go ahead," he whispers against my skin. "Get some rest."

When I enter the condo Oliver is crouched on the edge of the sofa, texting. He doesn't even look up when I'm four feet away.

"That's costing us a fortune," I say. "Can you cut it to a minimum?"

"What?" Suddenly the headphones keep him from hearing.

"Can you cut it to a minimum?" I repeat loudly enough for someone on the street to hear.

"Whatever," he says.

"Don't *whatever* me! Cut it short or I'm taking the phone."

There are moments, like this, when we fall back into to the role of toddler and exasperated mother. Those early days come rushing in with razor-sharp clarity, the way I lived for the noon hour when Oliver went down for a nap and I could stare out the bay window at the Japanese maple and get my mind to think. *Think.* Sometimes I just made up metaphors for things in the yard, imagining the way Joella Lundstrum might liken the maple's canopy of crimson leaves against the sun. Stained glass? Or something more, what was the word, *crepey*—a canopy of bloodred crepe? But too often, metaphors dangled just beyond my reach. My brain cells were saturated in hormones meant to shrink the world down to the size of my three-foot son. My vocabulary had consisted almost entirely of the plural—*we don't do that, do we want a cookie? we don't scream inside, we finish our food first, no we don't do that, should we go to the park? we say please, we use our words, didn't we talk about using our words?* The exception was the daily crack through which the seething "I's" and "you's" would appear like tiny wire cutters snipping the chains that bound us— *you do that again and I'm taking it away and if I take it away you will never see it again do you understand me if you understand me you need to say yes or at the very least nod your stubborn little head*—but always, always, holding back just before *you little shit* cut through. It was around this time that I began sleeping with Seth.

Oliver shuts his phone and tosses it across the sofa with a flourish.

"Thank you. I'm going to lie down for a minute," I say.

He shakes his head as if that's the single most idiotic sentence ever uttered in the English language.

"I'm hungry," he says.

I roll my eyes and go into the bedroom, and the first thing I notice is my clothes in the heap where I left them. Next to that is Jonathon's stuffed suitcase with everything still inside. What exactly had he been "putting away"? I peel back several layers inside his suitcase and discover a number of cold weather things—sweaters, socks, and pants. At the very bottom is his down winter jacket. The only place I've ever seen him wear it is on Mount Hood, in the snow.

3

I'm determined to enjoy myself. Mexico. Sunny. Eighty-five degrees. I just want to relax, to be free of whatever has grabbed hold of me lately. I'm sure Jonathon has a very good reason for bringing winter clothes. He can be a little eccentric. The kind of man who brings two blankets, extra napkins, and real silverware to what is meant to be a quick picnic. He's a carefully detailed planner, a cautious man with a tendency to prepare for the worst. But none of that matters anyway because by the time I wake and shower, Oliver's rollercoaster mood is on an upswing and Jonathon has picked up chicken and beans takeout and has made margaritas, and the three of us have been playing poker and laughing for hours on the balcony beneath the midnight-blue sky. I'm so relieved to be having a good time with my family that when I'm finally alone in bed with Jonathon, I kiss his cheek and within seconds fall asleep against him, drifting away to the pulse of cicadas and somewhere in the distance a woman singing to a guitar.

The next morning I get up before everyone else to go for a run on the beach. On my way through the kitchen I lift Jonathon's BlackBerry from the counter. The screen is locked. He's put in a pass code. Has he always had a pass code? He's president of a bank. Of course he'd have a pass code. I type in combinations of birthdays and anniversaries. Nothing puts me through. The sun and beach are waiting. I'm wearing my swimsuit beneath my shorts and tank top so I can stop for a quick swim in the ocean on the way back from my run. I promised to make orange juice and omelets for breakfast. Oliver might still end up in a sour mood no matter what I do, but I'm his mother, and seeing him well fed has a way of satisfying some primordial drive in the deepest trenches of my brain.

Outside a whistle blows and a man yells, "*Agua!*" as if he's dying of thirst. I peek over the balcony to see a pickup rambling down the hill, its bed loaded with jugs of sloshing water for the coolers like the one inside our condo. A woman across the street waves from her window, and the driver blows his whistle once more and stops and gets out and hauls a jug to her door.

The air fills with the sweet perfume of a tuberose blooming in a large glazed pot on the balcony. I gaze into the open blue sky. After months of hunkering down beneath a blanket of gray, it feels as if someone has yanked the cover off my head to reveal the true colors of the world. Indigo, cherry, lime. So warm, so intense, they seem to vibrate.

I place the BlackBerry back where I found it and hurry out the door.

The sand gives softly beneath my running shoes. Vendors are already lugging their colorful bowls and handmade lace down the glaring white beach. "Something for you, *señora*?" they call out. Restaurant employees have finished raking the trampled sand into smooth lines beneath the tiki bar *palapas*. Others haul red and blue umbrellas close to the shore, and then go back for the yellow tables and chairs to put beneath them.

An American tourist with binoculars is telling a small crowd he's spotted a whale. "Two!" he cries, and everyone vies for the binoculars as I run past.

The longer I run beneath the deep blue sky, the stronger and happier I feel. Why don't we do this sort of thing every year? It isn't that expensive, considering the dollar against the peso. It seems so ridiculous not to invest in a place down here and come every few months. Come on weekends even, just to get a jolt of this energy.

I feel my runner's high, my breath evening out. My thoughts turn to the time when Oliver was still Ollie. Our days filled with hugs and tickle fights, evenings spent reading after his bath—*The Giving Tree* and *Where the Wild Things Are*—taking in the sweet honey smell of his hair and skin. The first time we watched *The Wizard of Oz* he'd bolted upright on the sofa and claimed that Dorothy sounded exactly like me. "It's your same voice, Mommy, listen." I thought it was just Dorothy's long dark hair and light eyes that had fooled him into thinking we sounded the same. But when he said, "I love the way she sounds. I love the way you sound, Mommy," I looked into his giant gray-blue eyes and all those freckles dotting his creamy little nose, and I was thrilled to be Judy Garland's tonal twin.

Just because he's sixteen now doesn't mean he has to hate his parents. When I was sixteen my father had been dead for four years, and my mother was my lifeline, my savior, her arms a sanctuary against the cruelty of first loves and best friends turning on a dime into mean girls. The idea that my mother died before Oliver was born never stops feeling cruel. There are days, even now, especially now, when I feel like an orphan, the world too large and empty for me to feel that I belong. Oliver has no idea how lucky he is.

After several miles, the sandy beach becomes a rocky shoreline with no more access. I turn around and start back with the sound of waves rolling in my ears, a view of the mountains and jungle jutting out behind the "old town" where we're staying. Layers of white stone buildings and terra-cotta roofs line the hillside beneath the rich green jungle, and hovering above everything is a picture book sky. Another notch in my stress comes undone.

Halfway back I slip off my tank top, shorts, and shoes, and dive into the ocean. I lift my face to the sun and let the water cool the sweat from my pores. I see what looks like the fins of two dolphins in the distance. I've read that whales and dolphins keep sharks out of the bay. Funny how something so fierce could be afraid of something so docile. I imagine rushing through the condo to tell Jonathon and Oliver how incredible it is to see dolphins during a morning swim. "You're so right, Jonathon," I'm going to say. "We've been due for a change, and that change is *this*."

When I emerge from the water, a man is running across the beach toward me. I can't be sure, but he looks like the matador from the pool. *Benicio.*

He raises his arm. "Celia!" he yells. A sense of urgency radiates from his whole body. Whoever he is, he knows my name, and that alone causes my stomach to clench.

I draw my wet hair from my face, conscious of standing there in a bikini. I glance to check that my bottoms haven't slipped while getting out of the water. They're fine. Goose bumps prickle my damp skin in the breeze. I stop far enough for the ocean to still lap my feet.

It is indeed Benicio.

"I'm sorry," he says, sounding out of breath. He runs his fingers through his shiny hair. His skin is caramel in the sunlight, his eyes a deep amber. "There's been an accident," he says.

My stomach pulls tighter.

"Your husband needed me to find you. He said you were running on the beach."

My mind races in several directions at once. I have to get back. Jonathon has sent for me. Jonathon is safe. Oliver.

"What kind of accident?"

"It's your son. I don't know what happened. I just came as a favor to your husband."

"Where's Oliver?"

"I don't know."

I'm already slipping back into my clothes, my feet caked with sand inside my socks. Adrenaline causes my hands to shake so badly I can barely tie my shoes.

"Wait! No! Wait!" he yells as I take off running. "I have a car!"

I skid to a stop in the sand.

"I came here with my cousin's car. Over there. The white one." He points down the beach to a street where an old white Corolla is parked halfway onto the curb. "I've been driving back and forth looking for you. Please," he says. "It's much faster this way."

4

We round the corner and head in the direction of the condo. I recognize the streets from the drive from the airport, the Oxxo mini-mart with the giant Bambini Ice Cream ads, the old man on the corner posing for photos with his bored-faced donkey. Benicio tears down the streets the way the cab driver had, whipping in and out of curbs and people and traffic. He hasn't looked at me once since we got into the car.

"Tell me exactly what my husband said."

Benicio nods. "He just said there was an accident with your son and could I please find you on the beach."

The car careens around another corner. We're higher up the hill, and the white buildings are no longer piled on top of one another. Trees and grass begin to fill the spaces in between.

Jonathon was sound asleep when I left. Oliver, too. That couldn't have been much more than an hour ago, two at the most. What could have happened in that short time? Where would they go? Wouldn't Oliver still be asleep? My mind splinters with possibilities. Maybe Oliver hurt himself during some stupid teenage fit. Jonathon found him unconscious. Why would Jonathon go into his room this time of morning when Oliver always slept in? And even if he did find him unconscious, wouldn't Jonathon have rushed him to the hospital?

"Where are we?" I ask. "I don't recognize anything."

"It's a faster way. I cut around the outside so I don't have to stop so much." He wipes the sweat from his forehead while repeatedly checking the rearview mirror.

I glance back. A dingy white car like the one we're in follows at the same breakneck speed. There are three, maybe four men inside.

My whole body heats from the inside out. A memory shoots up of the time Oliver broke away from me and darted into the middle of Twenty-third Avenue. He was two years old, convinced it was a game. I screamed for him to stop. He laughed over his shoulder and headed straight into the oncoming cars. The sound of horns and screeching brakes finally brought him to a halt. He looked around and smiled at all the sudden attention. I was furious. I jerked him by the arm to the sidewalk and spanked him, hard, three times on the rear, something I had never done before or since. He howled, and I grabbed his shoulders and shouted in his face. *That wasn't funny! You could have died! Do you know what that means?* Of course he didn't know, but it would take another twenty minutes for me to realize this, for me to calm down, let go of the terror, allow my rational mind to catch up: he's safe, he's safe, he's safe.

I roll the window all the way down and tell myself that everyone drives this way here. I tell myself that if something is wrong with Oliver, I'll know deep down inside the way mothers know things. In fact, something inside does feel terribly wrong. But only in the sense that if I don't get out of this car right now, Oliver will never see me again.

"Stop the car."

"What?"

"Stop the car!"

"Why? Don't you want to get back?" The look of confusion on his face nearly makes me lose my resolve.

"Now!"

He hits the brake, and I brace against the dash to keep from pitching forward.

"Sorry," he says. "I'm not used to driving this car." He pulls to the curb and stops. An emaciated dog skitters out of the way. "What's wrong?" Benicio asks.

I don't answer.

"I don't think you should..." Again he searches the mirror.

I look behind us. The white car is gone.

He fidgets in his seat. "You're obviously a runner. Are you fast?"

I narrow my eyes at him. I open the door and realize I don't know how to find the condo from there.

"You sure you don't want me to drive you?"

I jump out.

"OK," he says. "Take that street right there, follow it back down toward the ocean, and go left at Badillo Street. You'll see the condo on the left."

I feel a wave of foolishness for being so untrusting, while at the same time I'm too uneasy to get back in. I hesitate, and my nose fills with exhaust and dog piss and the piles of garbage rotting in the heat. Flies buzz the car.

I'm about to shut the door when a commotion breaks out behind me. Brakes screech, car doors fly open, shoes trample cobblestones, someone yells orders in Spanish. From the corner of my eye I see the white car, and then the men who'd been inside.

There's no time to run. My mouth's already covered by a thick hand smelling of onions and soil, my own hands twisted at my back. Another man presses a sweet-smelling cloth over my nose. No! I scream, but barely make a sound. Everything happens so quickly. No! I struggle to breathe, fiercely sucking air, an instinct beyond the realization that this is what they want, for me to breathe as deeply as I can. No. I'm already woozy. My hearing fading away.

I've been an ungrateful, neglectful wife to Jonathon. A resentful mother to Oliver. They'll never know how sorry I am, how much I wish I could make it up to them. I'll never be able to tell them how in that moment, my love for them wrenches my insides more violently than the fear of what might happen next.

5

When I wake my first thought is that I've fallen asleep at the beach and am awakened by Jonathon coming to join me. My skin and clothes smell like the ocean. My face tight from salt. But it's dark, and my head and neck ache. When I try to move I realize that not only am I sitting in a chair, my arms are tied behind me, my feet are bare and bound to the chair legs. The reason I can't see is because I'm blindfolded.

I remember the car, the men, the struggle to breathe. The last thing I saw before I passed out was Benicio's amber eyes locked onto mine, and they were filled with a kind of terror I'd never seen.

Oliver. Where is Oliver?

My brain pounds against my skull. My mouth tastes of gasoline. I drop my chin to my chest, afraid I'm about to throw up. I haven't eaten all day. What I think is still today. I have no idea how much time has passed.

The room is quiet. The smell of sweat and sulfur. Someone cooking. The scent of burned tin on a hotplate. Cinnamon. I quiet my breath, steady the blood pounding my ears. I hear a distant car horn as if it's traveling up a canyon.

"Hello?" I say.

"Celia. You're awake."

Benicio.

"Untie me!" My mind races through all the reasons they kidnapped me. None of them are good.

"I can't," he says.

How could that look of terror in his eyes have been an act? I yank at my wrists and ankles, bound by what feels like hard plastic zip ties, the kind police use these days for cuffs. The edges tear into my skin. "Of course you can," I say.

A door opens and a ray of light creeps beneath my blindfold. "*Habla español, señora?*"

I go still.

"Hey." Someone kicks my foot. "I'm talking to you."

"My husband is president of a bank," I say, my voice barely a squeak. "If it's money you want, he can get it for you."

An argument suddenly breaks out in Spanish between two men. A mad firing of rolling tongues, and the only thing I understand is my name. The voices continue to attack one another until the sound of a harsh slap silences them both.

Hands grip the blindfold at the back of my head and tear it away. I blink in the dim room, trying to see clearly through tears I have no way of wiping. It appears to be dusk, though the sun might also be rising.

Where am I? White stone walls. A small bed with a red and yellow Aztec blanket, red and orange handmade pillows, the kind the vendors sell at the beach. The ceiling is a series of low beams. One door. Thick knotty pine and slightly ajar, leading into a hallway. Something small on the terra-cotta tiles through the crack. A toy. A child's alphabet block. D.

"So." Whoever has pulled the blindfold off behind me steps forward. I look up long enough to see it isn't Benicio. This man has short hair and a thick chest. The head of a howling wolf is tattooed on his beefy right forearm. Our eyes lock, and my first thought is that I've seen his face. It's clear to us both that I can identify him. This isn't a good sign.

"Celia," he says in a way that makes my skin shrink.

"Let me go. I won't tell anyone." It sounds stupid, even to me.

The man laughs. Hoarsely. Thick with cigarettes.

"Please. I have a son who needs me."

"We know what you have, Celia. We know everything about you."

He's just trying to get inside my head. "Then why'd you ask if I could speak Spanish?"

"You're clever, aren't you? Graduated at the top of your class. Reed College, wasn't it?"

Blood races to my brain to help unscramble the fact that he knows this about me.

"And pretty. Just like Benicio said."

My chest caves, wringing out my breath. "What do you want from me?" I steady my eyes on the bed. Tell myself to breathe.

"You know exactly what we want from you."

"I have no idea what you're talking about."

"Maybe it will all become clear when your husband gets here."

A surge of panic shoots through me. The bank was once robbed, and Jonathon held at gunpoint. By the time the police arrived, the gunman was weeping and Jonathon, a soft-spoken negotiator, had the gun in his hand. *It was lighter than I expected,* he had said that night, as if it were all in a day's work. But there is no way Jonathon is going to talk these people out of whatever it was they want. And the thought of them nabbing Oliver hits me with a force that nearly knocks me out. "You lay a hand on my son and I'll kill you!" I scream, pulling at my hands and feet.

The man laughs. "I think he underestimated you. You're going to be trouble, aren't you?"

"Who are you talking about?"

"You're a live one," he says with a small laugh. "I like that. Ready to defend your family with your own life. That's more than I can say for some people. Isn't that right, Benicio?"

To my left a small window cuts into the stone and is filled with iron bars, jailhouse style, set inside the sill. Among the trees outside, a clump of bananas dangles like a giant, vulgar tumor.

Left of the window is Benicio, tied to a chair, no more than ten feet away from me. His right cheek bears the red imprint of a hand.

I jerk my head back to the man at my side.

"What?" He laughs. "Surprised to see your boyfriend tied up?"

I'm more confused than ever. If Benicio isn't part of their plan, then he really was coming to get me at Jonathon's request. And if that's the case then something really happened to Oliver.

"Where's my son?" I plead with Benicio.

He raises his eyes to the man. He lowers them back to me and shakes his head. "I don't know anything about your son."

"What do you mean? Why did Jonathon ask you to find me?"

"He didn't," the man says, pulling my hair, tilting my face up to his. "I did."

6

The circulation in my arms and legs feels sluggish, my feet and hands painful and dead at the same time. My ankles have swelled against the bindings. The damp, sticky feel where the bindings cut cools every time the air moves in the room, which is seldom. It's hot. Eighty, ninety degrees. A faint citrus perfume floats through the window and quickly disappears. Benicio has apparently fallen asleep.

I read somewhere that the first twelve hours of a kidnapping are crucial. If the victim isn't found within that time, the outlook is grim. I have no idea how long I've been here.

My hands, my legs, my whole body shivers as if I'm immersed in ice. I can't hold still, even as some corner of my mind tries to soothe me with mundane thoughts of home. Sweeping the patio, ordering new topsoil for the garden. It's spring, and by the time we get back the lilacs and daffodils will be in bloom. The garden will be bursting with color. By the time we get home.

"Benicio," I whisper. His head hangs against his chest. "Benicio." He doesn't move.

I'm barely forty, and the fact that I haven't woken up naked, strapped spread-eagle to a bed, my veins saturated with heroin makes me think it isn't likely a sex ring. Then again, what do I know about sex rings? Is *sex ring* what they even call it? Maybe these people are revolutionaries. But I don't see any propaganda, no posters of who and what they're fighting for. The only other reason I can come up with is that they're part of a drug cartel. But what would they want with a copyeditor from Portland, Oregon? Ransom. Cash to fund some lost crop, pay off enemies, who knows? I've seen on the news how ruthless these people have become. Lopping off heads and displaying the bloody stumps on iron fence posts in the middle of city squares. I picture my own head plastered in the news around the world, and another wave of nausea passes through me. What kind of life can Oliver ever hope to have if this is his mother's legacy?

I shake so hard my teeth clatter.

They must have already known Jonathon is the president of a bank. They must have had us picked out before we even arrived. Benicio. He works at the condo. He could have gotten a hold of personal information.

My lips are dry and cracked. Thirst fills my insides with sand, fills my ankles, my wrists, the lining of my throat, the surface of my eyes. I haven't had anything to drink after my run. Let alone anything in the hours since they tied me to the chair. My body continues to tremble. The sensation of crying fills my eyes, but not a single tear can form.

If I'd just said no to this vacation. If I'd just stayed at the condo and read a magazine and made breakfast. If I'd not stopped for a swim or said hello to Benicio at the pool yesterday. So easy to pick out a seemingly insignificant move that could have made all the difference. Stopping to look through a man's binoculars, deciding not to swim in the ocean, tying a shoe faster, slower, tripping over a lace not tied at all.

"Benicio!" I whisper loudly. Why the hell is he tied up, too? He doesn't move, and I begin to think he's been drugged.

I hiss like a snake and he mumbles something in Spanish. He lifts his head and then drops it again, dozing in and out. It's only then that I realize I've been doing the same thing when I see the angle of the sunlight on the window ledge change and then change again in what feels like a matter of minutes but must be longer for the sun to travel that far.

The man with the wolf tattoo hasn't been in the room for some time. I hear him speaking now with a woman in another part of the house. The woman keeps saying, "*Sí, Leon. Sí.*" Every now and then they appear to be arguing, but who can tell? The first time I visited Germany, I was convinced that every conversation I overheard was a fight.

The woman laughs. Her voice sounds young, clear. Either they've just made up or I'm wrong about the arguing.

"Benicio. Wake up," I whisper. "Please."

His head suddenly flies back, and he sucks in a breath as if he's just woken from a nightmare.

"Hey," I say. "Why are we here? What do they want?"

Benicio looks confused, groggy. He bobs his head in the direction of the doorway and then at me. He shakes his head no.

"Who are these people?"

He winces as if pained by the question.

Just then a woman bursts into the room with a glass of water. She's wearing camouflage shorts and a black tank top and flip-flops. She can't be more than twenty years old. Just a kid, really. Not much older than Oliver. She's pretty, her long hair a few shades lighter than black. Her cheekbones are wide, and her eyes large and amber like Benicio's.

She lifts the glass to my lips and tells me to drink. Her accent is thicker than the men's.

I gulp so quickly that much of it spills down my chin and shirt. The cold feels good against my sweaty skin. My stomach immediately cramps. Is there something in the water? Or are my insides just so twisted with fear?

"Isabel," Benicio says.

The woman doesn't look at him, but the expression on her face makes it clear he shouldn't speak to her.

I finish the water and the woman lowers the glass.

"Can you please untie my hands?" I ask, hoping for some female empathy. "I've been like this for hours. It hurts. Please. You can lock the door or something. I just need to move for a second."

The woman slaps my face so hard my head shoots to the side.

"Holy shit!"

"Shut up," Isabel says.

"Isabel!" Benicio screams. I see a flash of resemblance between them. Brother and sister? Is the car Benicio drove really his cousin's? Is Leon his cousin?

Benicio speaks to Isabel in Spanish. She doesn't look in his direction, not even when his voice begins to strain. "*Por favor!*" That much I understand. The empty glass in Isabel's hand trembles.

A toddler crawls into the shadowy doorway. Isabel turns at the gurgling sound he makes, and just as quickly she turns back and flings the glass against the opposite wall where it shatters. The boy sits back onto his diaper. He puts the alphabet block in his mouth, peers into the room, and begins to cry before a set of hands scoops him away and slams the door.

Isabel pulls a pistol from the back of her shorts and points it at Benicio. Until then he's continued to plead.

The gun wobbles in her shaky hand.

"*No hablan!*" she says to Benicio. He's silent.

Then she points the gun at me. "No speak. Understand, *chica*?"

I nod. My life doesn't flash before me. I don't beg for mercy. I don't even think of my loved ones. Instead, I'm completely unfazed by the implications of a bullet aimed at my forehead. All I want to know is why they've taken me. Did they already know my husband's president of a bank? Does my being an American give them some kind of leverage? Is it just bad luck? Wrong place, wrong time? It must be more than that. They know who I am, where I went to college; apparently they even know my grade point average. That brings the story right back to Benicio. He could have gotten a hold of this information from our address, credit card numbers, *something*. But if he's part of all this, then why is he tied up, too?

I'm sure now that something has been mixed with the water. I feel drunk and even a little relieved, but more than anything I feel as if my marrow has been replaced with lead. The room seems to gel around me and slowly close in. It's as if the deepest part of night has arrived in the middle of the afternoon and the only thing to do now is sleep.

7

When I wake again it really is night. The window is so black that at first I think someone has covered it with a cloth. Then I see the bulbous outline of the bananas and figure it must be two, maybe three in the morning. This far south, the sun is already beginning to rise around five thirty. I'm guessing they took me nearly twenty-four hours ago. Maybe more.

Leon enters the room and begins untying me. "Shh," he says, smelling of coffee and cigarettes. I don't dare open my mouth. Maybe he's making the transfer now. Handing me over for whatever he's getting in return. I imagine Jonathon at the end of some sandy deserted road with a briefcase full of cash. I'd give anything to see Jonathon in those ridiculous sandals. To watch Oliver shut me out behind sunglasses and music pounding in his ears.

Leon hands me a piece of dense bread. My mouth is tacky, but I don't ask for water. I eat quickly, forcing the lumps down my parched throat. I can sense his impatience.

"Get up." He pulls me to my feet, and my knees give beneath me. Every muscle in my body aches, my vision spins. My feet have been asleep for hours. They're useless stubs on the ends of my legs.

I try to look in the corner for Benicio, but Leon jerks me toward him and forces me to stand. When I show the first sign of balance, he pulls me into the hallway and from there into a small bathroom. Sand coats the cold stone floor, and the tiny granules feel like glass in my feet. He goes in with me and shuts the door. We stand only inches apart in the dark. The cold toilet bowl touches the backs of my legs. The room reeks of sulfur from the drain.

"Pee," he says.

I don't move.

"Now."

I lower my pants and sit on the toilet. Barely a drop drains from my dehydrated body. I wipe myself and pull my shorts up as I stand.

"No," he says. "Take off your clothes."

I don't move.

"Now," he says.

I begin to cry.

He yanks my shorts and bikini bottoms down my legs. He tears my shirt over my head, and I cry out even as I try not to. He slaps me in the face, though not as hard as Isabel. "Shut your mouth," he says. He pulls the string on my bikini top and in one swoop it's lying on the floor. My whole body trembles. I can't stop crying.

"Quiet!" he whispers loudly. And then he just stands there. More mind games. Let me sweat. Get the full picture of what's coming next.

"*Muy linda*," he says with a grin.

We're crammed between the door and toilet. I shudder so badly my breasts brush his shirt.

He runs his finger from my temple down my cheek and neck and across my collarbone. It may as well be a poisonous snake for all the terror it sends through me. He grabs my arm and spins me toward the shower. With his free hand he flips the faucet on and shoves me beneath an icy cold stream. He smacks my bare ass with a single whack like I'm a cow being prodded into a slaughterhouse.

I stifle a cry into a sickening moan.

"You make one more sound and I will shoot you."

Somewhere in the house, a scuffle, and then a thud as if someone has hit a wall. A man screams in pain. I stuff my cries back down and pray. I've never wanted anything more in my life than for that scream to be coming from someone other than Jonathon or, God forbid, Oliver.

"Get the soap and clean yourself," Leon says.

My hand trembles across my body. The soap stings my raw wrists and ankles. It doesn't give much lather, and I hope Leon can see it's the soap, not me. I'm trying.

He shuts the water off before I've fully rinsed my skin. He pulls me out and hands me a towel. As I dry myself nervously, awkwardly in the cramped space, he lifts a pile of clothes from a shelf I haven't seen until now. "Put these on."

They're my own clothes from my suitcase. Underwear, bra, shorts, and a white sleeveless blouse Jonathon has always loved on me. I open my mouth to cry, to beg for an explanation. But the horror of possibilities keeps me silent. I do what I'm told, relieved and terrified by the familiar scent of my lavender laundry soap.

Leon shoves me back into the room, but this time he doesn't tie me up. He goes out and shuts the door and pushes the locks in place.

A rooster crows in the distance. The sun has broken the horizon and fills the room with a milky orange light.

"Benicio?"

I step into the corner and see the empty chair. "Benicio?" I'm alone. They've taken him away, and I understand now that he's the man I heard scream.

I curl onto the bed and cover myself with the blanket. I shiver as if in the throes of a seizure. It's shock. A character in a Joella Lundstrum novel survives an earthquake only to find her only child has been crushed to death right next to her beneath a beam. The woman thinks she'll never stop shaking. She'll never again be still.

I gaze at the beams on the ceiling and swear if they let me go I'll change everything about my life. I'll never again raise my voice to Oliver. He's just a boy trapped in the complex pangs of adolescence. I'll never let a day go by where I don't tell Jonathon that I love him, because I really do love him even if it isn't the kind of love that makes my heart race. I'll initiate more sex. I'll keep a cleaner house. I'll volunteer for some charity, spend more time thinking of ways to give back to the world instead of seeing what more I can take.

I nod off into another round of trancelike sleep, my brain half in, half out of consciousness. I'm at the pool. Benicio laughs with the little blond dog. This time I go for a swim. Benicio watches as I dive into the deep blue water, down to the tiles on the bottom. I caress them with my fingertips as I glide by, their centers slippery smooth, their corners pointed and crushing one against the other between the grout. And then for some reason I don't know how to swim. I don't think I've ever known how to swim and am furious with myself for having jumped in.

There are voices. They can help me. Then quiet, the only sound my own gasping breath. I'm unsure which is the dream. The pool, or sitting on the bed.

I glance at the window. The bananas, the room exactly the same, though I'm seeing it now from the opposite side. The chair I was bound to remains empty, the ties and blindfold strewn across the seat and floor. Benicio's chair is still empty in the corner.

The voices are real. Several men, a woman, maybe two.

The door flies open and Benicio stumbles inside. A set of thick arms slide a food tray across the floor behind him. There are pastries and two cups of coffee, most of which splashes over the sides. The door shuts and locks.

Benicio's cheek is swollen and red, his nose bleeding from one side. Blood trickles down his chin onto his shirt. He's still so strikingly attractive it's as if he's posing instead of standing in the center of the room—an actor playing the part of a warrior who's just lost a fight.

He works his jaw from side to side and touches his cheek.

My mouth has fallen open. I'm still getting past the thought that Benicio has been beaten instead of Jonathon or Oliver. I swallow my guilty relief and cross the room to take his arm and lower him to the mattress next to me.

He sits and feels around his head as if for lumps.

I lift the edge of the blanket and wipe the blood from his chin. "Are you all right?"

He stares across the room at the chairs, and I wonder if he has a concussion.

"They untied us," I say. "And made me shower. Does that mean they're going to let us go?"

Benicio laughs and his fingers shoot to his nose. It's bleeding again. He tilts his head back, exposing his smooth throat beneath the flecks of whiskers. "No," he says. "They aren't going to let us go."

I wipe the blood again. His Adam's apple dips and settles at my touch.

"Tell me what they want with us," I say, though if Benicio had answered in that moment I'd have never heard the distinct sound of Jonathon's voice coming from another room. I'm so ecstatic, so overwhelmed with relief that I nearly miss the fact that Jonathon is speaking Spanish.

8

Jonathon and I met within days of my mother's death. I'd gone into her bank, Pacific Savings and Trust, to sign the paperwork concerning her accounts. My eyes ached from crying. I was officially alone in the world. No family to speak of. I'd broken up with my boyfriend only one month before—a move I found myself regretting in the days leading up to my mother's funeral. The man hadn't been right for me, I knew this, but he'd had three brothers and two sisters and I liked them all, better than I liked the boyfriend, and I couldn't stop thinking how nice it would have been to have them gathered around me during the holidays. To have them gathered around me in the bank.

I signed everything after a blurry-eyed, cursory read. The sight of my mother's jagged signature was enough to throw me into another round of weeping. My vision was hazy, my eyes too tired to see. I was distracted, unable to shake the odd feeling that someone was watching me. I thought it was my mother looking down from the great beyond, trying to get my attention, advise me on playing a market I had no interest in—and, according to her lawyer, she hadn't been very good at playing herself. But as I rubbed my achy eyes, I noticed out of the corner a man in a dark gray suit. He massaged his temple at regular intervals as if soothing the thoughts inside his head. He shuffled papers unconvincingly. When I stood to leave, he stepped out from behind a long desk and introduced himself as the president of the bank. He told me how sorry he was for my loss. He'd known my mother, Gilion, only slightly, of course, but he wanted me to know that he'd always looked forward to her jaunty personality and all the conversations they'd had about the market. My mother *had* been jaunty, a word I never attached to her before that moment. She was jaunty and bighearted and full of intense, motherly love; and without warning, a greedy, savage cancer had ripped her away.

Jonathon and I were married four months later in a small ceremony in the backyard of the Victorian we'd bought for its history, adopting all the families who'd lived there over the centuries as if they'd been our own. It was summer, everything in bloom, the air filled with jasmine and honeysuckle, the bold red Canna lilies trumpeting along the south side of a house so snowy white that my dress would appear sallow in the photographs. Jonathon was an only child like me. An orphan, too. There'd been no family to encourage us to take our time. No one to suggest we get to know one another better before committing. No one asked if we were sure this was what we truly wanted. Friends, both his and mine, were overjoyed that we'd found someone of our own. Someone who was kind and decent and knew how to make a living. Someone who would keep us from being alone.

✦ ✦ ✦

I leap for the door. My heart bangs so loudly inside my ears I can barely hear what's being said. But I'm sure it's Jonathon out there, the frequency of his voice unmistakable after eighteen years of marriage, his signature throat clearing as obvious to me as a red flag waving in a crowd of white. My insides freeze. What the hell is going on?

Benicio picks up the tray of food and brings it to the bed.

"It's Jonathon!" I say. Maybe he really can take their guns the way he'd taken the robber's in the bank.

Benicio sips his coffee.

"Did you hear me?"

"*Pero concordamos,*" Jonathon says, or something like this.

"Come here!" I say. "Tell me what he's saying."

Benicio crosses the room and sets his ear to the door.

"*Pero concordamos.*" There it is again.

"What does that mean?"

Benicio holds a finger to his lips.

The conversation continues in Spanish, a detail that for the moment takes a backseat to the fact that Jonathon is in this house, right here, right now. Another man does most of the talking. After a minute the conversation stops.

"What did they say?" I ask.

"Why don't we sit down and have something to eat first?"

"What? Tell me what they're saying!" I jimmy the doorknob. "Jonathon!" I can no longer contain myself and pummel my fists into the door. This is all about to end. I can already feel myself in his arms, the stubble of his chin against my forehead, the familiar smell of his aftershave drifting on his breath.

"Jonathon!" I regret not screaming earlier to let him know I'm safe. He might not even know I'm there.

Benicio strolls back to the bed and sits. He takes a bite of pastry.

Silence. The voices are gone. There's only the clang of what sounds like an iron gate, and after that a car motor growing more distant. "Jonathon!" I cry. "I'm here! Get me out!"

"Please," Benicio says. "You need to eat something."

I rush to the window and peer outside. There's nothing but banana trees and palms and wily grass and a hillside in the near distance. Down below a dry riverbed trickles a weak stream. Chickens peck along its bank.

I march back and stand above Benicio with fists on my hips. The sun has fully risen, and his eyes light up like a cat's. "That was my husband. I'm sure it was his voice."

Benicio chews and nods without looking at me.

I grab my hair at the roots and pace a wide circle, avoiding the broken glass from Isabel. My mind is rusty cogs, straining to function, my thoughts slowly, painfully slipping into place. Jonathon hasn't studied Spanish since high school. We had this conversation when Oliver took Japanese last year.

I stop in the middle of the room and turn to Benicio. "Tell me everything you heard."

A small smirk rises in the corner of his mouth. Perhaps it would be bigger without the swelling in his cheek. Or perhaps it wouldn't appear like a smirk at all. It could be a look of pity gone lopsided with pain. "Please," he says, patting the space next to him.

What choice do I have? He knows a hell of a lot more than I do. I take a deep breath and resign myself to sit.

He hands me a blue mug full of coffee. "It'll taste terrible once it's cold." His fingers linger beneath mine. They're warm and surprisingly soft for a gardener's. Our eyes lock, and something electrical passes between us. I shove it aside. It doesn't mean anything. This isn't the time or place. But the circuitry between us zaps me again. I turn to the window and gulp my coffee.

"These pastries are from the French baker here in town," he says.

"Goddamnit!" I turn to face him. "Tell me what they said!"

"All right. We can eat and talk at the same time."

It's like hanging off the side of a cliff, suspended between one reality and another. I glance at the apricot Danishes, the congealed layer of sugar on top. My mind may be wrapped in an agonizing mix of confusion and fear, but my body is desperate for food. That first bite of pastry is the best thing I've ever tasted in my life. I wash it down with the strong coffee. I bite the pastry like a dog.

"How well do you know your husband?" Benicio asks.

I stop chewing. Jonathon is a smart man. But high school Spanish? If I go by the unbroken rhythm in his speech, I'd have to say he sounds fluent. Is such a thing even possible? I swallow a lump of apricot that nearly chokes me. "What kind of question is that?"

Benicio shrugs.

I swallow again, feeling a wedge in my throat. "We've been married for eighteen years."

"Long time." He takes another bite.

"Yes."

"But that's not what I asked."

"I don't understand."

"Your husband is not who you think he is."

Dread wraps like a worm around the pastry in my stomach. Jonathon has gotten himself into some kind of trouble. The bank. Investments. The news arriving on his BlackBerry, thrown across the room.

"You're pretty presumptuous about two people you don't even know." Heat rises to my temples. I take another bite and chew furiously on one side of my mouth.

"I see the look in your eye," he says. "Something has occurred to you."

I plop my mug and the rest of my pastry onto the tray and cross back to the window. It must be eighty degrees, but the breeze in my wet hair makes me shiver.

"Whatever is going on here has nothing to do with my husband," I say, even as my mind races through all the strange things he's done lately. This could be exactly what Benicio wants. For me to make connections where none exist.

There has to be an explanation. I snatch up an unused zip tie from the floor and fasten my hair into a ponytail, a small gesture that makes me feel more organized, more in control. I return to the window and speak as if to someone outside. "You're playing a mind game with me. Or maybe I'm playing one with myself. Maybe I just imagined the voice belonged to my husband." I turn to Benicio. "Is that bruise on your face even real? Or did you let them do that, tie you up, hit you in the face, just to gain my trust or some such shit?"

He nods at the floor. "That was your husband outside. You weren't mistaken."

"You've never even read Joella Lundstrum, have you?"

He leans back and places his hands on his knees. "Alice Brown single-handedly brings an entire corporation to justice."

"You could have read that on the back cover."

"'And the men who hold high places will be the first to come to their knees.'" A quote I recognize from the middle of the book. "Are we really going to argue about this now?" he asks.

"My husband doesn't speak Spanish. And even if he did, why would I still be in here if he'd already given them what they wanted? Come on. What's the plan? Shoot me, rape me, cut off my head, or all of the above?"

Benicio sets his cup down and crosses to me, slowly, stopping only inches away. "Your husband has been here before."

"What?"

"He's been coming here for years. As recently as two months ago."

"You're lying."

"Where did he tell you he was going at the end of January? A business trip?"

"He's president of a bank," I say, my voice breaking at the realization. "Of course he takes business trips."

"The end of January. Where did he tell you he was going?"

I feel faint. The American Bankers Association in Vegas. But maybe they already knew this about him, that he'd been out of town, and now Benicio's trying to convince me that Jonathon had actually come down here instead.

I regain my footing. "What does *pero con*-something mean?"

Benicio draws a long breath.

"Jonathon, if it *was* Jonathon, kept saying that."

"He was making sure that Leon hadn't hurt you."

This sounds so right to my ears that my body loosens with relief. Even if Jonathon really is mixed up in something, and I'm not fully convinced this is the case, but if he is he's come here to negotiate. He wants to know I'm all right. He's working to get me out.

"What I mean is, his exact words to Leon were, 'We agreed last week that you wouldn't hurt her.'"

Maybe something is lost in translation.

"He also mentioned something about going to Switzerland."
Switzerland.

Benicio grips my arms to keep me from slumping to the floor.

The warm clothes in Jonathon's suitcase. Perfect for Switzerland this time of year. Is Oliver going, too? Or is he being held somewhere like me?

"Listen to me," Benicio whispers.

I take a small step back. He follows with a step forward, still supporting my weight. Then something crosses his face. It seems to throw him off from the words he intends to say. He searches my eyes. "I don't understand how a husband could do this to his wife," he says.

I hang there a moment longer thinking of how unusually relaxed Jonathon was the morning we left. A man headed off on a vacation. It doesn't make sense. I struggle free and grip the iron bars. "Get away from me. You're making this whole thing up. That's not what he said out there."

"Listen." His voice is a deep whisper. "I tried to stop them from taking you. That's why they put me in here."

I squint and jiggle my head trying to make sense of what he's saying. "I was in your car, Benicio. You kidnapped me."

"My aunt and uncle own the condo you're staying in. Leon is their son. He told me your husband needed to find you. It was an emergency. When he gave me the keys to his car, your husband was standing outside the condo door looking half out of his mind. This is why I picked you up. They fooled me the same as they fooled you. And when I realized what was happening, when they pulled you from the car, I tried to make them stop, but the next thing I knew they put the same cloth over my face, and when I woke I was tied to a chair like you."

"Why didn't they just grab me themselves? Why send you?"

"It's complicated."

"I'm not stupid," I say, but the irony of my words hangs in the air. Oh but I am, just look at how easily I've been fooled.

"Leon has been trying to get me to join the family business for years. No matter how this looks, he cares about me. He wants me to do well, have a big family, all that."

"What does that have to do with—"

"The last thing I want is to join the family business."

"Right. Still not following."

"He thought if he made me an accomplice to kidnapping he could blackmail me to do what he wanted, and someday, when I was living this great life, I'd be thanking him for it. I know. It's impossible to believe that this is what people do when they care about you. You'll just have to take my word for it."

"What does this have to do with anything?"

"If you'd somehow escaped, you'd be a witness to me trying to kidnap you. They were driving right behind us. They'd back up your story, and I'd spend the rest of my life in prison. That was how Leon planned to blackmail me."

"I still don't get it. Now they've tied you up instead?"

"There were other guys. Leon answers to someone else on this. He's in over his head. I got the impression that this was mild compared to what was coming next."

I'm more confused than ever. "Just tell me how my husband is supposed to be involved in whatever the hell is going on here."

"He cheated them."

"Who? How?"

Benicio leans closer. Dark flecks in his amber eyes make them look like raw honey in the sun. His teeth are bright white against his smooth, café au lait skin. If it were just his good looks, he couldn't distract me like this. Couldn't make me transcend, if only for a second, everything that's happening. I'm not easily swayed by looks the way some women are. Whatever Benicio has goes beyond that. A visceral impulse buzzes between us, and I see the recognition of it in his eyes.

"Your husband is a businessman," he says as if forcing something, anything from his mouth. "An investor."

I let him continue.

"My family is always looking for investors. At some point the two met up."

"What kind of business?"

"I don't know a whole lot about it."

"What do you know?"

"What do *you* know?" he snaps.

"Me? I don't have a clue about any of this!"

He works his swollen jaw from side to side. He blinks.

"Is that what you think? Is that why Leon said I knew exactly what he wanted? That I've got some part in all this?"

"Are you saying you don't?" he asks.

I laugh and shake my head at the floor. This just isn't happening. *Wicked and Wanting* has storylines more believable than this.

"Yes," I say. "That's exactly what I'm saying."

"Fine." He stares at the wall. "I believe you," he says, softer. "It didn't sound right from the beginning."

"What didn't sound right?"

"That you had taken their money."

"All right. Wait a minute. Let's get something straight here. What are we talking about? Money from what? Drugs? Because there's no way my husband, or me for that matter, could possibly be involved in something like that."

"I wouldn't be so sure."

"Clearly you don't know my husband."

"Clearly neither do you."

Rage sears my skin. "Fuck you."

The room turns unbearably hot. I wipe my forehead. It instantly flushes again with sweat.

"I'm sorry," Benicio says. "It's not what you think."

"You have no idea what I think," I say, though in the back of my mind I know he's reading me like ticker tape.

"What if he thought he was helping people?"

I nearly laugh. I shake my head. "What?"

"People dying of cancer, heart disease, AIDS."

"What are you talking about?"

"Pharmaceuticals."

I stop, allowing the idea to sink in.

"Black market. Everything from oral chemo to high blood pressure."

Now I do laugh. A single, hysterical bark. "You're trying to tell me my husband is peddling prescription drugs?"

"Yes."

"To whom?"

"Clinics, dealers in the States. Thousands of people who couldn't afford them otherwise."

"I don't believe you."

"You don't have to. But if you can find a better reason for being in here I'd like to hear it."

"You're awfully cocky, aren't you?"

"Chalk it up to extenuating circumstances."

"Extenuating circumstances? Where did you learn to speak English?" Before he can answer I say, "What you're telling me here is absolutely absurd."

"I don't doubt it sounds that way."

"It's ridiculous."

"I'm no happier about the facts than you."

I picture the man I married, the man at the pool with the pale legs and humorless face, the man who instantly falls asleep at night, the man who cupped my breast and whispered that he loved me, the man who found Oliver's flip-flops and asked me if I'd forgotten what it is to be sixteen. I try to connect this careful, meticulous man to, *what*? The messy underworld of prescription drugs?

"From what I've overheard this past year, I think your husband made much more money than he was expecting to."

I barely have time to stop spinning from what he's just told me. "This past year? How long has he been doing this?"

"I've only been back in town for two years. But I got the impression it started long before that. All I know is the money just kept coming. More people down here got involved. He's got quite a payroll. Or did. For some reason it stopped."

"What made it stop?" I'm on autopilot, in search of nothing but the facts.

"I don't know. Maybe he wanted out. Maybe he invested some of it in the stock market and lost it. Or stole it. I have no idea. All I know is that he owes my cousin and the people he works with a lot of money. And they think you had something to do with it."

"Why in the world would they think that?"

Benicio doesn't meet my eyes.

"Why!"

"Because that is what your husband told them."

9

For months I've had the feeling that I was lying in wait for something that had no name. Something that I yearned for and dreaded at the same time. This feeling wasn't attached to reason. What little I shared of it with Jonathon always received the same careful response. *It doesn't seem to be grounded in fact. Please pinpoint what it is and I'll try to make it better.* But facts have been elusive little details beyond my reach. All I knew was that something was wrong, and the only thing I had to go on was a feeling, an intuition, a flimsy, namby-pamby notion from meditation class.

"What else?" I ask Benicio.

"Pharmaceuticals aren't their only 'project,' as they like to call it. They've got their hands in other things I don't care to know about. Business is business, especially for the guys Leon answers to. It's a lot of money, and they handle one the same as the other. Even if it were only prescription drugs, we're still talking millions of dollars. And people who go from having nothing but dirt to owning millions can get very angry if you take it away."

"Wait a minute. All right. Let's just say for argument's sake that everything you're telling me is true. Why would Jonathon bring Oliver and me down here with him?"

"I don't know."

"You're lying."

"Celia," he says, and my heart thumps against bone.

"I deserve to know," I say.

"I suppose you do."

"Tell me."

"It's only a guess."

"So guess!"

"All right." He takes a deep breath. "I think the money has been missing for a while and things reached a point where they no longer believed your husband was going to pay up. My guess is they told him to bring you to prove he meant what he said about paying what he owed, or else. They take the money; you enjoy your vacation. They don't get the money; they take you instead."

"I don't understand."

"You're collateral. To show he was true to his word."

"Collateral."

"Right."

"That doesn't make any sense. If he brought them the money, then why did they still kidnap me?"

"Maybe he didn't bring it."

My lip quivers. How did Jonathon remain so calm, knowing what was going to happen as we headed out the door of our home? He was unusually serene. Had he taken something? Some antianxiety drug? Or was his intention all along to get rid of me?

I begin to hyperventilate. How can any of this be true? If Jonathon knew he didn't have the money, then why else would he bring Oliver and me? Putting me in harm's way is one thing. But Oliver? His own son?

I shake the bars on the window. I growl and scream, even as Benicio tries to calm me.

"I could be wrong," he says.

"Get away from me! Don't touch me! I want out of here!"

The door flies open and in comes Isabel, screaming in Spanish, brandishing her gun.

Benicio raises a hand to stop her from coming any closer. He pumps it as a signal to calm down.

"*Por favor*," he says, and something in his twisted face convinces her to stay back.

She yells in Spanish. She repeats herself several times, jerks her head at me.

"Isabel wants me to tell you that this is what you get," Benicio finally says without taking his eyes off his sister. "It's your fault. And you're lucky she doesn't kill you right now."

Isabel steps closer. I turn away, focusing on the palms across the hillside, feeling the presence of the gun behind me.

She spits in my hair.

After a moment of excruciating silence, she walks off and locks the door behind her.

I wipe my hair with my shirttail. I hang my head between my shoulders and weep, my fingers clinging to the bars. Oliver is a two-year-old running into traffic all over again, but this time I can't reach him. This time Jonathon is driving the oncoming car.

Benicio puts his hands on top of mine and slowly pries my fingers from the bars. He draws me against him, pressing my cheek to his chest and closing me inside his arms.

I realize just how different truth sounds from lies. It isn't the words that are used. It's the sound of them, a frequency, a vibration, chords striking deep within the chest. I imagine trying to explain such a thing to Jonathon: "But the frequency of your words is all wrong when you tell me you want to make everything better."

I start to snicker. I haven't been crazy after all. All along my intuition has been gnawing a tunnel inside my head to let the truth in, and until this moment I've tried blocking it with everything I have, including my own sanity.

How long has it been since I've cried like this while someone held me? How long have I needed this? I sob until the front of Benicio's shirt is soaked in tears and snot. It's ridiculous. Embarrassing. I don't even know this man, and yet he feels more familiar to me than my own husband. "I'm sorry," I croak, wiping my face with my hand.

"What do you have to be sorry for?" he asks.

"Your shirt, for starters."

"Don't worry about it. It's warm in here. Nothing like a pool of tears to cool you off," he says, stroking my back.

I let go a small laugh and look up into his eyes. "I need to know about Oliver," I say. "Have you heard them say anything at all?"

He shakes his head. "I wish I had something to tell you."

I close my eyes. The room closes in again. It's hard to breathe. I wrap my arms tightly at Benicio's back and hold on to the solid feel of him, the ropey muscles beneath my fists. His heart beats inside my ear.

I'm well aware that novel experiences bring people together in ways nothing else can. Trauma bonds the hearts of those who experience its suffering together. I also understand that shock and pain make people do and believe things they otherwise aren't capable of. I don't know if this is what's happening to me. But as

Benicio strokes my hair, the sandy smell of his skin, the strength of his arms, the touch of his breath down my neck make me feel safer than I've felt in years. Safer than living in my own house where the biggest challenge I might face in a day is what to make for dinner. I'm not foolish enough to believe I'm out of harm's way, and yet the thought crosses my mind that as long as he's here with me everything will be all right.

The rhythm of his heart lulls me into a warm, stunned, daze. "You should finish your Danish," he whispers into my hair.

I stay where I am for as long as he lets me.

10

Hours go by and no one comes for us. During that time Benicio and I move apart and barely speak. He chews his nails at the window and gazes back and forth between the outside and his shoes. I flop across the blanket and stare at the ceiling, my hands linked across my middle as if I'm dead.

The truth doesn't necessarily equal relief.

Fourteen years ago I couldn't bear to lie anymore to Jonathon. I had set my wineglass down on the dinner table and confessed that I was having an affair. Jonathon lowered his fork next to his plate. He squeezed his linen napkin in his fist. I braced to be hit with the piece of cloth, not that it would have landed a heavy blow, but still, I blinked in anticipation. It seemed a whole minute passed with nothing but the gloppy sound of Oliver creaming his peas in his highchair, while Jonathon's shaky hands let go the napkin, brushed crumbs from the table, and lined the silverware next to his plate.

Seth Reilly had been the neighborhood bookseller. His smile coy, ironic, lopsided as if everything he said was a double entendre. There was something familiar about his Celtic good looks from the beginning, and one day it dawned on me how much he resembled a young Robert Redford. Very young. Younger than the Redford of *Barefoot in the Park* with Jane Fonda, but with the same sexy, sardonic wit. You couldn't live in our little enclave of historic homes and local restaurants and antique shops and not know Seth with his strawberry hair messing in the wind as he rode by on his Dutch bike with the red panniers. Not if you were a woman. Seth was a page-turner himself. Always leaving you wanting for more.

Jonathon was East Coast prep school, blond hair and square jawline, broad shoulders and tie. He was smart, a deep thinker, you could see it in his eyes, but he was never one to share too many thoughts. He was adequate in bed, knowing where to go and, more or less, how long to stay. He was quiet and kind, and there was a time when this sort of personal space bubble appealed to me. There was a time when I liked to say I was married to the president of a bank, especially when I thought of my mother. Then there was all the time after.

Jonathon never did throw his napkin at me. He got up and used it to clean Oliver's hands. He lifted our son from his high-chair and set him on the floor where the symphony of squeaky plush toys had scattered.

He returned to his chair in what appeared to be measured steps. He took a deep breath, cleared his voice, and said, "I suppose I haven't been a very good husband."

I couldn't speak. His words felt like a lightning rod to the chest, jolting me back to my husband and little boy who was now giggling in the most charming way on the floor of our Irvington Avenue home.

"Crap," Oliver said. His new favorite word. "Crap, crap, crap," with a monkey grin until I raised an eyebrow and gave him the look of mock discipline he was waiting for. He laughed and moved on to the animal nesting blocks.

I turned to Jonathon, flushed with shame. "I'm sorry," I said, and at the time, I meant it.

"How?" Jonathon asked me.

"How?"

"How did you manage it?"

I fumbled for an answer. "Tara, the high school girl down the street." Was that what he was after? The logistics of how and where the affair took place? "She babysat while I was…out."

I hated myself then. The shame was unbearable. It scratched and burned my insides like shards of broken glass.

Jonathon took his wallet from his rear pocket and set it on the table. He picked it back up and returned it to his pocket, a gesture that has always struck me as odd. "Don't leave me," he said.

Don't leave me.

Oliver must have sensed the standing hairs on my arms and neck. He looked up from the floor as if waiting to hear my reply. And what was it going to be? The course of Oliver's childhood, the course of his entire life, of all of our lives, was about to be handed down like a sentence.

"I won't," I said, turning my watery gaze from Oliver to Jonathon.

I would cross town to purchase books. I would never see Seth again.

That was fourteen years ago. It's far too late for me to be asking why Jonathon wanted me to stay, why I myself promised not to leave.

Now I lie here thinking how everything I convinced myself was one way has turned out to be another, and I feel an almost physical sensation of coming apart at the seams.

Things I never questioned seem so obvious now. I've conveniently taken no interest in the phone bills. It doesn't seem necessary. Jonathon handles all the bills. He's a banker. He likes that sort of thing. But when I *have* taken an interest in Jonathon's flurry of texts and e-mails, sometimes during the middle of a meal, times when Oliver isn't allowed to have his phone at the table, Jonathon shuts me down with that smile of his. I've dismissed everything, chalked it all off to my stress and the importance of Jonathon's work. His ever-important work. Because it is important, isn't it? People's lives are at stake, their life savings, investments, direct deposits, and bill pays, all happening on Jonathon's watch. But that smile. I can see it as clear as if he's standing in front of me now. It's menacing. How have I not seen that? Oliver saw it. He once commented after Jonathon got up from the table with his BlackBerry that if *he* ever gave me a look like that he'd be grounded for a month.

There are other things. The way he eagerly puts away his luggage and washes his clothes after every "business" trip. I've always thought he's just being neat and organized, and I'm grateful he's so considerate. It never occurred to me that he's hiding something. But he also keeps his passport, all our passports, locked inside a home safe, the combination of which I've never even asked about. I've thought the safe was silly, a bank toy, small enough to carry out of the house if someone really wants it. And besides, if I were leaving the country, it wouldn't be without Jonathon. Let him open the thing and get the passports out. Which is exactly what he did. But that isn't the point, is it? The point is to keep *me* out of the safe. What else does he keep in there? I've never even thought to ask.

I lie there bearing the brunt of the fact that all of this could have been avoided. In this very moment Oliver and I might be at home, going about our day, completely unaware of an alternate life where something so terrible could happen to us. If only I'd opened my eyes and not been so afraid to feel around in that vapor of nothingness that had become my marriage.

I think about what I gave up years ago. The breathless chases up the stairs to Seth's apartment. I felt so alive then, so happy— falling onto his unmade bed, having sex in the daylight, curtains wide open, long wispy shadows from the giant willowlike fingers stroking the walls, the bed. Seth's smooth body suspended above me, inside me. Just days before I left him, he'd put his mouth to my ear and whispered that he loved me. And even though it was right before he came, I didn't doubt it was true. I'd pulled his mouth onto mine to keep from hearing it again. But now I wondered if it wasn't to stop myself from uttering the same.

I suppose I haven't been a very good husband. That single sentence had managed to reach inside and tear away my heart. Tear away everything that made up who I was or might have been. That single sentence allowed Jonathon to have control, to lead the way, to somehow convince me we needed to stay together. All I had to do was glide through the days and years without questioning, without feeling, without wanting for a single thing outside of what I had. And if I did all that, the world, Oliver's world, would remain intact.

But Jonathon never said any of those things. He didn't even suggest them. All he said was that he hadn't been a very good husband, and he asked me to stay. How is it then, that I've devised all the rest?

I gaze at the beams and caress the dried blood on the inside of my wrist, a place once marked by perfume, by cold rain, and by Seth's warm lips. I nearly laugh at what I sacrificed in order to keep the world intact, a world that in the end has abandoned me and Oliver down a well so dark and dangerous that before today it could have only existed outside the realm of my imagination.

I glance at Benicio as if he might be reading my thoughts. He appears lost in a world of his own, making a fist and flipping open a finger at a time, counting something out.

Forces of chaos beyond my understanding or control swirl beyond this room. But here, closed up inside, my mind is becoming a stream of icy calm clarity.

Isabel opens the door and slides in a tray of food. Benicio turns from the window and calls out to her, but she closes the door and locks it without looking his way.

My mind feels open and clear, observant, sensitive to tricks, turning over every little thing for clues to get out of there. I consider the objects on the tray, a chunk of soft cheese and dense bread. Four unopened bottles of water. I observe Benicio cutting across the room, an actor on a stage, lifting the tray stage right, moving to stage center, throwing a soft—and, yes, call it what it is—sexy glance my way.

He sits on the floor in the center of the room. He motions me to join him with a gentle toss of his head.

I'm operating on a different level. I'm above it all, observing, calculating moves. I join him as if it's a picnic.

He twists open a bottle of water and hands it to me. He opens one for himself and drinks it down without stopping. We take turns tearing into the bread and cheese. Somewhere the baby cries. The iron gate clangs closed.

It occurs to me that I've never fully grown up. Jonathon has taken care of me in so many ways, ways a parent takes care of a child. I don't have to give any thought to the mortgage or utility bills or investing my earnings, nor have I ever given much thought to saving for Oliver's college. These are all grown-up responsibilities, all taken care of behind the scenes. When Jonathon asked me to stay instead of threatening to leave the way another man would have, I somehow interpreted this as if he were the one seeking forgiveness. *I haven't been a very good husband. Don't leave me*, like begging me to keep the man who'd done me wrong. How could I let him disappear from my life? Vanish suddenly, and forever, like my father? Like my mother?

My leap in understanding causes me to draw an extra breath. The only part I don't understand was why Jonathon wanted me to stay after what I did. This question has woven in and out of my thoughts for years. I wonder if it has something to do with all of this.

"There's something else," Benicio says.

His voice startles me.

"I think the reason they had you shower and change was because you were supposed to get on a plane. Something must have happened."

"What do you mean?"

"I think your husband brought them your passport. At least that's what it sounded like."

"What *what* sounded like?"

"I didn't hear the whole thing clearly. And your husband has an accent when he speaks Spanish. But what I thought I heard was him saying that he wanted them to keep your passport here with you, just in case."

I wait for him to finish.

"That's the part I didn't quite hear."

Doubt trickles down my throat like spoonfuls of cloudy soup pooling in my stomach. What if I have this all wrong? What if Jonathon has become involved with these people by mistake, and by the time he realized what was happening it was too late? What if he's just going along with them as a means to get me out of here?

"Maybe you're meeting him in Switzerland."

"What would make them think I would agree to get on a plane without screaming for help?"

Benicio stares at me. He's too kind to say the words.

I suddenly lose my distance, my vantage point from on high. I slide back down to the level of participation, the place where everything hurts. I turn to the window. "Let me guess. Threaten to kill someone I love more than anything in this world."

Benicio rests his hand on my shoulder. I turn to meet his eyes. Someone this attractive usually has it easier in life than most. Beautiful women probably throw themselves at him. Men probably offer him jobs. It occurs to me that he could have children, a wife somewhere, worrying herself sick.

"Are you married?"

Benicio drops his hand and shakes his head. "I was engaged once. To a woman in Los Angeles."

"Is that where you lived?"

"L.A., New York, Chicago, Miami."

"That's why your English is so good." I assume crop or factory work. I almost don't ask. "What were you doing there?"

Benicio is the one who looks out the window now. I sense the memories spinning behind his eyes. "Making people laugh."

"Making people laugh."

"Yes. I was a comedian."

"You're joking."

"Good one," he says.

"Wait. You mean, like a stand-up comedian?"

Benicio nods.

"That's hilarious. I mean." I give a slight laugh. "You know what I mean." I think of how playful he was at the pool with the dog. *You cheat, Pepe.* How agile and smooth his body cut through the air. I can easily picture him on a stage. "I've never met anyone who entertained people for a living. Everyone I know is pretty serious when it comes to work."

"Yeah, well, apparently you've never heard how comedy is serious business."

"Guess not."

A quiet sadness fills the air. We drift off in silence. I don't doubt we're both feeling the sway of loss, the bottomless dangling that never quite solidifies under the feet.

We finish off the bread and cheese. The water is nearly gone.

Then Benicio suddenly picks up where he left off. "The whole point is to make it look easy. There's an art to it. You have to build up tension and make it pay off. Timing is everything, as they say. And the surprise twists. Not easy at all."

"Is that why you quit?"

He shakes his head. "Now there's the funny part. If you're in a country illegally, you probably shouldn't be doing something that draws attention to yourself."

"You got deported?"

"Live. On the six o'clock news."

Countless newsreels flash in my head of immigrants in hand-cuffs marching past a chain-link fence, the wide-open doors of a paddy wagon waiting to swallow them up. I now know what it is to be locked inside a small, confined space, waiting to be handed one's fate.

"I'm sorry."

"It was my own fault. I made a name for myself by poking fun at the stereotypes. The tattooed gang stuff, migrant worker, taco maker, guy in cuffs getting deported."

"No."

"Oh, yes. And someone found out that I was busted in a raid, and there it was, the six o'clock satire. Life imitating art. The last laugh on me."

"I'm so sorry."

"Actually, I'd say *this* is the last laugh. Caught in a prescription drug ring." He shakes his head as if to say how ridiculous it all is.

We both give a gentle laugh. I drop my hand on his knee without thinking. The mood shifts. There's a moment when I know I should take it back, withdraw it quickly as if I haven't done it at all, but I allow the moment pass.

He stares down at my hand, and after a moment he places his own on top of it.

Clouds roll in and obscure the evening sun. A dull pressure fills the air. A thick breeze carries the far-off smell of rain.

Our eyes remain glued to our hands, one on top of the other, a tacky wedding photo pose.

"It's hard for me to think of them as bad people," Benicio finally says. "Leon has been like a big brother to me. And Isabel. My baby sister." He stops.

"Does the little boy belong to her?"

He glances up and swallows, and I see the hurt in his eyes. It's followed by something else. Something that seems to me more complicated, thorny. "Benny," he says. "She named him after me. There's no father. Another cliché for the books. But you have to understand. We didn't grow up with any of this. Poor, yes, but not this."

"What happened?"

"Long story made short. My parents were killed when a bus they were traveling in was forced off the road into a ravine. They had debts we didn't know about. I snuck into the States to help pay them and got a job in a frozen food factory in L.A. I sent every dollar home that I didn't need to survive. I'd always been the class clown, and one night at a comedy club I started this banter with a comedian on stage, and it turned out I was funnier than he was. One thing led to another and I became part of the comedy scene. I even had a couple of small parts in movies you've probably never heard of."

"Try me," I say.

"*Austin's Willing Execution.*"

"A comedy?"

"Hilarious."

"Never heard of it."

"Told you. The other was *In the Company of Harold's Daughter.*"

"You were in that? My God. Oliver has that. He's watched it a hundred times."

"And you?"

"No."

"I rest my case. Anyway," he continues with a smile, "I sent even more money home, and after a while I figured the debts had been paid. What I didn't know was that Leon had taken some of the money and started a business on the side. You get my drift. He hired my sister. I got deported, and the rest you already know."

I flip my hand over and squeeze his fingers. We both glance at my scabby wrist. "What happened to the woman you were engaged to?"

This seems to catch him off guard. "Emily. Yes, well, Emily went on to marry a guy I did shows with. I always thought he was one who called the INS."

"My God."

"Yes. But I also think the joke's on him. It doesn't pay to be a rebounder."

The word *rebounder* sticks in my head. I try to imagine myself rebounding. There'd be issues. Serious issues. How could I ever get close to someone again? How could I ever trust anyone after this?

"Emily doesn't really care about him," Benicio says. "At least that's what she says in her e-mails."

In the quiet his expression changes to something raw and achy, his eyes narrowing as if in the dark.

"Anyway," he says. "What about you? What do you do back home?"

The thought of home causes me to pull my hand away, retreat into the place where I don't want to be touched. "I'm a copyeditor. Very exciting stuff. It's my business to leave behind clean, perfectly understood worlds." I stop short of telling him what kind of worlds. "Clearly that's only on paper."

"Clearly." He smiles.

"These days, between creative writing workshops and spell-check, manuscripts come to me so polished I spend most of my time looking for words that spell-check doesn't catch. Like homophones."

"What's that?" he asks as if he truly wants to know.

"Words that have the same sound but different meanings and spelling."

"Ah, like beach on the shore, and Chico said that woman is a *beech*?"

I roll my eyes. "The resident comedian, ladies and gentlemen."

He smiles again, and it suddenly feels like we're on a first date, our voices low and close, the palpable awkwardness of being examined for a possible future.

"Wait," he says. "Like a beech tree instead."

"Exactly." Even I didn't think of that one.

"Tell me some good ones."

It's getting late. The room will soon be completely dark. Any moment there'll be rain.

"Let's see," I say. "She hadn't noticed the claws until he held the paper to her face."

Benicio appears confused.

"Clause. It's part of a contract. And bear claws." I curl my fingers in the air.

It doesn't seem to register.

"Never mind," I say. "How about, her ring was made of three carrots?" I munch an imaginary carrot.

Benicio laughs. "Nice."

"Could he be the cereal killer? As in corn flakes."

Benicio laughs again. "Good one. But I can't get past the size of that ring. He must have used baby carrots."

"Yeah. Hard to bend, though," I say.

How can we be joking at a time like this? It's as if nothing is real. Not my past, not the kidnapping, not whatever is waiting on the other side the door.

Benicio holds my gaze a few seconds too long, and I expect him to say something about laughter being the best medicine, but what he says is, "I love the sound of your voice."

I press my hand into my chest to stop it from pulling so tight.

"Has anyone ever told you that?" he asks.

I can almost feel Oliver's tiny fingers threading my own. "Yes."

"Well. It's true. Whoever told you that was telling you the truth."

I take a deep breath. "It wasn't my husband," I say. "Naturally."

We lock eyes and laugh. It grows stronger until it feels if we've pulled a cork on all the agony. We can't stop ourselves. He rolls one way and I roll the other. Our lungs empty of dread, then refill with air so fresh and blue it's intoxicating. My stomach, which has endured crunches for months, begins to feel sore. I venture into hysterics, my ears filling with the cadence of Benicio's infectious laugh, causing me to stagger over the line between laughter and tears.

I finally resign myself to the offer of his hand. When he pulls me up to sit, a thin tear spills down my cheek, and a heaviness descends back on the room.

He wipes away the teardrop with his thumb and leans close. Is he going to kiss me?

It seems he is.

11

I wasn't prepared for the rush of desire that flooded throughout my body the first time Seth leaned over the counter and pressed his mouth into mine. I wasn't prepared for my inability to resist. We'd just been discussing the latest Phillip Roth novel, which I didn't like and he did, when I looked up from Roth's book and met Seth's eyes. Until that moment I hadn't realized how full of need I had been. How lonesome my marriage to Jonathon had been, how much of a mistake. All along my secret yearnings for Seth had trickled inside me, one by one, though until that moment I'd thought them nothing more than a series of harmless daydreams. But that day at the counter I realized those yearnings had unknowingly built up in my system like a poison with a concentration that becomes critical over time.

The rush from Seth's kiss overwhelmed me. There was no other word for it. I pulled away, stunned. Phillip Roth fell to my feet and tore a page.

"So many pages," Seth said, his lips no more than an inch from mine. "He could lose a few and still tell the same story."

My chest rose for air. "So you agree with me then?"

"No doubt I agree with you, love," he said. And then he leaned away and called out to Noah, the forgotten young employee stocking books in another room. "I have an errand to run!" Seth pulled me out through the jangling front door, past the rows of potted bamboo, the red dahlias in full bloom, out around the south side of the house, and up the cedar back stairs.

✦ ✦ ✦

When the heat from Benicio's mouth presses into my lips, that first time with Seth comes flooding back. But there have been no months of buildup. No hours lost inside daydreams. This is a truck barreling through a red light, crashing into me without warning.

The stroke of our tongues gives me a jolt, and my need for him swells. Every move is tender and earnest. He releases the tie from my hair and cradles the back of my head. He pulls away and gently kisses my cheek, forehead, temple, the side of my neck. When he slips his tongue back into to my mouth the ache between my legs intensifies. He caresses my breast through my thin blouse.

Then he pauses and meets my eyes.

"This can't possibly be a good idea," I say, which even to me sounds like complete nonsense. I'm about to burst. It's a great idea. The best idea I've had in years.

He sits back without taking his eyes off me. His chest rises and falls in heavy waves.

These could very well be the last moments of my life. A brutal reality I need to face. I've made so many bad decisions. Is this just another in the series? Or is denying Benicio the real mistake?

I take his hand and lead him to the bed. He removes his shirt, and the air between us fills with the scent of sun and sweat and skin. Beneath my fingers his body feels smooth, his muscles hard, defined, dipping into the valley of his spine. Everywhere his hand comes to touch me—shoulder, breast, cupped around my mouth—a soft, slow, heat rises to meet it.

When he slides his hand to the waist of my shorts, I gasp. Is fear the force that's driving us? Is my sense of reason completely distorted? What the hell are we doing?

The need for him claws from deep within me. Animal. Carnal. Primal. This strikes me as funny, so very Dee Dee Dawson. Laughter reaches the base of my throat and works its way into my mouth.

Benicio stops and draws back, panting. "What is it?" His smile slowly mirrors mine.

My mind tunnels back to when I first saw him at the pool, how the blood charged through me. What I feel now began the moment I laid eyes on him. What I feel has nothing to do with shock or fear or not being able to think clearly. It's him. It's the two of us, together. "Nothing," I whisper. My laughter burns off and disappears, and along with it, my resolve to continue what we've started.

"I'm sorry," I say, rolling away.

After a moment he pulls my back into his chest and spoons me tightly. I can feel his heavy breath on my neck, his heart pounding against my spine. The first drops of rain fall past the window, and a minute later Benicio's heart eases its way to normal.

12

Rain lashes down. Lightning flashes through the room, then a crack of thunder, loud and jolting as a gunshot.

"I wasn't expecting that," Benicio says.

My back is still against his chest, his arms still holding me close in the hot, clammy air. My heart beats into his hands.

"The storm?" I ask.

"Yes. But not the one outside." He squeezes me.

"What were you not expecting? For me to stop what we were doing?"

Benicio kisses my temple, his lips warm and dry. "No. I didn't expect it to feel like that."

"Like what?" I ask.

"I think you know."

I let go a small, nearly imperceptible sigh.

Rain drums against the wide leaves and palms. The riverbed fills and rushes downhill. I close my eyes and begin to drift, thinking how I've been living like a paper cutout, a flat, one-dimensional image of a wife and mother. No change in perspective under different lighting. No lovely hue along the edge. No shadows thrown from the depth. In fact, there is no depth. And I have no one to blame but myself.

I can feel layers forming inside me, trenches being dug for me to climb into and fight. Jonathon isn't the only enemy here. I've been well armed in the fight against myself. I've carried around a pool of simmering hostility for years. It's eaten my insides like acid, and yet I refused to put it down. What's happened these last few months to finally blow the lid off? Why have I suddenly begun to fill with rage?

The answer hits me like a cuff to the back of the head. Oliver. It has to do with Oliver, though not in the way I once thought. His normal teenage angst, something I should have seen for what it is and let it be, has instead triggered my own feelings of anger and distress. Day after day, fight after fight, I see myself in Oliver. I can no longer escape who I am. He's become my mirror. The angrier he turns, the more my fury reflects back, and on we go, mirroring one another so many times that my whole life has become distorted, a superimposed reflection, a thing so unrecognizable it's hideous.

My lids fly open at Benicio's scream.

Isabel and Leon burst in yelling something I don't understand.

I sit up and jump to the end of the bed. Isabel catches me by the hair. She pulls me over to the chair and makes me sit.

"What?" I shout. "What's happening?"

Isabel slaps me again. This time, gun or no gun, I'm about to hit her back, but Benicio jumps up and grabs Isabel from behind. He jerks her away so hard she crashes against the edge of the bed and lands on the floor.

A look flashes between them. Some kind of knowledge I can't put my finger on. Do they suddenly see themselves as brother and sister instead of enemies?

Leon draws back a fist and hits Benicio, hard, in the face. An audible crack fills the room. Benicio screams in a way that tears my chest. He grabs his nose as blood streams through his fingers.

I try to get to him, but Isabel pushes me back into the chair with a pistol in my face. This time I feel the implication. This time I'm right there, present for my own execution.

With her free hand Isabel pulls a set of zip ties from her pocket. She steps behind me and fastens my ankles to the chair legs even tighter than the first time.

"Please," I cry. "There's no need for this."

"It's your fault!" Isabel says.

"What is? What did I do? I haven't done anything! He's lying. Jonathon is lying to all of you!"

Isabel jerks my arms with exaggerated force. Hatred radiates off her skin. It's unmistakable. This woman despises me. She finishes fastening the ties and pokes the top of my head with the side of her gun.

I tell myself to stay calm. As much as I want to kill her with my bare hands, I know fighting her will only lead to something worse.

Dark blood glistens down Benicio's face and hands. He chokes and spits a mouth full of red to the floor.

I'm going to be sick.

Leon shouts at Isabel. She leaves the room and comes back with a towel. He snatches it from her and hands it to Benicio, who tilts his head and covers his face with the towel. Blood coats his neck.

Leon backs him into the chair. He seems to be soothing him in Spanish, his voice suddenly soft. He clasps Benicio's ankles to the chair and then allows him to get his nose under control before he takes the towel away and ties Benicio's hands.

Benicio turns to me, his right eye badly swollen.

"I apologize if that comes out crooked," Leon says in English.

Benicio moans.

Leon shakes his head. "*Deberias haberme escuchado.* You should have listened to me," he repeats in English, apparently for my sake. Then he waves Isabel out of the room and locks the door behind himself.

I can't control my panicked breath.

"It's all right," Benicio says.

"It is *not* all right."

"It will be." His head sounds stuffed with cotton.

"Why are they doing this?"

Benicio seems to be searching for air. "I think I know how we can escape," he says. "What day do you think it is?"

"You're not making any sense."

"Just tell me."

"Why are they doing this?"

"Please!" he says.

"Christ. Your eyes are turning black."

"Please!"

"I don't know! Sunday or Monday. Who knows how long we were out in the beginning."

"I'm not sure either. But we don't want to get it wrong."

"Why?"

He spits another mouthful of blood to the floor. He pants as he speaks, clearly struggling to breathe through his nose. "Tuesday is Leon's morning to help his parents check in a group of tourists at the condo. Paulo, one of the goons outside, has to help him with the luggage. His brother, Roberto"—he stops and spits more blood to the floor—"goon number two who messed up my face the first time, has to run the *agua* truck for his father so he can take his mother for her cancer treatments."

"What are you saying?"

"Tuesday morning is the only time Isabel is left alone."

"For how long?"

"An hour, maybe two. And we don't have a watch."

"What do you plan to do, talk her into letting us go?"

Benicio appears to stifle a laugh. The swollen space between his eyes makes him look like a lion. "Isabel has very big plans." He coughs up blood, spits it away from me. "She's not going to let us go without a fight."

"What plans?"

"The kind only money can buy."

"Isabel is insane."

Benicio tilts his head back and breathes heavily through his mouth.

"You need a doctor, Benicio. Badly."

"I think I know how we can get past her."

I try to picture how all of this is going to play out. All I can see is a gun going off in my face. The idea that Oliver is going to grow up without a mother begins to fully sink in. I can't bear it. My thoughts race away and for some reason land on Benny. "What will happen to Isabel if we escape on her watch?" I ask.

Benicio moans.

"I don't know why I asked. She held a gun to your face. You may be her brother, but I can't imagine she'd get too broken up if something happened to you."

I think of the look that passed between them. It meant something. I follow my instinct, even as it tells me what I don't want to hear. Benicio knows more than he's letting on, and he's made a conscious decision not to tell me.

He turns toward the storm. The air is filled with the pleasant midsummer smell of wet soil from the warm rain. For a moment I'm thrown by the incongruity of it all.

"How do you plan to get us out of here?" I ask. "How do you plan to get us out of these chairs?"

"The broken glass."

"What about it?"

"You need to fall over and scoot toward it. Wedge a piece in your hands and use it to cut the plastic."

"Really. That's your plan?"

"I'd do it myself if I weren't afraid of hitting my face and knocking myself out."

"You need a doctor."

"That's what you said."

I imagine myself on the run, dodging bullets, getting hit, getting caught, raped, decapitated. A shiver runs through me.

"I don't know if it's worth it," Benicio says. "I don't know if I want to take the chance that we'll be killed trying."

"And if we do nothing?" I ask. "What do you think our chances are?"

"I think something has gone wrong somewhere. And the longer they have to wait, the madder they're going to get."

"Let's say we do escape. Where do we go? The police?"

Benicio tries to laugh. "I have a whole routine about how corrupt the Mexican police force is. You want to hear it?"

"Not particularly."

"And don't forget Leon has your passport."

"Shit."

"I think there's only one thing for us to do."

"And that is?"

"Make our way back to the border and sneak in."

"What?" I pull up a map of Mexico in my mind. "We're hundreds of miles away from the border. How the hell are we going to cross half of Mexico and then sneak into the States without getting caught?"

"It's not as if I haven't done it before."

Nights in the desert, hours locked in the back of a semi, crawling beneath barbed wire. There are people to be paid. "What are we supposed to do for money?"

"I don't know. I have about three hundred pesos in my pocket to get us started."

Three hundred pesos will buy us each a sandwich. I have several thousand dollars in my checking account. I think I might have tens of thousands in an investment fund. But now I'm not so sure.

"This is ridiculous," I say. "I'm an American. I'll just go to the consulate and explain everything. They'll help me. I know they will. Or do you also have a routine about corrupt U.S. consulates in Mexico?"

Benicio doesn't answer. Lightning flashes and thunder roars behind it. It takes a moment before the truth of what I've said dawns on me. Of course they will help me. But what about Benicio?

"There's a small consulate in Nuevo Vallarta about five miles from town," he says.

"What about you?"

Again he's quiet.

"And Oliver," I say. "Shouldn't I go back for him?"

"I have a feeling Oliver isn't waiting for you at the condo."

"Where is he?"

"I don't know. But he wouldn't be there. That would be stupid of them. He's probably wherever your husband is. Or maybe he sent him home."

Home? Who would be there to take him in? Maggie's family? I've managed to completely isolate myself over the years. There are acquaintances, a couple of neighbors, but no one I can imagine Jonathon asking for such a favor. We've become the family written about in the papers after the fact. They seemed very nice but always kept to themselves. Jonathon has talked about people from the bank, but the only time I ever see him with them is at the annual picnics and obligatory holiday parties, their awkward body language a clear indication of the lines drawn between them.

How is Jonathon explaining my absence to Oliver? Does he tell him I've been kidnapped? If so, won't Oliver wonder why Jonathon isn't he going to the police? And what about Switzerland? How is he explaining that? I grit my teeth, and my entire body fills with a dark and savage hatred.

"I have no idea who or how many people are connected to this," Benicio says. It appears to be getting more difficult for him to speak. "I would hate for you to get out of here, only to be trapped by someone else."

How likely is that? I can't help but wonder if he's concerned for me or just concerned about being left behind.

The rain is softer now, the storm moving past, the pleasant smell of wet soil drifting away.

"I'm pretty sure that tomorrow is Tuesday," he says. "We'll have to stay awake until the sun comes up." He spits more blood to the side, markedly less than before. "That will be close to five thirty in the morning. Once it's up we'll have to estimate the time. Count the seconds into hours until it feels close to eight. We'll listen for the sound of movement in the house. The cars leaving." His breathing is clearly labored. "I'm not sure how else to do it."

"Stop talking," I say. "Put your head back and take the pressure off your nose."

He does what I ask.

I imagine counting, one Mississippi, two Mississippi for hours. It'll be like counting sheep, impossible to stay awake for so long. "We'll have to take turns counting. One rests while the other counts and then we switch off."

He gives a moan I take for a yes.

Moments pass in quiet.

"How are we going to get past Isabel?" I finally ask.

Benicio lowers his head. The bleeding appears to have stopped. "First we need to decide where we're going," he says. "We can't just run out of here without a plan. That's suicide. They'll find us if we're not smart."

I imagine myself on the streets of Puerto Vallarta, making my way to the consulate. Won't that be the first place they look for me? I don't speak the language, don't know my way around, and can't trust a single person. Then again, what are my chances of getting within a few miles to safety, compared to the hundreds it'll take to reach the border?

"I think your best bet is to take a chance on the consulate." He seems to be reading my mind. "Make your way back into the city and hail a cab. After that you'll be there within half an hour."

"What if they're corrupt, like you said? What if they know who I am?"

"Make a scene. Scream your name. Attract as many witnesses as you can. Most people on the street will at least be able to understand you. There are Americans all around there. I think you'll be all right."

"And you?"

"I don't know." He sounds worse than ever. "I may have no choice but to get back over the border and do whatever I have to to survive."

And where will I go when I'm free? Make my way home, sleep in my own bed, carry on a life with Oliver, the two of us thick as thieves after all of this? And Jonathon? Where is he? In jail? Dead? Or just lying low until the next time he offers me up for another of his mistakes? I might never be able to go home at all. These people know where I live. Their reaches go far beyond this house, this country. I feel tangled in a worldwide net.

Then I think of Benicio, the two of us on the bed. My heart squeezes as if wringing out all the rest. There's no getting around the fact that if it's difficult for me to elude these people, how difficult will it be for someone who's grown up here? Someone whose handsome face is likely to be recognized by everyone in town?

I have to think of Oliver.

"I can't leave here without seeing for myself that Oliver is not in the condo."

"Celia. Of all the choices you have I wish you'd forget about that one."

"You don't understand. You don't have any children."

"I've seen things that have happened to children and their parents that you couldn't even begin to imagine."

That shuts me up. I'm out of my league. I know that. I have no idea what Benicio has lived through. And yet, I have to get to Oliver. There's simply no question.

"Do you have any idea what they'll do to you if they catch you a second time?" Benicio says. "I guarantee Oliver will never see you again."

That does it. I throw myself down, taking the chair with me. I hit the floor with a sickening thud, my arm and shoulder bearing the brunt. Pain strikes my neck and back. I bite down hard and refuse to scream. I will my body not to break. I breathe like a bull through my nostrils.

"Celia," Benicio says. It's almost a cry.

I struggle to find momentum, jerking my bound feet forward, then my shoulders, then my feet.

"Celia." His whisper is coarse from the blood in his throat. "Celia," again as I kick my legs and inch my way toward the glass.

13

After what must be thirty minutes of scratching the triangle of glass against the plastic tie and cutting the meat of my palm in the process, my wrists finally pop free. By the time I release Benicio my body is so pumped with adrenaline, I feel as if I could lift him right out of his chair.

Rain has gathered on the sill, and I use it to wet the towel and gently wipe the crusty blood from Benicio's face. He twitches in pain, his eyes black and purple, one swollen shut. He's in no shape to run.

I walk him to the bed and prop pillows beneath his head. He gives me his best smile and squeezes my hand. His nose is enormous. It's hard to tell just where it ends and the rest of his face begins.

I hold the towel through the bars on the window and dip it against the cool, wet leaves. I bring it back and lay it across Benicio's nose.

He groans.

"Pretend it's ice," I say.

The sun is beginning to break. "Rest." I cross the room for the shard of glass I used to cut us free.

I sit next to him, the glass closed in my hand like a lucky rabbit's foot. I count inside my head. One Mississippi, two Mississippi. No need to worry about dozing off. I've never felt more awake in my life.

With every ten minutes, I mark the concrete with the glass; like nails on a chalkboard, every scratch sets my teeth on edge. I remain focused for hours, never allowing myself to veer from the task, every thin white line a step closer to saving us. Every hour brings me closer to Oliver.

Benicio sleeps with his mouth wide open, snoring, gurgling with every breath he pulls in, lets out.

I estimate it's around seven o'clock when doors begin to open and close in the house. But Benny's cries obscure the sounds I need for cues. We need to act fast.

"Wake up!" I whisper loudly in Benicio's ear. "Hurry."

I rush over and place my chair back where it stood.

Benicio struggles to sit. He moans. He brings his hand to his face.

"Get in your chair," I say. "Quick."

It probably hurts too much for him to speak.

"Come on," I say, and help him into the chair.

I snatch up the old zip ties and cup them at his ankles to make them appear fastened.

Benicio places his arms behind the chair as if they're bound.

I gather up more ties, slide onto my own chair, place the ties around my ankles, and wait.

When the locks begin releasing I throw my hands behind me.

Benicio murmurs something. A prayer, I guess, and wish I could think of one myself.

"Isabel!" Benicio is suddenly wide-awake, up to the task. He spouts off in Spanish.

Isabel appears confused at first, but it doesn't take long to get her riled. She crosses toward him and screams something of her own.

Benicio's forehead beads with sweat.

Isabel pulls out her gun. It's hard to tell if anyone else is in the house. This is why Benicio is causing such a fuss, to see if someone will come running in. Benny's unanswered cries are a good indication that we're alone.

I scream. Isabel turns and Benicio leaps from the chair, grabbing her from behind. He ropes his arms down around both of hers and jerks her to the side to free the gun.

It's all happening so fast. Isabel stumbles but holds the gun beneath Benicio's grip.

I dive to the side just as the gun goes off. I land on my arm and scream in pain. I scream again in anger.

Benicio grasps Isabel's wrist and the gun goes off again, shooting the seat of the chair I just sat in. The sound is deafening. Everyone's screams are just as bad.

Isabel's arm continues to flail. She's trying to kill me.

Only seconds have passed from the time Benicio jumped from his chair to the gun going off once, twice, and now a third time.

A sting, and then a deep wrenching seizes the side of my calf.

Benny wails down the hall as if he's the one who's been shot.

Benicio flings Isabel against the wall, chopping her wrist so hard that the gun tumbles to the floor. Isabel screams. He snatches up the gun and points it at her face.

Her mouth fixes into an *O*. She's crying now, holding the wrist he's cut down.

"Celia?" Benicio says without taking his eyes off Isabel.

I'm still on the floor, the shots ringing in my ears. I'm afraid to look at my leg.

"Celia!" he yells.

I look. Blood streams down my calf. The sight of the hole intensifies the pain. I swipe at the blood, but it continues to flow.

Benny continues to wail.

Isabel shouts at Benicio.

Benicio screams for me. He moves to see my leg without taking his eyes off Isabel. "Shit, shit, shit," he says and glares at his sister with a look of pure hatred.

"I'm fine," I say. "It didn't go in. I could use a stitch or two, but I'm fine."

"Quick," Benicio tells me. "The medicine cabinet in the bathroom beneath the sink. There should be some gauze."

I catch my breath and hop to the bathroom, reminding myself of the pain of childbirth as I retrieve the gauze and a brown bottle of rubbing alcohol. I hop back with the pain shooting into my hip.

Benicio and Isabel remain in a standoff. Benny continues to cry.

I sit on the edge of the bed. I bite down and pour the alcohol on the wound like a soldier. Spit escapes through my clenched teeth. I tear a piece of gauze and tie it tightly around my calf. Then I hop across the room and get in Isabel's face. I want more than anything to smash it the way Leon smashed Benicio's. The shrill of Benny's cries stop me short.

"Hurry." Benicio motions for Isabel to move into the hallway in front of him.

The bedroom we enter smells faintly of urine but is clean and spacious with the same glossy terra cotta tiled floors. The furniture and décor are similar to the condo, warm, colorful, tropic.

The double bed is neatly covered with a white down blanket. Above the crib a mosquito net hangs like a white spotlight cone around Benny.

He can't be more than a year old, standing there in a diaper. He grips the bars of his crib and quiets when we walk in. His legs give a small bounce.

Isabel starts toward him.

"No!" Benicio says, and she freezes.

He lowers the gun but keeps it directed toward her. "*Hola,* baby," Benicio says sweetly.

Benny bounces his legs again.

I limp around Isabel, my leg on fire. I open the net and see the boy's face is red and soaked with tears. His hair is surprisingly light. He barely looks Mexican, though his lips are undeniably Isabel's.

"Hurry!" Benicio urges her.

I lift the boy from his crib like we planned. Benny seems cautious at first, staring deeply into my face. He looks at Benicio and then me. He reaches out and feels my hair. And then he smiles, and that's when I know.

Even if I hadn't been shot my balance would have wavered beneath me. I turn to Benicio. "He's not," I stammer when Benicio looks away. "Oh my God. My God," is all I can say.

"Put him down!" Isabel shouts.

Benny starts to whimper.

"Ssh." I bounce Benny on the hip of my good leg, stifling tears from so many kinds of pain.

Then I turn to Isabel. "You don't call the shots anymore, *chica.*"

I lift a satin baby blanket and a small floppy yellow bear from the crib. I smile at Benny and he smiles back, his father made over. For as much as Oliver resembles me, Benny resembles Jonathon.

He wraps his things into his arm and buries his face against the bear. I pat his cheeks dry with the blanket and instinctively kiss the top of his head.

"*Pasaporte*," Benicio says to Isabel. "*Dónde está su pasaporte?*"

Isabel stares at Benny in my arms.

Benicio gets down in her face and growls something in Spanish. Isabel shrinks beneath his words. She walks over to a dresser and pulls out my passport and hands it to Benicio.

He snatches it from her and sticks it in his back pocket.

Then he orders her to do something else. Isabel opens another drawer and takes out a violet tank top and jeans. She tosses them to me.

"Come," Benicio says and motions everyone into the next room. It isn't nearly as well kept, the queen-size bed is unmade and curtains still closed. Isabel pulls a pair of men's jeans and a black T-shirt from the drawer and hands them to Benicio.

I glance down at the gauze on my leg, already soaked red. The hot pain increases with every step.

Benicio orders Isabel farther down the hall, and I can hear the anger and determination in his voice.

Isabel crosses the room and takes a seat in the very chair she helped tie Benicio to. I'm so tempted to ask her how it feels to be the one trapped in here, but Isabel doesn't take her eyes off Benny. She's a mother concerned for her son, and in that moment I can only think of Oliver.

Benicio walks backward to the door.

"Here you go," I say, and set Benny down with his blanket and bear on the floor in the place Isabel slid in the trays. I notice my sneakers for the first time at the end of the bed. I set the clothes down and slip on my shoes, wincing at the pain. I remember the broken glass and snatch up the bloody towel and use it to sweep away the shards. I scoop the pieces inside of it and then throw the whole thing out the window.

Isabel watches with a dazed expression.

Benicio pats Benny on the head, and the boy peers up at him and grins as if this is all part of some game.

I gather the clothes and the remaining gauze and rubbing alcohol. Benicio and I back out of the room and lock the door.

In the kitchen Benicio pulls a plastic grocery bag from a drawer and stuffs it with chips and bread and bottled water and salami from the fridge. He rummages through other drawers, collecting a knife, lighter, flashlight, and several more plastic bags. He rushes into the bathroom and comes out with insect repellant and an assortment of medications cradled in his arm.

I've grabbed another bag and thrown all the clothes inside. I search for car keys and cell phones but find neither. Then a sickening thought occurs to me. I hobble down the hall and meet Benicio rushing toward me. "Does Isabel have a cell phone?"

"Shit!" Benicio runs back to the room. I stumble behind. When we open the door Isabel looks up from her cell phone with a grin. She snaps it closed, already finished with her call.

Benicio rushes toward her with such violence that I scream for him not to hurt her. He grabs Isabel's phone and throws it out the window. He screams some more, but I coax him out by shouting that we're running out of time.

"They couldn't have gotten very far by the time she got a hold of them," I say, feeling the weight of the oversight that may have cost us our lives.

I lock the door behind us while Benicio rummages through drawers in the second bedroom. I meet up with him again just as he pulls out a pistol and a large wad of dollar bills.

"Here." He hands me a black handgun. Jonathon is right. It does feel lighter than you expect. "You know how to use one of these?" Benicio drops open what I know from TV to be the magazine, and check for bullets. It's full.

"I'm a quick study," I say.

He clips it shut and tries to smile. His face is so distorted I can hardly make out what his features are supposed to look like. "Ready?" he asks.

"*Sí*," I say with a grin.

The plan we've made will no longer work. It didn't include Benicio's broken nose and my getting shot in the leg. The speed we hoped to have by running downhill is now stalled. Someone is going to return any moment. Besides, Benicio has been right from the beginning. It's all too risky. The condo. The consulate. The police. Going about things in a way these people would expect.

I keep telling myself that someday I will know Oliver as a man. I will know his children, my grandchildren. No one is going to take that away.

We can't go near the road, not even down the hill through the trees. The only way to survive will be to go up the mountain, through the jungle, and come out the other side.

14

When I was twelve and on my way home from school one after-noon, a boy named Michael Mahon came riding down the side-walk on his bike toward me. He stopped and skidded a black mark across the concrete. He turned and studied it, apparently impressed.

"There's an ambulance at your house taking your dad away," he said.

Michael was full of shit. He was always telling stories about how he and his mom were millionaires in hiding. How they pre-tended not to have money by living in that small, lopsided house so that Michael's father wouldn't come back from wherever he'd gone and take it all away. Michael claimed to be royalty, a black belt in karate, a keeper of secret codes, and when he went away in the summer he bragged it was to France. "*Merci beaucoup*," he'd said to everything until another boy slugged him on the play-ground.

I walked out around him.

"I'm not joking," he said.

"You're a liar," I said, and kept on.

"Am not."

"My dad is at work right now, you idiot."

I could hear him turning his bike around behind me and starting to follow. I was at least four blocks from home.

"I knew you were walking here. I saw you when I passed by earlier."

"So."

"So, I know where you live."

I didn't like the sound of this, even though everyone knew where everyone lived in those days. "And?"

"And I know what I saw at your house."

"Leave me alone," I said. "Or I'm going to scream rape."

"Fine, Miss Freak. Have it your way. But it sure looked a lot like your dad on that stretcher."

My stomach turned. I was now three blocks away but it felt much farther. My father had complained of feeling tired that morning. My mother had pointed out that he didn't look well and suggested he stay home.

Either Michael was playing a sick trick on me or an ambulance was taking my father away. Either way was bad.

I made a run for it, grappling with my giant math text and two English books covered in Mylar from the library: *To Kill a Mockingbird* and *A Tree Grows in Brooklyn*. My hands sweated around the plastic. I had to stop three times when they tumbled to the ground.

I heard the commotion of voices before I rounded the corner, saw the flashing red lights reflecting in the neighbor's cars. I reached my yard just as an ambulance was pulling away.

Neighbors had gathered around my mother in the street. Mrs. Barbery stroked her back. She saw me approaching, and turned my mother in my direction.

My mother held her fists against her chest, her cheeks wet with tears. Her hands shook when she fastened them onto my shoulders. "Get in the car. We need to meet Daddy at the hospital."

"What happened?"

"I think he had a heart attack. Hurry now. I don't want him wondering where we are."

"But I thought he was at work," I said, my mind trying to make sense of what was happening. My father had dropped me off on his way to work that morning, his briefcase tossed between us in the front seat as always. He had gone to work, and therefore, the man in the ambulance could not be my father.

"He came home sick at lunch," Mrs. Barbery said, as if reading my mind.

If only I'd listened to Michael Mahon. If only I'd run home the second he mentioned the ambulance, I wouldn't have missed the last chance I'd ever have to speak to my father. That morning he had yelled at me to hurry up. Yelling was not something he often did. He wasn't feeling well. But I wasn't listening. I didn't care. I changed my shirt for the tenth time, making us both late.

I wanted to apologize. I wanted him to know how much I loved him. I wanted to hear him ask, "What's my little raven-haired doll up to?"

His heart stopped for good before he even reached the hospital. For the first time, maybe the only time in Michael Mahon's life, he had told the truth.

I think about this as I trudge uphill behind Benicio, through the trees and brush along a river gushing with rapids. I try thinking of anything other than Jonathon's lies and the pain in my leg. My shins itch and sting from the million micro-scrapes in my skin. I've never finished either of those novels. To this day, I can't even look at them without feeling a pang of loss. I've never been good at math, but after that day I couldn't crack open a math book without thinking of how it'd kept me from my father by continuing to slip from my hands. I hate math. Hate its cousin, finance, too. It doesn't help that my mother became interested in the stock market back then. I understood as I got older that she'd been forced to do something without my father's income. But back then it left a funny feeling in my throat when I saw her hunched over the paper on Sunday mornings, excitedly checking the Dow.

Mosquitoes puncture my skin, heat and blood loss leave me lightheaded. Tropical caws, screeches, and barks shudder my nerves. Hot pain flares in my leg with every step, and in the midst of this I think of numbers, of money and finances and the power they have to make or break a person's life, and I hate them even more.

I recall the times Jonathon sat at the kitchen table frowning at his laptop, and how quickly he turned on a smile when I walked past. Like hitting a switch. On again, off again. Had he been e-mailing Isabel? He's probably already taken the money from my checking and savings accounts, the fund from my mother, which is so small I can only appreciate it for its sentimental value, something Jonathon would easily dismiss. But that fund is one of the few things I have left from my family. One of the few pieces of proof that I once had a place where I belonged.

Jonathon had lied to me about so many things and then had crawled into bed with me, made love to me, told me that he loved me, and made it seem as if all he ever wanted was my happiness and all I ever did was stand in my own way.

After an hour of pushing through the jungle, Benicio and I stop for water.

"You need to change that bandage," he says. Earlier he gave me antibiotics and Tylenol with codeine, which has barely made a dent in the pain.

The gauze is blood-soaked. My whole calf, swollen.

"Have a seat," Benicio says, his face even more hideous outdoors. What a sight we are. Gruesome creatures escaping through the jungle like half-eaten prey.

I remove the gun from the waist of my shorts and lower myself to the ground. Pain throbs deeper when I release the pressure.

"Watch out for snakes," Benicio says. He elevates my foot on a log.

I think he's joking but then realize that of course there are snakes, among many other things I have no idea about.

He unwraps the bandage to reveal a gouge the size of a grape on the outside of my calf.

"That bullet took a chunk out of your leg," he says, absorbing the tiny pool of blood with the fresh ends of the gauze.

I bite my knuckle to keep from crying out. Even the slightest touch is unbearable.

"You could use some stitches," he says.

"I could use a cork."

"You're funny," he says.

"You're the first person to think so."

"Maybe it's a side of you that only comes out in Mexico."

"After kissing a comedian. Who can say? It's all a first."

"Right. Maybe it only comes out when your husband has you kidnapped."

He holds my gaze for a moment, clearly trying to smile. Dried blood has settled into thin creases on his neck and begins to soften and drain from sweat. "I'm sorry," he says. "You didn't deserve that. You didn't deserve any of this."

I lie my head on the ground and gaze into the canopy of trees, remembering the days of staring at the Japanese maple in my yard, convinced my life couldn't get any worse.

Benicio takes out the fresh gauze and rubbing alcohol. I know what's coming and turn my head and grit my teeth. Hot lava pours inside my leg. I cry out and pound my fists.

"I'm sorry," he whispers. "I'm so sorry."

I cover my eyes and take several deep breaths, my chest heaving with tears. I focus on our plan to reach the kiosk near the canopy tours by dark. I'm losing faith. Our only other choice is to hide out another full day until it closes again. It isn't as if we can walk up and buy food and ice and not be noticed. We have to break in during the night. Maybe even get a few hours of sleep in the locked bathroom.

Benicio gently wraps my leg.

I open my eyes and think of Isabel and Benny. "Your sister was determined to kill me," I say. Insects gather in the air around us. I reach for the bug spray in the bag. "I saw it in her face. She was aiming for my head." I spray the air, my arms and neck, and then I spray some into my palms and rub it over my face.

Benicio doesn't look up. He tears the end of the gauze down the middle like the tongue of a snake, and makes a tourniquet. He fastens it just above the wound.

"At least I understand now why she hates me."

"She just wants the money."

"Why didn't you tell me?"

"What good could possibly come from telling you?"

"I would have known what I was dealing with."

"What would you have done differently if you'd known?"

"I don't know."

"You should forget about my sister. She's the least of our worries. At the rate we're going I don't think we'll find the kiosk before sundown." He stands and offers his hand.

I snatch up my gun and allow Benicio to pull me to my feet. "That boy is my son's brother."

"I'm sorry." He places his hand on my cheek. "I'm just trying to keep us alive, and I'm afraid we've lost too much time."

I turn away and shove the gun in my waistband. The pressure on my leg shoots pain into my back. It robs me of my breath, but I make every attempt not to show it.

"They most likely think we headed downhill," Benicio says. "But I don't want to underestimate them."

"I can't go any faster," I say.

Benicio locks eyes with me. "It's not your fault. Let's see how your leg holds out. You're still losing quite a bit of blood."

We both stare at the gauze already dotted with red.

"Shit," I say.

Benicio turns his head as if chasing some far-off thought.

"Come on. I can do this," I say, lying.

"I'm not so sure."

"What about your face?" I ask. "Shouldn't we be doing something about that?"

"I need ice and a surgeon. Not a lot of those in the jungle."

"It looks worse than you can imagine."

"I'm sure it does."

He digs a hole with his heel and drops in the bloody gauze from my leg. He kicks dirt over the top and takes my hand. "This isn't a competition," he says, and I think of how I cried against his chest, the heat of our kiss, his heart pounding against my back. He touches my cheek again. "For good or bad, we're in this together."

15

Benicio distracts me from the pain by pointing out vanilla vines and coffee trees as if the two of us are on a day hike, strolling along, taking in the sights. He points out parakeets flying to and from a termite nest they are raiding to feed their young. He tells me about all the animals we're likely to run into. Badgers, armadillos, and squirrel monkeys. Lizards, iguanas, countless varieties of birds with shocking green and yellow feathers.

"Just tell me what's going to eat me," I say.

"Jaguars, though no one ever really sees them. But there is the poisonous beaded lizard. I've seen plenty of those. Tarantulas, of course."

"Are you serious?"

"Lots of snakes."

"If we don't make it to the kiosk, where are we going to spend the night?"

"Here somewhere. We don't have a choice."

I glance around at the thick brush and what I now know is an enormous parota tree, which the indigenous people use to make canoes. I imagine lying on the ground with snakes and tarantulas crawling across my prone body. Some kind of insect nesting in my wound. We may as well have tried to make it to the consulate. We seem doomed either way.

It isn't long before we need to rest again. I make an effort to hide the pain, but Benicio is clearly on to me, asking to stop for just a moment while he doles out another round of Tylenol with codeine. He swallows another round himself.

Rapids rush by on the river, making it difficult to hear our own voices. But the unmistakable sound of laughter suddenly carries on the waves. We stop.

Benicio tucks me behind him and pulls out his gun. I grab my own from my waistband but am suddenly unsure what to do with it. I can imagine using it to threaten people the way characters in movies do, bossing them around, getting them to do what I want. But shoot it? Even now, after everything that's happened, after being shot myself, it seems out of the question.

We duck behind a clump of bamboo. Benicio takes my gun and shows me where the safety is. "The only thing left to do is cock the hammer, line up the rear and front sights in your aim, and pull the trigger."

He talks of shooting a gun like it's nothing more than mixing a drink. Add that, then that, then this.

A new round of fear passes through me.

The laughter on the wind is now followed by screams.

We ready ourselves behind a parota tree. My hand sweats around the warm metal of the gun.

Yellow-helmeted tourists come rushing down the rapids on a yellow inflatable raft. They jab yellow oars into the choppy water, laughing as they work to keep the raft facing forward. Once they pass, two more rafts charge by the same way. After that there's nothing but water hurling against the rocks.

Benicio clicks the safety and shoves the gun into his jeans. He releases the breath from his chest.

I realize I'm no longer holding my gun. I've dropped it to the ground with the safety off.

"We may be closer to the kiosk than I thought," Benicio says. "Let's rest a while longer. Take the pressure off your leg."

I shake my head no.

"If we keep pushing it, you'll end up not being able to walk at all."

I know he's right, but I don't like handing over the decision-making. Handing over too many decisions is what got me into this mess in the first place.

Benicio clears the ground at the base of a tree. He sits down with his back against the trunk. "Here," he says, patting his lap. "Lay your head down and rest."

I've been up all night counting, and before that I was tied to a chair.

I lower my head onto his thigh, feeling a warm surge of feelings in my stomach. He brushes a tangle from my face and strokes my hair with a single finger until I drift into a dissatisfying sleep, dreaming the universal dream of running in place.

I wake to him watching me.

"Your fingers were twitching," he says. "You moaned a couple of times, too."

"How long was I out?"

"An hour and a half at the most."

"What!" I sit up with a wince. "Why did you let me sleep so long?"

"That leg needs to heal."

I swallow dryly and turn away.

He stands and brushes the dust from his shorts. "We may be closer than I thought, but that doesn't leave room for something that might go wrong along the way."

I offer my hand and Benicio helps me stand. My leg has swelled even more. "Oh God," I say, before I can catch myself. How much codeine do I need to make it go away?

Benicio wraps my arm around his shoulder. "Let's get over to the water," he says. "The cold will feel good on your leg."

"But we'll be out in the open."

"We'll be quick."

My leg is now hard and hot as an iron grill.

I lower myself onto the rocks, determined not to cry. The pain is worse, if that's even possible. I feel light-headed, a little high, afraid of passing out.

Benicio removes my sneaker and I dip my leg, slowly, into the water. The corkscrew current is so painful I pull my leg back out.

"Here." He wedges a log between two rocks and makes a small eddy. The water still spirals but without the speed and strength of the rapid.

I grit my teeth and lower my leg, determined to leave it submerged. After a few minutes the cold slips inside and chills the red-hot nerves. I finally feel some relief.

Dragonflies zip across the river. The humidity is thick without the ocean breeze. My skin is covered in layers of sweat and dust and bug bites. The dime-store repellant is no match for insects of the jungle.

Benicio rummages through the bag of food. He cuts salami into small pieces and stuffs them between chunks of torn bread. He hands the makeshift sandwich to me.

He tears small pieces of bread and chews them with an open mouth so he can breathe. A crooked bump at the center of his nose appears bigger in the sunlight. Some version of it will probably be there forever. Every time he looks in the mirror, every time someone asks where it came from, he'll think of me. And every time I swipe a razor down my calf, I'll think of him. We've made a mark on one another, scars like tattoos, bearing one another's names.

"Wouldn't it have been a lot easier for you to just join the family business?" I ask. "I mean, here you are running for your life in the jungle with a broken nose instead of kicking back in your estate on the beach."

He lets go a small laugh and nods but says nothing.

My leg is slightly numb. The codeine and cold are finally kicking in.

We eat in silence, keeping one eye upstream, the other on the trees behind us. We're open targets for someone coming from either direction. The rushing water makes it nearly impossible to hear approaching feet.

"We better hurry," I say, even as my words begin to gel in my mouth. *Relax*, my body begs. *Hush*.

Benicio takes off his shirt. The carve of his muscles beneath his smooth dark skin is so beautiful against the rocks and sun, the white foam whirling behind him, that I forget to chew the food in my mouth. My heart thumps, and then a piercing dart when I think of lying with him on the bed.

He stands and drops his shorts.

My face flushes.

"I promise I'll be fast," he says.

It's only now that I remember to chew. He maneuvers across the large rocks like a crab, the muscles in his arms and legs twist and flex under his weight. He drops feet first into the river behind a clump of rocks that keep him from being swept away. He tilts his head back to wet his hair and swipes the dried blood from his face and neck.

Codeine is a beautiful thing. It's easy to imagine the two of us here under different circumstances. Lovers taking a dip in paradise. My lids open and close like a camera's aperture, capturing the moment forever.

Benicio rises from the water and scoops his clothes from the rock. I hold up a hand to stop him from getting dressed. I've drifted away from the pain in my leg, away from my rage, my inhibitions and fears. I'm a kite cut loose from the life I've been tied to.

"Come here," I say, scooting behind the partial wall of brush. I lift my blouse over my head and undo my bra.

Benicio unravels his clothes across the ground for me to lie on. He moves beside me, quickly aroused.

"This is crazy," he says.

"I know."

"The codeine?"

"Maybe."

I can feel Benicio's body fill with urgency.

I push my shorts down and take him into my hands in the same moment his fingers slip between my legs. The ground beneath us doesn't seem strong enough, and I half-expect to crash through the earth and disappear.

This is a different kind of quick than the one I experienced with Jonathon. I'm so ready for him, and he's about to explode in my hands. It isn't out of habit, routine, and efficiency. I'm swept inside a current. There's nothing to ground me, nothing to grab onto, nothing to keep from being pulled farther and farther away.

I moan. Claw fingernails into dirt. Sweat stings my eyes, drips to the ground, pools with Benicio's. The pain pulses deep inside my leg, and yet I've never felt so euphoric, my core so unmoored in all my life. Gone are the agony and loneliness and lies. Gone the rage. I've punched my way through to happiness.

I want to make it last. I ease off on the pressure, turn my lips away, but our bodies are so far gone, so irretrievably lost inside a force so powerful, that in my hesitation only seconds are spared.

Afterward Benicio lies back and laughs at the sky. He seems to be reading my mind. Yes, it's ridiculous. All of it. Our pasts, the way we found each other, the fact that the two of us should meet now when we might not live to see another day. It's the best thing that's ever happened to us on the worst day of our lives.

Benicio closes his eyes and I sit up, my body swaying with tipsy contentment. I'm punch-drunk, naked, covered in sand, a pink chicken rolled in Shake 'n Bake.

I jostle Benicio's shoulder.

He opens his eyes with a start.

"Do you know what Shake 'n Bake is?"

He sits up and looks around.

"It's Shake 'n Bake, and we helped!"

Benicio pulls on his shirt, clearly not knowing what he's laughing at, other than me.

"Didn't you have those commercials when you were a kid?" I ask.

"No."

"There were these two kids." I stop. "Are there wild dogs out here?" I hear a bark. Not the kind that comes from a squirrel or a monkey. The kind that comes from a barrel-chested dog.

I turn my ear to the jungle. There it is again.

Benicio yanks on his shorts and shoes.

I dress quickly.

"Get behind the big tree," he says.

I'm already moving, looking to see what I should grab. The tree's at least twenty yards away.

"I'll get the stuff, just go," he says.

I slide the gun into my shorts and hobble behind the tree, grunting and cursing beneath my breath as the pain, the memory of the bullet, comes grinding back.

Benicio's no more than fifteen feet behind me, out in the wide open with the bag of food when the dog barks again. It's close. Very close. Benicio runs, ducks, and scrambles across the ground.

Then the loud crack of gunshot. Another. I look in the direction it seems to be coming from. The dog barks nonstop, a desperate refrain.

Branches above me quake and flop; small, long-legged monkeys leap from tree to tree, croaking and twittering in panic.

When I turn back I expect to see Benicio behind me, his amber eyes and cracked nose, my shoulder bracing for the touch of his hand, the breeze lifting a trace of river water from his skin. But there's no one. Benicio hasn't come any closer. He lies facedown in the grass. His arms and legs splayed open as if he's embracing the earth. No matter how long I stare he just lies there, still as a corpse.

16

First my father. Then my mother.

"She's gone," the nurse said to me.

But I already knew. My mother's withered hand beneath mine was cool and light as a dead baby bird. We were alone in the hospital room when I whispered, "It's all right, Mom. You can go now." I didn't mean this. There was nothing all right about my mother leaving me, and I wanted to take it back. But the wispy sound of her final breath was unmistakable. The absence of her spirit had deadened the air in its wake.

Something black and wretched took hold of me. I drifted wordless past the nurse. Outside the sun hovered in a flawless sky. Men and women ducked in and out of shops and cafés. Children cried, then laughed. The trolley wheels slogged metal on metal. Somehow life managed to go on. But nothing looked the same through the waxy lens of grief.

For weeks I walked by the hospital half-expecting the sliding doors to jerk open and my mother to step out laughing, telling me how it was all just a silly mistake. A blunder, a goof, a screwy mishap. *Oh, Cee-Cee, you won't believe it!* Weeks turned to months.

I got married as if through a screen, a gauzy veil allowing only the tiniest things to sift through. I kept waiting for the grief to go away. For something to take its place.

+ + +

I fumble the safety off the gun. There's movement in the brush. A German shepherd lunging on its leash, a man in a gray T-shirt and khaki shorts—leash in one hand, gun in the other.

My sights race between the man and Benicio on the ground. Somewhere in the back of my mind I believe Benicio won't allow himself to die. I believe he can control such a thing. It's idiotic. It's foolish and childish and insane, and yet the idea that Benicio won't leave me no matter what slows my wild pulse and makes sense of the chaos in my head.

From where I stand I don't think the man can see Benicio in the grass. I don't think he knows I'm behind the tree. But the dog knows. He smells the way, lunging straight for Benicio. Within seconds he'll be on us both.

I steady my hand around the gun. There shouldn't be any question. No moral dilemma. His life or mine. Even so, the fact that I'm about to kill another human being tugs the gag reflex in my throat. I lower the gun. A collage of images flash before me. Oliver's tiny body running into the street. Benicio facedown in the grass. Jonathon's smile, that *smile*, and then his voice like a steady whistle in my ear, in my head, a piercing that will not go away. *Please pinpoint what it is and I will try and make it better.*

I raise the gun and cock the hammer near my cheek.

The dog lunges. The man pulls back on the leash and crouches into the edge of the clearing. He calls Benicio's name. He yells in Spanish while I hold my breath, lining up the rear and front sights, taking aim.

I glance once more at Benicio. His gun is just out of reach of his hand. I will him to feel me there, to make a sign to let me know he hasn't left me. Not yet. Not here. Not today.

The man takes another step. "Benicio!" he shouts.

And then I see Benicio's fingers curl into a fist. He unfurls his forefinger and thumb until his hand takes the shape of a gun. He pulls an imaginary trigger.

I aim at the man's chest. The heart? The head? My God, I think, my God, and pull the trigger.

What happens next happens inside a bubble of eerie, high-pitched silence. Senses shut down. No sight, no sound, nothing to feel or smell. The pain in my leg is gone. Fear is gone. Time and place cease to exist. I disappear.

Then the blast of my own gun suddenly rushes my ears long after I've pulled the trigger. The man has disappeared into the grass, and the dog is charging Benicio.

Time resumes, along with fear and pain and the horror of what's happening.

Benicio jumps for his pistol, turns, and fires two rounds. The dog yelps and twists sideways, flipping in the air. He yelps once more, then stops.

I drop the gun as if it's seared my hand. I hobble out to Benicio. He meets me halfway and wraps his arms around me. I can barely breathe. The man I shot is sprawled on the ground not far from where we stand. I turn away, but not before seeing his blood-soaked body from his neck to his belt, a black hole gaping at the base of his throat, his eyes open and dead to the sun.

I lean to the side and throw up.

"Roberto," Benicio says. "Fucking Roberto." He paces the grass near the man's body. He looks to be crying. He mumbles in Spanish.

I throw up again, sure I'm going to pass out. I stumble back to the tree. I can't erase the bullet hole from my eyes.

When nothing is left in my stomach, I spit my mouth clean and press my hand against the tree. "We need to get out of here," I say. "They could have heard those shots." But in my mind all I can think is Roberto was someone's son, brother, husband, father. He drove the *agua* truck for his father on the days when his mother needed cancer treatments.

Benicio nods at the ground.

I accidentally lean on my bad leg, and an explosion of pain erupts all the way into my jaw. We're stuck here for the night. I cannot, will not move another inch.

I pick up the gun and click the safety. "It was either him or us," I say, with a coldness that surprises me. After that it's as if a heavy drape is pulled over my eyes. Light evaporates. The entire day fades away.

17

Scraping. Something digging in dirt. I open my eyes to see Benicio at the edge of the clearing, thirty feet away. He's shirtless beneath a ray of sunlight slanting through the trees. For a moment I float in ignorance, thinking I'm at the pool and Benicio is working in the garden. I savor the cut of his shoulders, the curve of his back. Then I remember how intimately I know his hands. His mouth. His body inside me.

Then the memory of Roberto floods in. I ache everywhere. My muscles are wet rags wringing beneath my skin. I don't even try to move.

Benicio is digging a grave with a large branch. The ground appears stiff, dry from the winter months. He chops at it like a farmer with a pickax. How long have I been out? How long has he been digging? The sun sits lower in the sky. It appears as if Benicio has managed nothing more than a shallow rut in the ground.

I make an effort to sit, but the side of my head feels as if it's been slammed with a cinderblock. I must've whacked it on the ground when I fainted. I unclench my fists and lay my head back onto the bag of clothes Benicio has slipped beneath me.

I watch as he tosses the branch to the side and empties Roberto's pockets of a cell phone and cash. He stuffs them into his own pockets, and then he wipes his forehead across the back of his forearm and drags Roberto by his wrists into the shallow hole. He rolls the dog next to him, and then he covers them both with dirt and vines, branches and leaves, creating a mound that animals are sure to tear apart in the night.

He sees I'm awake and holds up a finger to say just a second. He jogs to the water and washes his hands. Then jogs to my side.

"How's your head?" he asks, helping me to sit.

"Fine." I lie, wondering just how much pain I'd be in if it not for the codeine.

"How about the leg?"

The pain seesaws from moment to moment. I take several deep breaths. "Better. I think."

He appears skeptical.

"Really," I say.

He lowers himself beside me. Neither of us mentions what's happened, and the silence mushrooms between us.

"I'm sorry about Roberto," I finally say.

"It's not your fault." He glances toward the river. Does he finally regret not joining the family business? Anything has to be better than this.

An armadillo saunters through the clearing. Then another. Exclamation points to a life so surreal it's beyond belief. We're living on the outside of logic. Anything seems possible.

Benicio takes out Roberto's cell phone and flips it open. "No coverage up here." He snaps it shut.

The minute we're in range I'll use it to call Oliver. The thought of this fills me with the urge to get up and run.

"When Roberto doesn't return they'll come looking for him," Benicio says. "They'll figure it out by tonight."

"What should we do?"

"Not stay here."

"How far are we from the kiosk?"

"Too far for you to walk. We need to think of something else."

"What else is there?"

"We could go back down."

"And walk right into them?"

"Of course not."

Benicio empties a plastic garbage bag.

"What are you doing?"

"I'm going to run ahead and make it to the kiosk. I'll grab a raft and some supplies and meet you back here."

Fear rises to my throat. My skin begins to itch. My arms and legs are covered in horrible red bites. Ants? Mosquitoes? What else is there? "How long will you be gone?" I grab the insect repellant and spray myself again. I spray the air and ground, but there isn't an insect in sight.

"No more than a few hours."

"A few *hours*?" I can't imagine the kind of dark that comes to a jungle in the middle of the night. "I'd rather come with you."

"You know you can't. You need to stay here and wait."

He's right. But still. "What if someone comes?"

"If I don't spot the kiosk before they close I'll never find it in the dark."

I look around, sick with fear, trying my best not to show it.

"Keep your gun close. Here's an extra just in case." He hands me Roberto's gun, a small smear of blood on its side.

I turn away. He places the gun on the ground.

"I want you to wait by the river just after sunset," he says. "I'm going to tie this garbage bag to a tree so I can spot it on my way down."

I have little faith that any of this is going to work. It seems far more likely that one of Leon's men will find me, and even if they don't something will eat me alive before dawn.

"Where does the river lead?" I ask.

"We won't take it all the way. We'll cut across a few miles before the end and follow a trail to Mismaloya."

Mismaloya. This is the town I read about online when Jonathon showed me Puerto Vallarta. It's the place where *Night of the Iguana* with Richard Burton and Ava Gardner was filmed. It looks exactly the way paradise is supposed to look.

"What are we going to do there?" I ask.

"Hide in plain sight."

"With that face and this leg?"

"Yes." He loads some things into another bag, explaining how everything will unfold.

"Are you sure about this?"

"You'll see," he says, and I sit back, settling into a feeling I can't name. "I'll take care of everything," he says, and I wish he hadn't said it. It sounds so much like something Jonathon would say that I can't help recoiling when Benicio leans down and softly kisses my cheek.

He says a few more things about a plan when he returns, and then he's gone.

18

Exhaustion, like a cast, sets my bones, making it harder and harder to move. Everything I've endured over the last few days has collected inside me. I've lost track of how much codeine I've taken. I drift in and out of a trance, never quite losing my awareness of the mound near the trees. With every rustle of leaves or crackle of branch I'm sure someone or something is unearthing the man I killed. The man I killed. The idea is so unthinkable that I question more than once if Roberto isn't really alive after all. If perhaps the sounds I hear in the jungle are actually Roberto coming up for air.

I force my arms and neck into a stretch, though neither gives much. I drink water and think in a thickheaded, nonsensical way of how so many years of my life have passed and yet very few memories can be retrieved. How have I filled the hours? I don't know. How you fill your days is how you live your life goes the adage.

Coming here has changed everything. If I live through this I'll always be able to recount nearly every second of what's happened since I got off the plane. Much like my days with Seth. For all the years I had stopped thinking about our time together, I can still reach in and pull up moments, days as clear and easy as plucking shiny apples from a bowl. I can recall the smell of his dish soap (lemon), the color of his bath mat (aqua marine), and dozens of conversations we had about life, about books—*I would not, could not, become a fan of Vonnegut*, I told him, which sounded so much like Dr. Seuss that he replied—*Would you, could you, on a train?* I recall the timbre of his voice, the soft lilt of his accent, especially when close to my ear. I recall the first time I heard him say, "Dude's paralytic" (drunk) as he looked down from his kitchen window at a man on the sidewalk doing a slow search for his balance between the street sign and the bike rack. I recall a particular shirt Seth wore (coffee-colored, short-sleeved with bone-white buttons) in the bookstore on a day when he told a group of twelve-year-old boys to quit acting the maggot (fooling around), and I could recall, too, that it was raining outside, a light Portland mist, the daylight already vanished by four o'clock in the afternoon when Seth smiled his lopsided smile near the paperback stand as he turned to put another log on the fire. Ironically, I could recall the many times he'd said, "Your only man," as in the thing one can most rely on, the thing most appropriate to one's need. "If you want to get around town, a bike's your only man," he'd said, unloading his panniers of the chocolate chip cookies he gave away on a white saucer near the register. "If you're looking for melancholy," he'd told me, rolling a mint inside his cheek as he rested in the faded purple armchair near the Mystery aisle, "then *What We Talk about When We Talk about Love* is your only man."

"I love you," he'd said, breathless in my ear.

Goose bumps rise on my skin as if I'm hearing it still.

The woman who took over the old house that used to be Reilly's Books— where wedding cakes now bake on one side and wedding dresses are sold on the other—told me that Seth married a woman named Julia in Minneapolis, where they had two daughters and together opened another Reilly's Books. Reilly's II. I recall the exact moment I heard this, the crisp sunny morning, the dry sidewalk, the cold feeling in my chest as I wandered away.

By contrast, my years with Jonathon have been like one long predictable day of breakfast (cereal and yogurt and one-and-a-half cups of coffee), followed by work (mine—*primal, sultry, hot, moist*. His—well, who knew a thing about that?) followed by dinner (pasta or chicken, a burger every now and again) followed by the weekend when the lawn needs mowing (summer) or the gutters need cleaning (fall), and then maybe there's something good on TV.

And yet, I can't forget the months after my mother died when Jonathon couldn't have been more caring, more sympathetic to my constant tears and distraction. And the way he cried the moment he laid eyes on Oliver. He used to race me to the crib when Oliver woke, never hesitating to change a diaper or give him his bath. When Oliver was four, he had a series of imaginary friends, including a white dog named Poopsie. Oliver had insisted that Jonathon put him in the back of the car when he drove him to preschool. Once there, Jonathon had to open the hatchback, take the dog out, and leave him tied up outside the door where he waited all morning for Oliver. When Jonathon arrived at noon he had to untie Poopsie and let him back into the car. The pediatrician had told us that imaginary friends were a sign of intelligence and imagination, and Jonathon was happy to play along. When he once forgot to put Poopsie in the car, he didn't hesitate to turn the car around in the midst of Oliver's screams and kicks against the back of the seat, and return to the preschool, jump out, untie the invisible dog, open the hatchback, and coax him in. The dog needed convincing, Oliver had told Jonathon in so many words, because he was sad and mad that they'd left him behind.

I had stood in the kitchen while Jonathon told me this story, my eyes welling with tears of love and gratitude. In that moment I was so thankful I'd cut things off with Seth. I thought I was the luckiest woman in the world.

"I love you," Jonathon had said the night before we left for Mexico, and I'm beginning to think, even now, even after knowing what I know of Benny and Isabel, even when it doesn't make a bit of sense, that some part of him actually meant it.

Above me, long-legged monkeys croak and bark in the trees as if signaling one another that I'm still there on the ground. The jungle is beginning to take on new sounds as if preparing for nightfall. Clicking, squawking, and every now and then a long, haunting squall like a peacock. Benicio never mentioned peacocks.

The wait drags on as the heat blossoms. How much longer can I stay awake? I'm worn to the point of delirium. How much codeine is too much? I've taken plenty, and it seems to be toying with my mind and my emotions. I'm high, though not so high that I'm unaware of it. Still, with every passing minute it becomes easier to convince myself that Benicio has no intention of coming back. He's kind enough to care what happens to me but realistic enough to think of me as the thing I truly am. Dead weight. A thorn in his side. An albatross around his neck. Too many adages to count. I'm all those and a murderer, too.

I flip the phone open and check for coverage. None. The battery is dangerously low. I turn it off. I need to get out of here and call Oliver. Maybe even Jonathon. What would he say to me? I love you? It sounded like the truth. Doubt creeps like vines, twisting, strangling the thoughts I want to have, giving voice to the ones I try pushing away. What if he's actually a victim in all of this just like me? What if Benny is the result of a one-night stand? A mistake he was trying to fix. I should have run back to the condo first thing. He's probably pacing the floor with Oliver, the two of them worried sick, police searching for me everywhere. For all I know the State Department is involved. The cable news networks have been running my story for days. People all over the world are going to let out a sigh of relief when I stumble out of the jungle alive. It'll be the miracle they're all praying for. Why have I so easily put my trust in Benicio?

"Once we get into town we'll get a room at a villa called Casa Romero on the edge of Mismaloya," Benicio had said just before he left. "You'll be wearing Isabel's jeans to cover your leg, I'll wear sunglasses and a hat. We pay cash upfront. Believe me, they won't ask any questions."

"I hear hiding in plain sight didn't work out so well." The words had slipped through my lips before I could stop them.

"Live and learn," he said, and jetted across to the water's edge where he tied a large white garbage bag with a red tie onto a branch sticking out across the water. It's still there, flopping in the breeze, signaling him that I'm waiting.

Before he ran off he knelt down close and said, "You'll be fine. But just in case, I mean, it's not going to happen, but if we somehow get separated…" He reached into his pocket and pulled out the lump of cash he'd taken from the drawer. The hundred dollar bills. He handed me what looked like half. Then he told me he'd take care of everything. "I'll be back," he said, in a way that mocked the mocking of Arnold Schwarzenegger. I had smiled but nothing seemed funny. By the time he was walking away, even as he turned and waved, my mind was already filling with the possibility that he had no intention of ever seeing me again.

If I have a shred of sense I'll get up right now and follow the river back down the way I came. But I'm high on painkillers. Is this really the time to be making that kind of decision?

Yes. Maybe. Doing something seems better than doing nothing. I stand, light-headed in the heat, dizzy in my codeine haze. White sparkles at the corners of my eyes take a moment to clear. I hobble back to the river and soak my leg in the space Benicio fixed for me. Small lizards dart in and out of the large rocks on the bank. I close my eyes and listen to the rushing water, feeling the jungle as if it's a living, breathing thing, something that could choose to leave me alone or eat me alive.

My eyes are still closed when I feel the prickly sensation of being watched. At first I refuse to give into it. But the tingling grows into a burn. Where's my gun? In my daze I left both guns by the tree.

My eyes spring open to find a four-foot iguana staring at me from a rock a few feet away.

I yank my leg from the water and scoot sideways into the dirt. It's like staring into the face of a dinosaur. Scales and spikes, long, ancient-looking claws. The creature flicks his tongue as if tasting me on the air. Is this one of the poisonous iguanas Benicio told me about? After all this I'm going to be eaten alive.

I'm too vulnerable down on the ground like that. I look for a stick, anything to hold in my hand, but there's nothing but dirt and boulders the size of chairs. He flicks his tongue, takes a step forward, and then freezes.

Am I supposed to make myself look large the way one does with cougars and bears? Or stay small and nonthreatening? I rise, slowly, preparing to run. I step backwards to see what it will do. Nothing happens. I step once, then again, taming the jerky movements caused by codeine, fear, and pain.

I can't even stand the sight of a spider on the ceiling. A raccoon once burrowed its way into the attic and I nearly jumped out of my skin when it scratched the insulation.

"Nice iguana," I whisper, now slightly farther away. "Good boy."

I continue to slog backward, the iguana to the right of me, a dead man's grave to the left. I finally reach the safety of the tree, and it appears that the creature has no other intention than to sun itself on a rock.

I sit down near my gun and let go of the breath I didn't realize I was holding. I remove the sloppy bandage on my leg and without hesitating pour the rubbing alcohol onto the wound. It sizzles like white fish on a grill. The pain is losing its hold on me. I think again of giving birth to Oliver, how badly it hurt, the shock causing me to scream with every contraction, and yet by the end when it should have been worse, when I was so exhausted I could no longer speak, I'd come to accept it for what it was. Another wave of pain, another push, and it would soon be over.

One way or another, this will soon be over, too. I rewrap the wound, using the last of the gauze. I tie the final knot, and that's when I look up to see the iguana hissing in my face.

I knock the safety off the gun, cock the hammer, and pull the trigger.

The next thing I know it's raining sticky rags of green and red and brown. Chunks land in my hair and on my face, across my arms and legs. A smell quickly follows, vinegary, sickening. I have no idea if it's coming from the strewn iguana or the bad taste in the back of my throat.

I scream. Loud and for as long as I can. When I run out of air, I do it again. Scream until my lungs burn. I pass over into a place without reason. I don't care about my leg. I don't care about the gunshot ringing in the jungle. I don't care if someone hears it and comes to find me. I don't give a goddamn if Benicio hears the gun, hears my screams, and thinks someone shot me. I'm getting the hell out of this jungle before I pull the trigger on myself.

19

I can't remember the last time I felt this kind of fatigue. There's a physical weight to it, a cloak made of iron around my shoulders, and I can't shake it off. Still, I trudge down the path along the river, eyelids bobbing, my mind caught in a state between slumber and daydream. My feet continue to move as though I'm on a death march. Move or be shot.

It isn't until I'm well underway that I remember Benicio has my passport in his pocket. I stop in my tracks. My eyes fling open. This is turning out to be a big mistake. I haven't quite thought the whole thing through, and now I'm already too far down the mountain to turn around and find our spot before dark, if I can find it at all.

It took us nearly two hours, maybe a little more, to reach the place where we stopped. That's going uphill, which is harder, especially with my leg. Going downhill should take no more than an hour. That's the good news. The bad news is it'll be dark by the time I reach the house on a desolate road, and I have no idea which way to go from there. How am I supposed to get past the house and down the rest of the mountain without being seen?

How far down the mountain is it past the house before I reach the city? It's looking increasingly like I'll spend the night in the jungle after all.

I keep to the river, hoping to find the path to Mismaloya. My neck is sore from turning to search for Benicio. I can't rid myself of the foul smell from the iguana. I'd jumped in the river and rinsed the creature's flesh from my skin and hair, and then changed into Isabel's jeans and shirt, and yet the odor persists. It coats the lining of my nose. I can feel pieces of iguana in my hair, but when I reach up I can't find them in the mass of tangles.

I keep on. By dusk I hear the echoes of civilization. A car horn, siren, the rumble of a large truck. Tinny, distant, perhaps miles away.

Wait by the river just after dusk, Benicio said. If he's coming, it will be any time now.

I rest with my back to a tree, staring at the hypnotic flow of the river, its breeze a welcome relief from the heat. Exhaustion wrestles me to the ground. My eyes sting with salt and fatigue. I close them for a second, allowing myself to float beneath Benicio's hands. Just a second. Just one more second of this.

I wake to blindness. So complete is the dark. A chorus of crickets, cicadas, and frogs pierce the night. More insects have feasted on my skin. I fight against a knot in my neck. Whatever time it is, dusk has long since come and gone.

A rustling through the trees behind me. Voices. This is what woke me. Then movement caught by a light. I feel around the ground for the gun. I click the safety off and hold it near my face. A flash of white in a cluster of leaves. A woman's face? It's gone before I can see.

Twigs snap. A weak moon slides from behind a cloud. In the dim light it's impossible to see through the thicket of trees.

Then comes the light again, a giant flashlight bringing a man and woman into focus as they work their way through brush. Beams of light swing like spotlights through the dark. They plod slowly, examining the ground. I can see now that they're dressed like ancient explorers in khaki pants and vests. What are they looking for? No more than fifty feet away. A woman with a blonde pony-tail. A man who doesn't appear to have much, if any hair at all. They speak in whispers. Spanish? English?

I hold my breath and drive all my energy into my ears. The couple is headed straight for me.

The woman tilts her head back and laughs at something the man says. They seem so normal. The light swings across their white socks and hiking boots. Backpacks, thick wristwatches. The woman has what looks like a phone clipped to her belt. She can call someone. This might be my only chance.

Then the man stops, and the woman's flashlight glints off something on his belt. A gun?

My pulse races.

The couple appears completely unaware of my presence. They edge their way along the path, combing the ground with their flashlights. I draw my body in, making myself smaller near the bottom of the tree where the trunk widens out.

The woman stops abruptly and points to the ground. The man leans over to inspect something while the woman scans the dark with her light, a hand on her hip. They crouch toward something, nodding, whispering.

I pray them into being some kind of scientists in search of rare, nocturnal animals. But I know. Blood pounds my ears. I know what it is they've found.

Their beams of light come to a point on the bloody gauze in the man's hand. The piece Benicio half-buried with his shoe.

Their heads shoot up and turn side to side, clearly searching for the owner of that gauze. The woman takes several steps with a hand on her phone. The man with his hand on what I now know for certain is a gun.

"Celia?" the woman calls out. "Where are you?" They're Americans.

"Celia!" the man echoes. "Say something if you can hear us!"

My heart pounds blood into the sore spot I hit when I fainted. I can't afford to make the wrong decision. What if they're here to help? What if the police have already arrested everyone at the house and a search team has been sent to find me?

I picture Jonathon at the kitchen table with his laptop. The smile, the frown. Truth. Lies. I don't even know who my own husband is, let alone perfect strangers. I think of Benicio taking off with my passport. Was that an oversight? How could he think to give me money and a phone but not my passport? My judgment is rubbery. I try but can't seem to grasp it.

They call to me repeatedly. Zippers open on their backpacks. They're just far enough away that all I can hear are the undertones of conversation.

"Celia! Can you hear us?" the woman yells.

I remain huddled behind the tree. I don't dare make a move. I'm being held captive all over again, and it takes everything I have to keep my wits about me, to not jump up and scream and shoot and run. Wait, wait, wait becomes my mantra. My whole body is shaking again. The sting and itch of insect bites intensifies.

Backpacks rustle, a flurry of words exchange, but I still can't make out what's said. I may have damaged my hearing when the gun went off near my ear.

The moonlight is now filtered by a cloud. These two must have planned to camp out here. There's no way they'd they be going up the mountain at this hour unless they planned to spend the night. Maybe they're meeting someone up the hill.

When they call my name again I know instinctively that they're not there to save me. Leon's people sent them when Roberto never returned. Why else would they come out in the night like this? Real rescuers only search by day. Isn't that what the six o'clock news always reports? The search is called off for the night and will resume first thing in the morning.

A clanging upriver startles me. Plastic pounding rock. The couple's flashlights cut swaths of light through the trees.

They stomp right past me to the river's edge.

I crawl to the other side of the tree. I'm shaking so badly I'm afraid I might accidentally fire the gun.

More clanging against the rocks. Beams of light swing faster.

Then a loud clatter, voices yelling, choking, words muffled as if stuffed down a throat, others coming out strangled and thrown, nothing making sense.

I can't see anything.

"No!" The voice is Benicio's traveling downriver on the wind. "Stop!" Then comes a terrifying, savage scream.

I draw my wrist to my mouth, stifle the cry down my throat. I choke back the sounds gathering there, but they escape in strangled gasps and groans.

"Celia!" he begs.

All I can think of is Oliver. I can't move. I can't take even the smallest chance that these people might do me harm.

"Celia!"

Hot tears stream down my cheeks.

I breathe deeply through my nose and hold the gun near my face, ready, expecting at any moment that they'll find me because how can they not feel me there? My whole body is bursting with emotion, a beacon pulsing through the trees.

Then silence. Crickets and frogs. The river gushing past.

I peek around the tree but see nothing. The gun trembles against my cheek. I could shoot into the dark and hope for the best. But I might shoot Benicio or miss everyone, and their lights will be on me, blinding me, guns firing within seconds.

Moonlight slowly returns, revealing shapes at the river. The flashlights lie on the ground now, catching the movement of bustling legs, a yellow raft, an oar on a rock, a torn garbage bag, scattered food, and finally a listless leg, the canted sole of a shoe. After a moment the foot slides across the dirt, stops, then slides again. Benicio is being dragged away as if by a creature into the dark.

PART TWO

20

I've slept in front of the air-conditioner for two days, my body sleepwalking at intervals to retrieve a glass of water and then return me to the bed. I had every intention of calling Oliver the minute I got to Mismaloya, but the cell phone died, and by the time I reached a shop with a cord to charge it, grabbed a few supplies at the corner Oxxo Mart, and checked into Casa Romero, it was all I could do to stumble onto the bed and plug the phone in and catch my breath. The last thing I remember is closing my eyes to try to think straight, to choose my words carefully. I didn't want to frighten Oliver. I didn't want to give anything away.

Now, here I am, waking to a crack of early blue light slanting through the drapes. My mouth is tacky, my tongue pasted to the roof. I blink into focus the spare, quiet space, the white stucco walls and simple kitchenette. Fruit stacked in a bowl on the counter. I don't know if it's real or plastic. I barely remember coming into this room.

I rise from the bed and realize how weak I am, my movements slow and light as if my arms are filled with air. My head is the only part of me with any weight, a bowling ball balancing on my neck. I turn the television on CNN to find out what time it is, what day it is. Six o'clock in the morning. A week since I first arrived in Mexico.

My room is on the second floor overlooking the Bay of Banderas. I stagger out to the balcony and stand in the bright morning sun. Blue water covers the earth as far as I can see. To the right and left green hills ascend into jungle.

A foul smell lifts with the breeze. It takes a second to realize it's coming from me. I'm filthy, covered in grime and sores and body odor. And somewhere still, the rotten, vinegary chunks of iguana.

I glance down at my leg. The wound has crusted over, its center a hard brown rock, the rim made up of pink skin, pulling, and puckering as it tries to renew itself. There's something vulgar and carnal to its shape and color. I squeeze gently and a bubble of puss oozes free. I need to get back on the antibiotics. I'm surprised it isn't worse.

I close my eyes. White stars float through my vision. I need to eat.

I step inside, relieved to find the fruit is real. Bananas, apples, mangoes. My hands tremble as I peel a banana and lift it to my mouth. It's too tacky to slide down my parched throat. I choke. I get a glass of water from the water cooler. *Agua!* floats through my mind. Roberto. The gaping black hole in his neck. The phone.

I force the water down, then the rest of the banana. I locate the phone on the floor, plugged into a socket between the bed and nightstand, flashing with fifteen new messages no one is ever going to hear.

I sit on the edge of the bed. My fingers tremble as I struggle to remember a number I've dialed several times a day for years.

After two rings a male voice picks up. "Hello?" the voice draws out as if confused by the strange number. Is it Oliver? How can I not know my own son?

"Who is this?" he asks.

"Oh my God," I say.

"Mom?"

"Yes, honey. Yes. Dear God. Yes. It's me."

"What's going on?"

"What's going on?" I look around the room, stifling my tears, searching for my voice, my mind. "Oliver." There doesn't seem to be anything else.

"What?"

"You're safe."

"Of course I'm safe. What's wrong with you? When are you coming home?"

Home? I shouldn't have called yet. Jonathon has told him something, but for the life of me I can't think of what it could be. After all I've been trying to sort through, all I've been forced to imagine, I seem to have exhausted my imagination.

"Oliver. Are you saying you're at home?"

"Um. Yeah. In my room getting ready for school. Why are you acting so weird?"

"Where is your father?"

"I think he's in the garage looking for another suitcase. What's going on? Did they put something in your Kool-Aid at that place?"

Jonathon is in the garage. Jonathon is home.

"What place?" I ask.

"Mom. You're not making any sense. The place you went. The retreat thing, whatever it's called."

Retreat thing.

"Oh," I say, not wanting to frighten or confuse him. He sounds so normal. So safe. "You know, they just, yes, maybe. I haven't been feeling quite myself since I got here."

"I thought that was the whole reason you went."

So that's it. Jonathon told him I ran off for some kind of spa retreat, a break for the mentally strained.

"Do you want to talk to Dad?"

One thing is clear. Oliver detests small talk. In fact, this is the longest conversation I've had with him in months without it turning into an argument. Oliver is still Oliver.

And Jonathon?

My whole body trembles with adrenaline. Think, think, think. I'm blundering around in the dark, ricocheting between elation that Oliver's safe, at *home* even, and horror and confusion over the rest.

I crawl under the blanket. "Yes," I say. "Why don't you put him on?"

"All right."

"But Oliver? Wait." I can hear him walking through the house, opening and closing doors, clunking down the stairs. "Did you get home all right? Is everything…good?"

"It's fine," he says, his pitch of sarcasm a welcome note. Everything is back to normal for him. I can't ask for more than that. "I don't know about Dad, though," he adds. "He's been pretty edgy since you've been gone."

"Has he?"

"Which, by the way, was kind of weird. You didn't even mention you were going. Or say good-bye." There's an unmistakable trace of hurt in his voice.

"I know, sweetheart. I'm sorry about that. It was kind of last-minute decision."

"Anyway, now he's going off on this business thing."

"What business thing?"

"You know. Work stuff."

"Oh, right. I forgot about that. When is he leaving?"

"Day after tomorrow. You'll see him before he leaves, right?"

"I don't think—what time did he mention I was getting in?"

"Jeez. You really did drink something funny. Don't you know when your own plane arrives?"

"Not, it's just, I mean, I don't have everything in front of me."

How can Jonathon tell him I'll be home before he leaves if he doesn't even know if I'm dead or alive? Is he planning on leaving Oliver alone when I don't show up?

"Here he is," Oliver says. "You can ask him yourself."

"No, Oliver! Wait!"

"Hello?"

The voice of my husband. The father of my child. The man who's nothing if not an endless well of reason. *I love you. Please pinpoint what it is and I will try to make it better.*

"Jonathon."

"Cee! I didn't think I'd be hearing from you so soon."

I can't speak.

"Did you call my phone first?" he says. "Sorry, I'm in the garage. I left it upstairs."

"What?"

Jonathon muffles the mouthpiece, but I can still hear. "I'll bring it right up to you when I'm done with it, Oliver," he says, apparently referring to the phone. It's all so normal. So ordinary that I have to look down at the crusty crater in my leg to remind myself of everything that's happened. I stare at the bites and scrapes and grime, and for a fleeting moment wonder if I've imagined it all. Maybe I fell and got a concussion, hurt my leg in some other way, wandered off with amnesia, or simply went insane. The true crazies have no idea they're crazy.

"He's gone now." Jonathon's voice takes on a frantic whisper. "I didn't want to scare him. My God, Cee. It's so good to hear your voice!"

I don't say anything.

"Where are you?"

"I'm safe."

"Where? What happened?"

"Why aren't you out trying to find me?"

"I was! I am! Jesus. I've been half out of my mind. I brought Oliver home to keep him safe and I'm going back, that's what I'm doing out here in the garage. Getting a bigger suitcase. I'm coming back for you."

It almost makes sense.

"Where are you?" he asks.

And then I see Benny's murky green eyes innocently giving everything away.

"I'm safe," I repeat.

There's a long pause that ends with a sigh. "Celia," he says, as if I'm trying his patience. "It's not what you think. These people—"

"Has this all just been some kind of misunderstanding?" I ask.

"As a matter of fact, yes. I've made mistakes, but I had no idea—"

"How the hell did you get away?" I ask.

"Get away? What do you mean?"

"Why did they let you go?"

"Who?"

"I know all about the trouble you're in."

"Listen. I don't know what they told you, but—"

"I'm lucky to be alive."

"Whose phone are you calling from?"

"I was shot in the leg!"

"Don't exaggerate, Cee. No one was going to kill you."

In that moment it seems as if anything at all might fly out of my mouth. So many thoughts run through my head at once. A funnel cloud of ugly, complicated thoughts spin through my brain. Everything swirls upward into a finely tuned point, a bayonet sharp enough to skewer me, which is exactly how it feels in my chest.

"How about I lay out the *real* facts?" I say. "Your girlfriend tried to kill me. You're in a shitload of trouble with these people. You're using my life and possibly Oliver's to try and get out of it in ways I can't even begin to understand. You have another son. Benny. An entire secret life you've been living for who knows how long. Well, guess what? You're not the only one who can keep a secret. The last thing I'm going to tell you is where I am."

I clasp my crusted wound, feeling the thick layers of old blood, blood that has worked so hard to repair me, to keep me alive.

"There's no need to make this any more complicated than it already is," he says, casually, flippantly as if he's trying to match a tie to a suit.

"You pathetic son of a bitch," I say.

"Cee. You need to calm down. If I wasn't worried about your state of mind before we left for Mexico, I'm sure as hell worried about it now."

To this I have to laugh. And laugh. And laugh until my face streams with tears and I can barely speak. I don't care that it makes me seem unhinged. I'm finally sure just how solidly together I am.

"She's what, twenty years old, Jonathon? What were you thinking? You'd start over with a new family? Replace Oliver and me with two others half our age?"

"You don't know what you're talking about," he says, from his place of imagined superiority, but I'm already laughing again.

"You won't think this is so funny after the Feds find out what you've done," he says.

"What *I've* done?"

"Really, Celia. Stealing my keys and codes. How did you think you could get away with embezzling from my bank?"

I throw the blanket off and stomp out to the balcony. I grip the railing and steady myself. Another giant cog clicks into place. He's been embezzling from his own bank and is setting me up for the fall. A million tiny scenes flash through my mind. Times I was sure I left my computer open, only to find it closed. Certain I left it on the edge of the kitchen counter, only to find it next to the fruit bowl. Whatever he's doing he's been doing it through my laptop.

"Just tell me where you are," he says in his reasonable husband voice. "I didn't mean what I just said. I'm sorry. I've made some terrible mistakes. Just give me the chance to explain."

And then another cog grinds through the grit.

"This is why you asked me to stay," I say.

"Tell me where you are."

"You've been stealing from your own bank for years, haven't you?"

"Cee. Please. We can fix all of this if you just tell me where you are."

"If I had filed for divorce, all of our finances would have been combed through by lawyers. They would have seen everything."

"Listen to me!"

"It's all been closing in on you, hasn't it? And your solution is to pin this on me." I have to laugh. "Who is going to believe that I knew something about embezzlement?"

"This is giving me a fucking headache."

"Are you so greedy, so evil, that you'd do this to your own wife, your own *son*?"

"I haven't *done* anything. Stop rambling. All these years I've taken care of you. From the moment you walked into the bank all torn up about your mother."

The mention of my mother stops me cold. My vision spins. I'm afraid I'm going to be sick. "I have no idea who the hell you even are," I manage to say.

"You're not exactly the woman I married either. How many men have you had since our vows?"

"How many children have *you* had?"

He's silent for so long that for a second I thinks he's hung up.

"He's dead, you know," Jonathon says.

"Who?"

"Benicio."

I dig my fingers into my thigh. It's just another one of his lies. I play along. "What are you talking about?"

"You know exactly what I'm talking about."

"You're a liar," I say. "You're sick, Jonathon. I had no idea just how sick you were. I didn't see it at all. You had me so convinced—"

"He was just using you. You didn't think he meant all those things he said, did you?"

I need air.

"I promised to get him back into the States if he helped me. He was in love with some woman in L.A. Didn't he tell you? He was in love with Hollywood."

"You're so, so sick."

"Listen. I need to give Oliver his phone back. You know how he is."

"What do you want from me!" I scream.

"Why don't you tell me where you are; then I can show you myself what it is that I want?" His tone changes completely. The menacing smile is coming through the phone.

"You know, Oliver got by just fine without you this week," he continues. "In fact, he ended up having a great time by the pool. But there's no telling what could happen to a boy over time without his mother."

Air squeezes from my lungs. Rage detonates my skull.

I steady my breath.

"I want you to listen to me very carefully," he says, his voice more menacing than ever. "You're distraught. After everything you've done you're calling now to tell us that you're sorry. We don't deserve what you've done to us. Your life isn't worth living after all the mistakes you've made. Soon after this phone call you're going to be found with a bullet in your brain. Or perhaps hanging from the curtain rod in some hotel room. A suicide. No doubt in anyone's mind."

This madman has my son. My worst fear has come true. Oliver has been taken after all.

21

My mind shifts into high gear, steering me toward my own survival. If anything happens to me there'll be no one to save Oliver.

I wash my clothes in the sink and hang them to dry on the balcony. I keep a gun near me at all times. I scrub my skin raw in the shower. The last of the insect bites softens and stings as I shampoo away the clumps of guts and dirt and oil from my hair. Several tangles at the base of my neck are so severe the only way I'm going to get them out is to cut them loose. I shave my legs and armpits with a used disposable razor someone left in the medicine cabinet.

Michael Mahon told the truth at least once in his life, and I didn't believe him. Is this Jonathon's one time to tell the truth? Is he really capable of hurting Oliver? I don't want to believe it. I can't. He's full of lies and manipulation. I need time to figure out what to do next. But how does he know about the woman in L.A.? Is Benicio really working with him to get back in the States? Is he dead?

I briskly dry myself and loop the towel around my wet hair.

Roberto's phone rings in the other room. It occurs to me that cell phones have pings. I have no way of knowing how far Jonathon's connections go, and I'm not going to take a chance that somewhere someone is able to trace this phone.

I place the phone, still ringing, on the hard tiled floor and smash it to pieces with the butt of the gun. It's remarkably resilient. I want to shoot it.

I stand with a head rush and brace myself against the dresser. On top of the dresser is the money. Next to that, my passport.

When I'd finally stood from behind the tree in the jungle, it was the first sign of morning. I almost didn't look back. I took several steps down the path before I could bring myself to look upriver at the scatter of things along the bank. A ring of dank monkeys sifted through the debris, fighting over and devouring the food from the kiosk. I pulled the gun out. The couple seemed to have left everything behind. Including the raft. They must have been in a hurry to get out of there with Benicio. I couldn't imagine where they'd gone or how they'd taken him away.

I lifted my arms and growled at the monkeys, hoping I wouldn't have to shoot. The monkeys scattered, and I sifted through the garbage with my foot, unsure of what I was looking for. Something personal. Some sign Benicio had left behind that would reveal everything to me. What I found when I nudged a torn box of crackers was my passport.

Now I stare at the dusty blue booklet on the dresser, the golden eagle rising up, fierce, in control, a superpower I'm somehow a part of but in a way that's so abstract as not to be real. It should be my ticket out of here. But it could also be the thing that gets me killed, or in the very least, imprisoned. What will happen if I try to reenter the States? Am I already listed as *wanted* in their database?

I have two thousand dollars. If Benicio's been using me he sure has a funny way of showing it. He's risked so much. Right up to the last second, calling out my name, trying to save me, trying to save himself. Could he have faked what I saw in his eyes when we made love? And that feeling radiating from deep inside him? *I had a couple of bit parts in movies you've probably never heard of.* He's an actor. But it's not as if he's won an Oscar.

I'm startled by a knock at the door.

I'm naked with a towel on my head. I grab the gun from the dresser.

"Miss Donnelly?" a woman calls out.

I don't answer.

"Are you all right in there? I haven't seen you since you checked in."

"Just fine!" I call.

"I have your breakfast here," the woman who might be coming to kill me says. "I brought some yesterday but you didn't answer. I thought I'd try again."

"Just a sec. I'll be right there."

"Should I just leave it at the door?" she asks.

I peek through the corner of a small window at the edge of the kitchenette. I vaguely remember the young Canadian woman who checked me in at the reception. She's now standing outside my door with a tray, glancing to the side with a look of boredom.

I'd planned to use a fake name but she insisted on seeing my ID. It's a wonder she let me check in at all considering the shape I was in.

I scramble into my damp shorts and blouse. I can't remember much of what I said to her.

"I can leave it here if you like," she says.

I place the gun in the back of my shorts, rewrap the towel on my head, and swing open the door. The woman reminds me of Oliver's girlfriend, Maggie, what she'll look like in fifteen years. The red in her hair is slightly faded; laugh lines have begun around her mouth. Still pretty. Maybe more so with the years. What's this woman's name? All that comes to mind is her insistence that I write down the number on my passport.

"Thank you," I say, taking the tray. "What did you say your name was?"

"Willow."

"Willow?"

"Hippie parents. I used to hate it, but it's grown on me as I've gotten older."

"No, it's lovely."

"You're looking much better," Willow says.

As skeptical as I feel, I'm still taken by the warm openness in her face and voice. A gentleness in the faint lines of her mouth. Her eyes are big green almonds.

"I was quite a mess when I checked in. Sorry about that. I'm actually a very normal person caught in the middle of some very abnormal circumstances."

"That's what you said when you checked in."

"Did I?"

"You don't remember?"

"Not exactly."

Willow glances down at my leg. The long, hot shower has caused the scab to puff into a mountain of marshmallowy puss. A crater of white, surrounding what looks like a shiny red leech. My whole leg is blotched with bruises, my arms covered in scratches and bites.

"Listen, Willow. Do you have a second?"

She meets my eyes. "Is there something you need?"

We're still standing in the doorway. I glance right and left at the stairway going down on either side of the villa, an antebellum entryway with coconut palms and a trickling fountain at the center. It's seen better days. The iron rails given to rust, the blue-and-white enamel-tiled steps chipped along the edges. The air is quiet. I lower my voice anyway. I'd invite her in if not for the gun and money on the dresser.

"How many rooms are there?" I ask.

She eyes me with a look of suspicion. "Five. Two on each floor and then the penthouse upstairs."

"Are they all full?"

"Usually." She sighs and shifts her weight, and then it's as if she's made a conscious decision to be friendlier. "But not these days. Things have been kind of slow with the economy and everything."

I'm only half listening. "I need a favor."

She glances at my leg again. "OK?"

"I'll be honest with you. My marriage has fallen apart. I mean, fallen apart is an understatement. Things are kind of messy. Really, really messy."

She nods.

"My husband doesn't know where I am. I just need some time to figure things out."

She glances at my leg once more. "Did he do that to you?"

I cover my eyes and think that, in fact, Jonathon *has* done this to me.

"Yes," I say, dropping my hand. "And he's planning something even worse. That's why I had to get away. I'm sorry. I don't mean to drag you into this."

"Oh please. No need to apologize."

"I don't want to burden you with the details of my ridiculous life. I just need you to assure me that I can get some privacy here. If anyone comes looking for me or calling to see if I'm staying here, can you please, I don't mean to ask you to lie, but I just need some time to work through this."

"I understand. No, listen, mums the word. Your privacy is my priority."

This sounds both rehearsed and sincere.

"So if anyone, I mean, my husband has a lot of friends around, if anyone comes looking for me you'll be sure to say you never saw me, right?"

"OK." She seems to be considering how it'll all play out.

She glances again at the hole in my leg as if she can't control the impulse. I don't blame her.

"Thank you," I say. "This is serious. I wouldn't even say anything if it weren't."

Willow shifts uncomfortably. "Did you go to the police?"

I feel a wave of weakness. I can't hold this food beneath my nose much longer. "I heard they were corrupt."

She laughs. "Not all of them. But sure. I'd say enough to make a person leery."

"I honestly didn't think there was anything they could do. And besides, I didn't want them to know where I was staying, in case my husband knows someone who knows someone on the force."

"Right. Well."

"I'm sure you don't want a scene around here, scaring people off with business so slow to begin with."

"It's not a problem. We're pretty out of the way as it is. Not many people come here who don't know of this place already."

And that is the very thing that worries me. I found this place without any trouble because Benicio told me right where it was. If he knows, who else does?

22

Large round sunglasses, flip-flops, straw sun hat, bandages, peroxide, clunky hair clip, blue plastic wallet, Spanish–English phrase book, sweat shorts, two tank tops, and a simple yellow cotton purse. I place the items on the counter at the discount store. The clerk barely looks up as she rings everything through. She takes my dollars and hands back pesos in change.

Outside, I pile my hair inside the clip, slip on my sunglasses and floppy hat, and throw everything else into my new purse. Cars rumble past, music blaring through open windows—accordions and trumpets, a celebratory rhythm reminiscent of German oompah bands. The smell of cooked meat, of discarded mango rinds going bad in the sun, hangs in the streets. Flies are everywhere. Two blocks down I duck into an electronics store, which smells, oddly, of vanilla from the racks of the local product stacked at the entrance. I purchase a prepaid cell phone and leave.

After that I purchase an hour at the Internet café across the street. First thing I do is check my e-mail. There's at least a hundred messages—work, spam, reminders of events at Oliver's school, parents responding back and forth, back and forth again.

One from Pacific Savings and Trust. They send periodic e-mails inviting me to sign up to view my accounts online. I've never even bothered to bank on such a simple scale, and yet somehow Jonathon is trying to implicate me in an embezzling scheme.

I need to see what he's done, if anything, with my money. I click the message and follow the steps for each account, savings, checking, money market, the fund my mother left me in her will. After I enter a password the final step is to wait until I receive confirmation by e-mail. At that point I can view my accounts. But the last line informs me it can take up to twenty-four hours to confirm. Twenty-four hours before I can sign on.

I comb through more e-mails and something catches my eye. Several subject boxes have been highlighted, which means they've already been opened. They're e-mails about work and each has small arrows next to them. Someone has gone in and replied.

I open the first reply, supposedly sent by me:

Hey Jane,

It doesn't look like I'm going to be able to take these on. In fact I've been considering moving in another direction all together. Opening my own business, something I've been thinking about for a long time. Sorry for such short notice. I hope you find someone soon.

Best,

Celia

Not only is Jonathon erasing me from his life, he's trying to erase me from my own.

I click on the others and see the same thing. One even includes the line, *I've fallen into something far more lucrative and just couldn't resist.* It's dated the day we left. The morning I raced through the house trying to get ready with only minutes to spare because Jonathon, for reasons I hadn't understood at the time, shut the alarm off and let me sleep in. It was so he could get on my computer. There's no way to prove I didn't send those e-mails myself.

At this point nothing should come as a surprise. And yet every new piece feels like another bullet in the leg—excruciating. Impossible to believe.

I sit back and focus on the distance to help relieve the dizziness forming behind my eyes. Across the street a man in sunglasses stands waiting at a bus stop. He cranes his neck up the street as if looking for the bus. But then he turns and cranes his head the other way. For what? A woman pushes her baby in a stroller down the sidewalk. She walks slowly, stopping for long periods to gaze in the shop windows behind the man who nods when she finally strolls past. It's a small town. They probably know each other. I'm just paranoid. I glance around the café at all the people hunkered over their computers. Students and middle-aged couples, Americans, Mexicans, Europeans. Every one of them strikes me as off, as some kind of prop in an elaborate scheme.

I'm an idiot! I have to stay sharp to get through this, and I realize with a jolt that I've just screwed up in a major way. Jonathon has been going into my e-mail. How often, I don't know, but chances are good that he'll see the password I set up for my bank accounts. He'll know I'm trying to get through. If he's trying to point the finger at me for embezzling, and the Feds, as he calls them, are really looking for me, can't they trace me to this computer in Mismaloya?

I take a deep breath and scramble to open a new e-mail account with another provider. I send Jane a message telling her to disregard the others and to please respond only to this new address. I'll explain later. There isn't much I can do about the bank except hope I catch the e-mail confirmation before Jonathon does.

Then I write an e-mail to Oliver.

Sweetheart. Bear with me. Things are not what they seem. I'm not at a spa, but I'm somewhere safe for the time being. I need to know you're safe, too. Your father is involved in some very serious things. Potentially dangerous things, and I'm afraid he's going to get even more desperate to see them through. I don't want to say any more than that, so you'll just have to trust me. I want you to find somewhere to go for a few days until I can get back. Is there a place you can think of where he won't come looking for you?

I stop for a moment and wrack my brain. Where on earth can he go? I read back what I've written. It sounds like the rantings of a madwoman. He already thinks I'm at some spa trying to get my head straight.

I delete everything and start over.

Oliver, e-mail me immediately at this address only. I love you more than you'll ever know.

I hit Send, hoping the message has just enough emotion in it for Oliver to want to keep it to himself.

I chew my nails, at a loss for what to do next.

I realize how absurd it is that I don't even know Benicio's last name. I do a computer search for *Benicio-Comedy-Scene-Los Angeles*. Nothing pops up that applies. I try, *In The Company of Harold's Daughter* "cast members." Pages of results appear. None include the name Benicio. He said it was a small part. So small he isn't listed in the cast?

Someone scoots a chair across the tile floor, and the scraping causes me to let out an embarrassing shriek. Everyone turns.

I cup my hands like horse blinders around my eyes and face the computer again.

A clock in the corner of the screen shows ten minutes left before I'll have to pay again. I check my e-mail to see if the bank has sent a confirmation but there's nothing.

Then I check my new e-mail address. One new appears in the inbox. It's from Oliver.

Nice try, Cee, it reads.

I draw my hand back from the keyboard and cover my mouth. He's broken into Oliver's e-mail, too. I lean back in my chair, feeling shot through the heart. I've already killed a man and know in an instant how easily I could kill another. I grab my things and race out the door.

23

I lock the bolt on hotel room door behind me and spend the next half hour fingering my passport, fixating on the arrows clutched in the eagle's claws, feeling as if each one pierces my heart. I pace the balcony, deciding what to do next. I need to get inside Jonathon. Think like he thinks. What's he trying to accomplish? I sense he wants me on the run. He wants me out in the open where someone will see me. This is why he tried to scare me into thinking someone could find me in a hotel room. What will he do if I call his bluff and sit tight? There's no way for him to know how this past week has changed me. What will he do if I do nothing at all?

Story. I have to think of this in terms of story. I've read thousands of books in my lifetime, not to mention the ones I've edited. If there's one thing I understand about the way something works, it's story. How is this one going to unfold? How will it end? More importantly, what needs to happen for my own ending to find its way into Jonathon's twisted plot?

A tiny thread begins to reveal itself. If I can just follow it through, allow it to map a path through the maze, then I can find my way out to the other side. I check the time. Oliver is at school, and there's no way he'd leave the house without his phone.

I pull out the prepaid cell phone and block the number the way the storeowner showed me. I dial Oliver's number and his voice mail immediately picks up. Does he turn his phone off during class?

I'm having second thoughts. Maybe Jonathon did something to his phone after we talked, convincing Oliver it no longer works.

I dial the number one more time, and suddenly my boy is on the phone. I can hear the bustle of a high school hallway in the background.

"Oliver!"

"Mom! What's wrong?" he asks.

"Are you at school?"

"Yeah, but I was just about to leave. Dad just called and said there was an emergency and I had to come home."

This is why the voice mail picked up. He was on the phone with Jonathon.

"Oh God, Oliver. You need to trust me, sweetheart. Something terrible is happening."

"That's exactly what Dad said."

"What else did he say?"

"For one thing, he said if you called to please not listen to you."

My heart flips. My free hands wrings through the air. I have to think quickly, but all I want to do is reach through the phone and snatch him to safety.

"Are you really calling from Switzerland?" he asks.

"Switzerland?" I'm sweating in the hot sun of the balcony. "Jesus Christ, no, honey, I'm not in Switzerland!"

"Dad said you were."

"I'm sure your dad said a lot of things, Oliver, and they're all lies."

He pauses and I know he's deciding whom to believe. The next seconds are crucial.

"Where are you?" he asks.

"I'm still in Mexico. I can't come home just yet—"

"Why not?"

"Oliver. I was never at a spa. I was kidnapped."

"What?"

"It's a very long story. I got away. I'm all right now. All I can say is that your father had something to do with it. Money has something to do with it."

"This is messed up. You said that you were at a spa when I talked to you this morning. Somebody's lying to me."

"I was trying to protect you. I didn't know, I mean, *really know*, how much your father was involved until I got him on the phone. You just have to trust me. I wanted to make sure you were all right, Oliver. Please, please believe me."

I can hear the chatter of young voices and slamming lockers in the background.

"Oliver?"

Nothing.

"Oliver!"

"He's here, Mom. I can see him through the door. He's parked at the curb waiting for me."

"Shit. Can he see you?"

"I don't think so."

My mind spins faster than my words can keep up. "Listen to me. I'm begging you, Oliver. Go to the opposite side of the building and out the back doors. I want you to run to the Lebanese restaurant we always go to. There's that small alleyway alongside with the hair salon and those other shops in the courtyard. It shouldn't take you more than ten minutes to reach it. Wait there and I will call you right back."

I can hear him moving through the halls. The background noise fades in and out. Then the thud of a large door being released. He's outside.

"This is crazy, Mom. Dad said we had to go to Switzerland to bring you back."

"He lied to you, Oliver. He lied to me and probably everyone he knows about everything. There is no business trip. This was his plan all along."

"Where are you then? I mean, where in Mexico?"

I stop short. I don't trust my own son. "I'm some place safe. Don't worry about me. Just get yourself to that courtyard. Now!"

The next ten minutes are the longest of my life. I imagine Oliver running through the streets of Portland while Jonathon wanders the halls of the high school, smiling at the kids, stopping to ask if anyone has seen Oliver. He might start to get frantic, check in at the office. All of which will give Oliver plenty of time to get away.

Then I imagine Jonathon spotting Oliver across the street. Picking him up in the car, playing the picture of calm, the voice of reason, convincing Oliver that I've lost my mind.

Switzerland. What the hell is in Switzerland? He must have hidden money there. What is it about Swiss bank accounts? I can't remember, except that people open them for nefarious reasons. Anonymous. Wasn't that it? Accounts that can't be traced?

He's planning to take Oliver with him. Is it because he has no choice? Is he planning on leaving him there? Why didn't he go straight there from Mexico? Why did he bring those warm clothes to Mexico and then turn around and go back home? My escape must have thrown everything off. Had he planned to take Isabel and Benny with him? Was that another reason why Isabel was so angry with me?

Nine minutes have passed when I dial Oliver's number again. He answers by breathing heavily into the phone.

"Are you in the courtyard?"

"I just got here."

I still can't allow myself to trust him, and it hurts like hell. Jonathon could have brainwashed him. He could be sitting in the car with him this very moment for all I know.

"Walk into the salon and tell the receptionist I want to make an appointment," I say. "Hand her the phone."

"What? Why?"

"Just do it!"

"This is really messed up."

"You have to trust me, Oliver."

After a moment of rustling a woman comes on the line asking what day will work best for me.

"You know what," I say. "I just realized my schedule is really crazy right now. Let me call you right back."

"Hello?" Oliver says, back on the phone and clearly annoyed.

"How much money do you have?" I ask.

"On me?"

"Yes."

"I don't know. Thirty bucks, maybe. Why?"

"How much do you have in your savings account?"

It crosses my mind that maybe Jonathon has taken that, too.

"Last time I looked at the statement it said about eight hundred. Why?"

Thank God, at least in this respect, that he takes after his father and actually pays attention to his statements.

I struggle to think fast. Where can he go? Who will take him in? There's only one person, only one place I can think of. And it's absolutely absurd.

"Listen to me very closely, Oliver. You cannot tell anyone where you're going. Not Maggie, not anyone. Least of all your father."

He's quiet. Too quiet.

"Oliver. Promise me! You have no idea what I've been through." I'm pleading now, trying not to cry.

"But why can't I tell Maggie? She's not going to tell—"

"I had a chunk taken out of my leg by a bullet that was shot by someone who works for your dad."

"What?"

I picture Roberto on the ground covered in blood. Tears lodge in my throat. "I wish to God this wasn't the truth."

"Are you all right?"

"Yes, sweetheart. I *will* be. So long as you do what I'm asking."

"Jesus," he says, suddenly sounding like the scared child he is. "What am I supposed to do?" Fear is now palpable in his voice.

"First of all, I want you to stay calm. Take as much cash out of the ATM as you can. Then get on the Max train and take it to Union Station. Buy a ticket with confidence. Don't draw attention to yourself. Don't let anyone see a nervous teenager fumbling at the counter. They might call the police and send you home."

"But where am I going? I don't even have any clothes."

The image of him as a toddler flashes before my eyes. He's waving good-bye from the babysitter's arms. I wave back over my head as if dismissing him, and in truth some part of me was as I rushed away, the taste of toothpaste fresh in my mouth, my pulse pounding, pounding, pounding all the way to Reilly's Books.

"Mom? Can't I go home and get some things first?"

"There's no time."

"The Max is coming right now. I can hop on it and make it there and leave before he gets home."

"Oliver, no! Whatever you need I'll buy new for you."

"At least tell me where I'm going!"

"You're going to Minneapolis, sweetheart. Just hang tight. I'm going to meet you there."

24

I crack the door and scope the stairway. Empty and quiet, the only sound is birds calling to one another in a two-part chorus. A couple of tabby cats dash across the courtyard then duck behind a hibiscus bursting with bloodred blossoms. It's ten o'clock in the morning.

I slip out and head down the stairs. Small wheels creak on the landing above me. I glance up. A cleaning cart is parked outside the penthouse door. A maid appears. A Mexican woman in her twenties. She instantly locks eyes with me.

"*Hola*," she says.

"*Hola*," I answer, dropping my gaze.

"You need towels today?" she asks.

I've kept the *Do Not Disturb* sign on my door since arriving. "Yes. Thank you. Some sheets, too, if you don't mind." I think I might never get rid of the stench I've brought into the room. "You can just leave everything outside my door."

"OK, *señora*."

When I glance up again she's entering the penthouse.

I find Willow behind her desk in the office speaking Spanish on the phone. Her eyes narrow when she sees me. She holds a finger to her lips. She looks away and nods at something the caller is saying.

I study the shelves behind the desk. An assortment of DVDs and books, several copies of *Night of the Iguana*.

Willow speaks a minute longer, and then spins back around and hangs up the phone.

"You won't believe who that was," she says, getting up from the desk and twisting the blinds closed on the glass doors.

I'm prepared for the worst. "My husband?"

"The local police, if you even want to call them that. More like *minders*, really."

"What did they want?"

"You, as a matter of fact."

"Shit."

"Actually, they already sent a guy round this morning asking a few questions."

My stomach turns into a fist.

"What did you tell him?"

"I said I never heard of you."

I lower myself into a chair.

"Didn't he ask to see the registration forms for the guests?"

"As a matter of fact, he did. But after our little talk this morning I decided to throw yours away. Well, I actually just hid it in a drawer."

"And he believed you?"

"He didn't even look around upstairs. If he had he would have seen the *Do Not Disturb* sign on your door, a room that's supposed to be vacant. These guys just go through the motions more than anything, make it look as if they're working. Frankly I don't blame them. They don't get paid enough to actually do much."

"Somehow that doesn't make me feel any better."

"I have to say, though, this one seems to be doing a bit of a job anyway. That was him on the phone just now. Something new had come in."

"What?"

"He asked if a man had checked in by the name of Benicio Martin."

I must look like I'm about to collapse. *Martin* is his last name. Willow studies me. "Someone you know?"

"Yes. Maybe. I don't know." I push away the image of his body being dragged across the sand. The sound of his voice screaming my name. I want to cover my ears right there in the office.

"The cop wants me to call him if this guy shows up."

How did he get away? "Why? What does he want with him?"

"I was just trying to get him to tell me. He wouldn't say. Just someone of interest in the case of a wanted woman."

My head jerks up.

Willow eyes me. "Apparently you're wanted for something."

I drop my head into my hands. I can't stay much longer without getting caught.

I look her in the eye. "I didn't lie to you, Willow. My husband set this up. It's his way of finding me. Please. You have to believe me." I imagine Oliver shaking at the counter in the train station. If he doesn't get away, if anything happens to me, he'll be returned to Jonathon.

"I believe you," Willow says, almost too easily.

"You do?"

"Yes. Why shouldn't I?"

"Why should you?"

"The other thing my hippie parents gave me besides my hippie name was a sharp instinct for bullshit."

"Who's in the penthouse?"

"No one, why?"

"I just saw the maid cleaning it."

"She only comes three times a week. Someone checked out two days ago. It's not as if there's a mad rush of people checking in here. You're getting a little paranoid."

"I could have used some hippie parents myself."

"Then I'd be calling you Sparrow instead of Celia."

"You wouldn't be calling me anything because I wouldn't be here. I never would have married a sociopath. Sparrow would've seen through his lies."

She smiles and gives a knowing nod.

"I have another favor to ask. Two, actually."

"All right."

"You're awfully eager to help me."

"Is that a question?"

"No. My question is how long have you worked here?"

"I bought the place about five months ago. Why?"

This might explain why she doesn't recognize Benicio's name. He made it sound like he knew the owners.

"Never mind. It doesn't matter. Listen. If this Benicio guy comes looking for me, I need you to stall him."

"How?"

"I have no idea. Tell him you're short staffed and he'll have to come back or something. Lock the office and pretend to go somewhere for a minute or two. Just let me know he's here and I'll figure out what to do next."

"What's he look like?"

"Very handsome. Mexican. Broken nose."

Willow's eyebrows lift. "Is he your boyfriend?"

"Maybe. I don't know. And my husband didn't break his nose, if that's what you're thinking. His own cousin did."

"This is making my head spin."

"Imagine what it's done to mine."

"OK. What's the other favor?"

"Do you have a laptop I could borrow?"

"I only have the one I use here for the office."

There's no way I'm going back to the Internet café.

Willow taps her finger on her closed mouth. "I go to lunch at noon and close the office for two hours. I suppose you could use it then."

"You don't mind?"

"Not at all."

"Is the Internet wireless? Will it work in my room?"

Willow nods. "I'll give you the password."

"Thank you. Do you mind if I check one thing really quick right now?"

Willow gestures for me to have at it.

I check the train schedule. Oliver should have already boarded the train to Minneapolis/St. Paul. He won't arrive there, though, for thirty-six hours. Why would anyone take a train these days if it takes that long to get somewhere?

I search for the address and telephone number in Minneapolis. Clicking on the picture of the storefront gives my fingers a strange tingling sensation. I write the information down on a sticky note from the desk and stuff it in my pocket.

"That it?" Willow asks.

At the last second I glance at the DVDs behind the counter. "You wouldn't happen to have a copy of *In the Company of Harold's Daughter,* would you?

"The movie?" Willow looks confused.

"Yes. Long story."

"Well, if the story is anything like the one you've already told me then you more than deserve to have a laugh." She steps behind the desk and runs her finger along the spines of the DVDs. She pulls one out. "I love this movie. It's a classic," she says. "People actually steal it."

"I promise to bring it back."

"You have a pretty honest face, according to my hippie senses."

"Thank you," I say, but as I race back to my room I can't stop thinking of all the lies I've been telling myself for years.

25

I pull the sticky note from my pocket. There's no point in rehearsing what I'm going to say. It isn't possible after all these years to come up with a right way to say something so preposterous.

I stare out at the ocean, asking myself if I were to boil down everything in my life, what would be the one thing I'd hope to wring out of it? The phone starts ringing before I can answer.

"Reilly's Books," a woman says.

"Oh. Hi."

"Can I help you?"

"Yes, I was wondering, well, I was in last week and Seth was telling me about a book and then I left without writing it down, and so, is he there? Can I speak with him?"

"Of course. Can you hold?"

My foot thumps like a jackhammer on the balcony. Gulls swoop in and out over the water. On the beach below children hit each other with pails and laugh. Time slows.

"Seth here. What can I do for you?"

His voice buoys up like a life ring in my chest. My heart latches onto it immediately.

"You see," I say, "I always thought I would not, could not become a fan of Vonnegut."

26

"Where are you?"

"Somewhere in Washington State," Oliver says. "I feel like I'm being punked."

"Oh, Oliver."

"I keep thinking everyone around me is going to burst out laughing at how stupid I've been."

His voice fades in and out. Each time it pops through I flush with relief.

"That's exactly how I feel. Like any moment the cameramen are going to appear from behind the palm trees."

"When are you coming to meet me?" he asks.

"Just hang in there. I'll let you know as soon as I figure it out."

"Why can't I have your number? How am I supposed to call you?"

"For one thing, I can't stay on here for more than a few minutes at a time. I've only got a limited amount of minutes on this phone, and I don't know when I'll be able to buy more. Besides that, I'm pretty sure your father can trace the number online through our account. Haven't you seen those commercials about parents checking to see who their kids are talking to? The numbers come up in a second."

"But who am I supposed to call if I need something?"

Good question. He has no one but me. "If you sit quietly on the train and feed yourself when you're hungry, you aren't going to need anyone or anything until you get there."

"Where am I going once I get there? You haven't even told me."

"I'll let you know soon. I promise."

Oliver sighs heavily into the phone. As afraid as I am for him, I feel comforted by the fact that Jonathon doesn't have a clue where he is, and with every passing moment Oliver is getting farther and farther away.

"Mom. Are you sure about all this? I mean, Dad said you were having a lot of trouble, like, in your head, and now I'm on a train headed to nowhere because you told me to. I mean, it sounds pretty far out there, and—"

"There is absolutely nothing wrong with my head, Oliver." I feel the panic rising in my voice. I'm losing him. He could get off at any stop and go back. Proof. He needs proof.

"He keeps calling like every two minutes. I haven't answered yet but—"

"No! God no, Oliver. Whatever you do, don't answer."

How am I going to make him understand? My leg. The camera on Willow's laptop. "I know it sounds crazy. You have every right to question your father and me. Just do me this one favor. Stay on the train and I will e-mail a photo of my leg to your phone. It's gruesome, but it's proof."

"Uh…"

"I'll have a computer in about an hour to take the picture. I'm sorry, Oliver. I have to go now. I love you, sweetheart. Sit tight and everything is going to be fine."

I'm so used to Oliver hanging up without saying a word that I almost miss his mumbled, "Love you, too," right before I hit the button. I fall facedown onto the bed and laugh until I cry. So this is what it takes to win the love of a teenager.

I strip the dirty sheets from the bed and replace them with the clean ones the maid left by the door. I pop the DVD into the player and crawl under the covers with the remote. The breeze ripples the thin white drapes into the room like ghosts standing guard at the balcony. It may be hot outside, but the breeze feels cool and I'm still having trouble regulating my body temperature from all the adrenaline rushes, the constant shock, a cocktail of medications coursing through my veins.

I go straight to the film credits. A list of actors I've never heard of. Down to the grips and gaffers, and still no Benicio Martin. Maybe he goes by a different name. I go back and start again. This time a name catches my eye. Emily. Emily Sandstrom. Shopgirl in comic book store.

I pick up the breakfast tray with the food I didn't finish and place it across my lap. I take a deep breath and start the film from the beginning.

I turn the volume down so I can scrutinize every face. There are so many street scenes full of people in the background that I'm like Jonathon on his BlackBerry, my fingers pecking away on the remote. Pause. Play. Pause. Play. Thirty minutes into the film and I haven't seen anyone who looks remotely like Benicio. Then the comic store appears on the screen.

I up the volume as a young woman (Harold's daughter?) walks in with a group of friends. They spend a few moments messing around in the aisles, making fart jokes and punching each other in the arm, and then the camera pans to the counter where the shopgirl informs them that the books in the store are actually for sale. The group of kids make another fart joke, and then the shop-girl turns to a guy stacking comics on a nearby shelf.

I hit Pause. I leap off the end of the bed and get close to the screen. I hit Resume.

"Good one," Benicio says sarcastically. *Good one.* The same way he said it when I asked if he was joking about being a comedian. I sit back on the bed, my body suddenly trembling at the sight of him. The scene moves forward with the group of kids leaving the store, and for a split second there's Benicio's back, his hands so familiar, his head shaking at shopgirl with an understanding. Emily, the woman Benicio nearly married, rolls her eyes.

I watch it again. The look between them is so familiar. It could be Seth and me in his bookstore on any given day, our secret world layered with jokes only the two of us understand.

Benicio is who he says he is. The film backs up his story. I scroll the closing credits one more time and search for anything resembling "shopguy." There it is. Shopgirl's assistant: Mateo Blanc. His stage name.

I shut the television off and walk onto the balcony with my phone. I think of Benicio working in the garden at the condo, of the life he left behind and how badly he must've wanted to return to it. *He was working for me in exchange for help getting back into the States. He was in love with some woman in L.A.*

How does Jonathon know this?

Emily doesn't really care about him, Benicio had said about the man Emily married. *At least that's what she says in her e-mails.*

27

Willow arrives with the laptop.

"Any news from anyone?" I ask. I hid the guns in the drawer of the bedside table before inviting her in.

"Nada."

I'm still shaken from the sound of Seth's voice, still reeling from the mixed emotions of seeing Benicio's face.

"I did see a weird story in the paper though," Willow says. "About a guy they found in the jungle a couple of days ago."

My heart hurls against my chest. "What guy?"

"It said he was in the hospital. At least at first he was."

It's not a body. It isn't Roberto. Treated in a hospital. "What was his name? What do you mean, *at first*?"

"Apparently the guy managed to slip out of the hospital by jumping through the window."

I lower myself to the edge of the bed. What's he made of, titanium? "Did you get his name?"

"They withheld it on purpose to protect his family or to notify them first, something like that."

I bite my lower lip.

"It's your friend, Benicio, isn't it? That's why the cop called here today. Because he escaped."

I breathe deeply and let it go. "There is still so much I haven't told you."

"Well?" She pushes her ears forward with the tips of her fingers.

I do it. I tell her everything. From Seth, fourteen years ago, to Jonathon and Benicio and the kidnapping and the scam Jonathon's trying to pin on me and poor Oliver on the train and something that has to do with Switzerland, and finally back to Benicio and the film and the woman in L.A. and me sitting there on the bed not having a clue what to do next.

Willow's mouth hangs open. "I'm sorry, but this is the most excitement I've ever had at this job. At any job."

We both laugh, and the tension, the strange shock of hearing and telling such a story, loses some of its weight.

"I was thinking of selling the place," Willow says. "Now I'm not so sure."

"Just don't sell it before I leave. I need you to help me get out of here."

Willow smiles. "What did you have in mind?"

"When did the paper say he escaped?"

"Yesterday, I think."

"He could have walked all night. He could show up here any second. Are you headed to lunch now?"

"I usually pick up something on my way home and then take a little siesta like everyone else."

"Is there a sign on your door showing when you'll be back?"

"A little clock set at two."

"Thank you for this." I pat the laptop and realize that Willow is the closest thing I've had to a friend in years.

"I'll pop in and pick it up when I get back."

After she's gone I take the laptop out onto the balcony and breathe in the moist salty air.

How can one person feel so many things at once? Doubt. Gratitude. Outrage. A steady drip of sorrow and love.

I remove the bandage and snap a photo of my leg. I throw in a couple more of my bruised and insect-bitten arms and e-mail them off. I think of taking one of my face but can't bear the thought of Oliver seeing the pain and fear in my eyes. This seems far worse than the gruesome hole in my leg.

A cruise ship sails in the distance. A tiny toy on the horizon but I know it's the size of a whole city, full of people, people having the time of their lives. What I wouldn't give to kick back in the sun and disappear inside a Joella Lundstrum novel, to have the luxury of lingering on beautiful phrases, losing myself in prose, to have everything that's once muddied transformed into something crystal clear.

My conversation with Seth replays in my mind. He paused at first, and then said, "Can you hold, please?"

"Seth? It's me."

"Yes, I think I put it aside. Let me check in the back."

Then he returned, his voice clearly shaken.

"Celia. Jaysus. Celia. My wife answered the phone. She was standing right there. I couldn't, Jaysus, I couldn't speak."

I hadn't thought the whole thing through. The last thing I wanted was for anyone else to be lied to.

"I didn't mean to cause any trouble."

"No apologies, please. It's been so long."

"Fourteen years."

"I can't believe it's you," he said in a voice filled with an excitement I didn't deserve.

There wasn't enough time for me to explain everything in detail. I simply stuck to the fact that Oliver was on his way there because Jonathon had done something awful and we needed to escape. We had nowhere else to go. This fact alone was humiliating enough. But there were so many other reasons for me to feel foolish. I apologized more than once. I didn't mention I was in Mexico. He listened carefully. If he thought I was crazy, if he was passing judgment on me I never sensed it. In the end he told me he was honored that I felt I could ask him such a thing. "Of course I'll look after him. Of course."

Then right before we hung up he said, "I don't blame you for doing what you did back then. You were a married woman with a family. I had no business doing what I was doing."

He was now a married man with a family of his own. Was this his way of saying nothing could happen between us again? Point taken.

"Do you regret the time we spent time together?" I asked, knowing I was crossing the line.

"No. Never. Not for a second."

I look across the ocean now, the sound of Seth's voice still humming in my ear. I may never know what Benicio's true intentions are. But what I do know is that it no longer matters. I know exactly what mine have been. And I don't have a single regret.

28

"That thing is sick, Mom." Sick meaning cool in the case of the hole in my leg.

"I'm glad it was sick enough to keep you on the train."

I explain where he needs to go and who will be there to take him in.

"I don't understand," he says. "Is he a friend of yours? I never heard you mention him before."

"He's someone I trust," I say. "Let's just leave it at that."

I explain how I hope to arrive not long after he does. I tell him to open a new e-mail account and write to me at my new e-mail address. Most of all he just needs to stay put. Wait it out. And of course, not tell a soul. "You didn't tell Maggie, did you?"

He doesn't answer.

"Oliver!"

"No."

My stomach hardens.

"Oliver, you didn't!"

"No. I said I didn't."

But long after I hang up the sensation lingers in my gut. It won't let me be.

I return to the computer, unsure what to do next. I type *Benicio Martin* into the search engine and rows of articles appear, everything from comedy shows as Mateo Blanc to the raid that led to his deportation. All of it is true. Everything he told me about himself is true. I hit "Images," and there he is smiling, his perfect nose, his face shaven and clean. I feel a pressure in my chest. It deepens when I see a photo of Benicio and Emily, his arm thrown around her shoulder, the two of them so beautiful together, dressed in black, their happiness palpable through the screen.

He loves a woman in L.A. He loves Hollywood.

I step away and tighten my hair inside the clip. I need to think. Ideas are competing inside my brain. How can I get through customs? How can I board an international flight without luggage? I'll have to get a suitcase. I'll need things to put inside. And the guns? I can throw them into the ocean. And then what? How will I protect myself from Jonathon once I'm back in the States?

I check my e-mail and see a message from the bank. It's the confirmation I've been waiting for. I plug in the passwords and log on. I brace myself for what I'm about to find.

What I'm not prepared to find is my checking account intact. My money is untouched. Fifteen hundred dollars and twenty-two cents, to be exact.

I check my money market. Ten thousand, plus. That's a lot of money. Why hasn't Jonathon taken it? It doesn't make sense. The only activity going in and out of this account in the last few months has been the automatic deposit from my checking, and a small amount of earned interest.

It doesn't make sense. He hasn't taken a dime.

"Goddamnit!" What the hell is he after?

I click on the portfolio my mother left behind. I know there won't be anything for Jonathon to bother with, and I'm right. More than right. Not even a dollar amount listed. No zero balance. Nothing. Just a series of numbers and codes. At the bottom of the page it reads, BALANCE UNAVAILABLE. There are no other options.

I'm about to leave well enough alone, assume that it's finally gone belly up, but something in the back of my mind tells me to slow down. My mother's voice. *Not so fast, Cee-Cee. Take another look.* I tap my pursed lips and let my mind wander. Maybe the lack of information on the account is due to the type of fund. Dividends originating from an investment account. I didn't pay much attention when I signed the paperwork from my mother's estate. That was years ago. All I remember is the lawyer saying that one of her investments had been virtually worthless, and yet my mother insisted everything she had be dumped into it and then put in my name. It came with preconditions, too. "Good thing it doesn't have much money in it," the lawyer had said, "because if you ever wanted to withdraw it, you'd have to go all the way to…"

Am I remembering this right? Did he really say Switzerland? I'll have to go all the way to Switzerland?

29

By the time Willow knocks on the door to retrieve her computer, I've been wringing my hands for an hour.

I swing the door back and pull her inside. "I need the fax number of your office."

"Whoa." She stumbles in. "OK. Hi there."

"I figured something out. At least I'm starting to figure it out."

"Can we sit down? Because it looks like your head is going to explode."

"It is. Listen," I say as I continue to stand. "I think this has all got something to do with an investment my mother left me in her will. It's from Switzerland. I'm sure that's what the lawyer said. I mean, he said it nineteen years ago, so I can't remember word for word, and of course I was pretty distraught at the time, my mother had just died—"

"I just had a nap. Can you start over?"

"This fund wasn't worth anything at the time, it hadn't been worth much of anything I don't think, for decades. The lawyer said that it came with odd preconditions and that it was too bad my mother insisted that all of her assets go into it because the shares had this terrible track record and even if it ever did amount to something I'd have to go to Switzerland to get it out!" I pace the room with my fists pressed against my clenched teeth.

"I'm not following you," Willow says. "If there's no money in it, then why is your husband after it?"

"I tried to check it online just now and nothing showed up except numbers, something that looked like codes. I don't know if there's money in it or not. It doesn't say what's in it. I'm just going on a feeling. He wants whatever it is, or maybe he just wants to use it for something else. Either way he can't get to it because of the conditions in the will, and that's why I need your fax machine."

"You're just going on a hunch?"

"I'm going on a vibe. A big vibe. A vibe as big as a wave crashing over my head."

Willow yawns and shakes her head. "Can't argue with a vibe." She agrees to run out and purchase another disposable phone with the cash I give her. "Let's just hope that for once business stays slow and no one notices the office is closed."

When Willow returns I immediately get the lawyer on the line, though it's now the lawyer's son, Marc Jacobson the second, who took over the business after his father passed away.

"How do I know you're who you say you are?" Jacobson says. "I can't just fax this stuff over without proof."

He isn't even trying to be helpful.

"Fine," I say. "I'll fax you my passport picture and Social Security number. Do you need anything else?"

"A signature. Something that has your signature beneath a written request."

"It's on its way. And do me a favor. Send the entire will. Every piece of information you have."

"We normally charge for this sort of thing."

"So send me a bill. I'll pay it the moment I get home."

"I could just charge it to your husband's bank account."

"Why would you do that?"

"It's just that I already have it. The one I used when I sent copies over to him."

"What copies?"

"Of the will. And the information about the trust."

"Why would you do that? Everything is in my name!"

"Um, no. Both of your names are here in my office. You gave him permission to have access, at least to the information."

"But my mother left everything to me. I wasn't even married when she died."

"All I can tell you is that his signatures are right next to yours."

"When was the last time he requested a copy?"

"I need your written signature before I can give you that information."

"You just gave me information without the signature."

"That's all I can give you over the phone."

"Fine. Fine! But make sure you include everything with the fax. Anything at all that pertains to my mother's will. I can't call back again."

Forty-five minutes later Willow arrives at my door with a stack of papers the size of a novella.

"I think he added some things just so he could charge you extra," Willow says.

I don't remember this much paperwork, though the truth is I barely remember anything about that day in the lawyer's office, and then later at the bank, moving through a fog, shaking Jonathon's hand, agreeing to have dinner with him. The whole thing took place as if in a dream.

"You're a gem," I say to Willow. "An absolute lifesaver."

"I can't wait to see what you find in there."

"By the way, any more phone calls from the police?"

"Nothing."

"Anything in the news about the guy who escaped from the hospital?"

"Benicio?" Willow teases.

"Yes. Benicio."

"I checked the local news. I didn't see anything but there may be more on the evening news so I'll check again." She gestures to the stack of papers in my hand. "Do you want me to come back after I get off work and help you go through all that? Bring you some dinner?"

"I would love that. Thank you."

I toss the pile onto the bed, thank her again, and lock the door. I don't even know where to begin.

I sit down and sift through the pages in the order they were sent. Legalese. I go back and start over. Slower. Like trolling through a river of mud. "Good God," I say out loud. How is anyone supposed to make sense of this?

Then the sight of my mother's loopy signature stabs me in the heart. It isn't sorrow I feel, it's anger. If she hadn't died, I wouldn't be in this mess.

There's a note from Jacobson apologizing for the fact that his father passed away before the file was fully completed. When he took over, the file had been overlooked. He's recovered several letters that were removed from a safety-deposit box but left forgotten in an attached file. He's enclosed copies of them in the fax as well. Again, he apologizes. It isn't like his office to make such mistakes, but surely I can understand what it's like in the aftermath of a parent's death. He also includes the dates when Jonathon made requests. There are two. The first, shortly after

Jonathon and I were married when I must have signed something giving him permission to the files. The second, several weeks ago, just before Jonathon suggested we take a vacation. I understand now that he was desperate to cover his debts. He started combing through anything he could think of, searching for a way out. He found a solution. That look on his face when we were heading out the door for Mexico was one hundred percent relief. He was drunk on his own cleverness, his own dumb luck. *Oopsy.* A small fortune has been right there the whole time, lying next to him for eighteen years. "I love you, Cee," he said with enough emotion for me to believe it. Maybe it wasn't a lie after all. I'm his ticket out. I'm going to save him. Oh how he loves me.

I sift through the papers until I come across what appears to be an investment fund. At the bottom of the last page is typed *See attached note.* It's a handwritten letter. I don't recognize the handwriting. It isn't my mother's. It looks as if a very old person wrote it using an ancient, abandoned style of cursive. On closer examination I see that there are actually two letters. One signed by Annaliese Hagen. The other, Sonja Hagen. Sonja was my mother's mother who died before I was born. I know very little about her. Annaliese would have been Sonja's mother, my great-grandmother.

I recall the few conversations I had with my mother about our ancestry. My mother was the first U.S.-born child in her family. She had no interest in the past and apparently neither did her own mother. According to my mother, all Sonja ever told her was that she herself had become an American; her husband, my grandfather, had lived and died an American; and my mother was American, too. There was no need to concern herself with the rest. The only thing my mother seemed sure of was the fact that women in the family have never had very good luck. Not in love, and not in business, which they seemed to take an interest in regardless.

I read the letter from Annaliese to Sonja.

Dear Sonja,

Let me start at the beginning, even as I've come to the end, even if you think you already know all there is to know. I promise you do not.

Growing up in Zürich I always dreamed of being a chemist. This, of course, is nothing new. Nor is the fact that my family saw this dream as little more than the fantasy of a foolish girl. My father insisted I become a teacher for grade school children. If a girl had any sort of intellectual promise this was what was allowed her in my day. She could teach boys to follow their dreams, while teaching girls to be girls, as if they couldn't figure out such a thing on their own.

I did what I was told. I never knew any woman to rise above teaching. I never knew any woman to even try. I was too young and naive to believe I could make a difference. But not a day has gone by in my life where I haven't felt the weight of that decision, the weight of such regret.

But what I've never told you is this: I came close to being recognized as a chemist when I invented a cold remedy together with a chemistry student, a young man I had known since we were children. We used a good portion of the money I earned from teaching for the research, and in two years' time the remedy was selling very well. It was obvious to everyone in town that I was a woman doing fine on her own. I was in no need of a husband, and this caused my family a great deal of stress, particularly my father who was embarrassed by me and who, in so many words, accused me of favoring women over men. The truth was I was financially better off than many of the men we knew. I was an unmarried woman with money in the bank. I didn't need a man, and for this they despised me. For this they believed I deserved to be punished.

One evening as I was leaving the Metzgerei, two men stopped me just outside. They shoved me back into the alleyway until I found myself in the lane where the Lautens left their trash. The men circled me like hungry hounds. They said it was time someone showed me what a woman was supposed to be doing. I could smell the liquor on their breath. I could hear shoppers the next lane over, and yet no one came when I screamed.

It pains me to share this part of my life with you, but to leave it out would be to lie, to pretend it never happened, to make as if it had no bearing on what came next.

My dear daughter. You know what they did to me. Afterwards, I stumbled out onto the street. Mothers saw me and clutched their children to their sides. Husbands hurried their wives in the opposite direction. I staggered home alone, my face bloodied and swollen, my dress torn and soiled. No one helped me to heal during the awful weeks that followed as I tried to come to terms with what those men had done to me. I became a disease others did not want to come near. The weeks of waiting to see if I might be with child were a torment. My own sister asked me where I found the will to live. But it wasn't my life I wanted to take. It was theirs. Why was I asked such a question while they walked the streets with their heads held high?

That was many, many years ago. It took time, but I moved past that day in both body and spirit. I did not give my life to those men. I did not let them take away my right to happiness. My right to love and pleasure. What they did was not my fault. And yet I admit that even after all these years I've never understood how two grown men could have done such a thing to an innocent young woman. Who knows what motivates the hearts of men? In this sense my father was right about me. I prefer the hearts of women.

I did not become pregnant then. Don't fear that one of these men turned out to be your father. But if my prospects of ever finding a husband before this happened were low, they were hopeless after that.

The exception was your father. I married my friend the chemist, Walter Hagen, or should I say, he married me, claiming to have loved me his whole life. In time I came to love him, too, even when he decided to take sole credit for our cold remedy and claimed to his colleagues that I had lied about my part in formulating it. The truth was he couldn't live with their chiding, nor could he live with the fact that I had never set foot in the science lab of a university and yet I knew what he knew. I devoured every science book I could get my hands on, including the ones he left lying around unread as he busied himself in the laboratory. I eavesdropped on conversations between him and his colleagues in the salon. I absorbed everything into the deepest parts of my being. And I forgave him for what he had done. I understood that he lived beneath the weight of the same establishment as me.

By the time you arrived, Hagen Pharmaceuticals was thriving. We lived better than anyone in our corner of town. I had few true friends outside of my own sisters and brothers, but my life, once you were in it, could not have been better. I was fascinated by your insatiable curiosity. You taught me the truth about the intellect. You were my scientific proof that we are all born with a strong, healthy dose of intellectual curiosity. Male, female, what does it matter? Your questions, your answers, were no different than those of your male cousins, though in some instances, I must confess, yours were far more complex than theirs.

Nearly ten years went by during which it seemed impossible that anything should ever go wrong. The townspeople had come to respect me, as our company employed so many of the families. They depended on us for virtually everything they had.

But of course, nothing truly lasts. People became mysteriously ill, and over time it was discovered that our cold remedy contained arsenic. How it got there I never knew. It was not part of the original formula your father and I had devised. Was he to blame? Or was it a mistake? I knew in my heart that he had put it there. Arsenic in small doses makes people feel very good, very alive, and they would no doubt come back for more of the remedy. It is when arsenic builds up over time that it becomes deadly. He knew this. I knew this. We were chemists after all. And he sold it anyway.

We lost nearly everything. The company would have gone bankrupt if not for the production of facial creams women were unwilling to go without. Even so, people in town spit on me. I hope you have no memory of this, as they did not spare me even as I held your hand on the street.

I can still feel the scowl of the tellers in the bank as I withdrew my monthly allotments. They liked to keep me waiting for hours under the pretense that there was a problem with the account. A problem that always seemed to resolve itself if I waited long enough. I was determined in my patience. I refused to let them win.

What I did relinquish was your father. For many reasons our marriage was beyond repair. Even so, I refused to relinquish my ownership in the company I had helped in good faith to start. I refused to let go of the shares. For the rest of my life those shares have remained nearly worthless, but they are priceless in principle, you understand.

In the end I was a chemist both in practice and in my heart. In the quiet of my own room I devised formulas never seen. But I devised them nonetheless. I was who I was regardless of what others tried to make of me.

It is in this spirit that I leave these shares to you under the condition that you will never give your husband control of them. And should there ever be healthy funds to withdraw from again, you must visit the bank personally to make a withdrawal, even though you live on the other side of the world where I myself have taken you. This inconvenience is small compared to what I have lived through to make such funds possible. It is important for all the sons and daughters of those who spit on me, for the children's children of the men who assaulted me, to see you walk in with your head held high, for it is they who have a legacy to be ashamed of. They will wait on you like servants, hand over to you what I hope will be more money than they will ever know in a lifetime, money that began with the hard work, the intellect of your mother, the chemist. You may remind them of this. You are my daughter. Never forget.

Your loving mother,
Annaliese Hagen

It feels as if a storm has blown in and set my hair on end. I rub my eyes and iron flat the goose bumps on my arms.

I need to get out of this room. Take a walk on the beach. Clear my head. But when I step out onto the balcony and peer over, the swimmers and sunbathers make my stomach flip. Everyone appears suspect in sunglasses and hats. Faces hidden behind clever disguises. Are they looking up at the seagulls and paragliders? Or are they looking at me?

I come back in and get a drink of water. I take a deep breath and return to the bed. My hands shake as I read the letter my grandmother Sonja wrote to my mother.

Dear Gilion,

Enclosed you will find a letter from my mother Annaliese written to me shortly before her death. I should have shown it to you long before now, but isn't that one of life's little tricks: to deliver clarity only when we reach death's door? It is in memory of her, of the grandmother you never knew and whom I regret not sharing with you, that I am writing this.

First things first. I invested more money in Hagen Pharmaceuticals years ago after receiving a letter as a shareholder informing me that the company's chemists had patented an innovative anesthesia they were planning to bring onto the market. I hid the letter and told your father nothing. At the time we married, women in this country had only been voting for twenty years. Merely a handful of elections to take part in, hardly enough to make a difference in the rule of law. In some ways it felt as if women had come such a long way; in others, it seemed they hadn't stepped away from the stove. In the eyes of the law my property belonged to my husband, but his property belonged to whomever he decided. Even my own body was considered his property. We fought about this and so many other points we could not agree on, and more than once he raised his hand to me to make his point. But there was one thing I had over him, and that was the Hagen shares left to me by my mother. Your father couldn't read German, and so I lied and told him the trust fund was nothing more than paperwork for an old house in the hills of Switzerland that had fallen into disrepair decades before on a small piece of useless land. He believed me. I was a bit of an actress, I must say.

But the Hagen investment. One of the chemists responsible for the development of the anesthesia was listed as Ulrike Tobler. A woman. If only my mother had lived to see the day! If you have read her letter, then you understand that for Ulrike Tobler alone I had to invest. The anesthesia was used for surgeries. Hagen Pharmaceuticals could barely keep up with the demand. They sent statements of the shares, which I claimed to your father were tax estimates of the land if we wanted to reclaim it. I told him it was best just to leave it alone and let the government take over and deal with it. It was one of the only times he told me I had a good head on my shoulders. As I said, I was quite an actress. I gave him a long spiel about Switzerland and their awful laws and high taxes. I threw away the statement with flair, only to retrieve it later from the trash and hide it with the others beneath the loose baseboard in the laundry room.

It is shameful to say, but World War II proved to be even more profitable. Where soldiers used to die en route to hospitals, many of the injured were now safely operated on not far from where they fell, and as a result had a greater chance of survival. Word traveled fast, even in wartime, and before long surgeons around the world were using the anesthesia. I became rich in secret while the husbands and sons of people I knew were dying at the hands of the Germans. I never wished such a thing on anyone, and was torn apart by my strange fortune.

They say history repeats itself. I believe this is true. By the time the war ended you were five years old, and I decided to leave your father, the same as my mother left mine, something that was still unheard of in those days. There was no one to talk to about this. No one who understood my tears and frustration. When I tried to speak with our family doctor, a man I had known for years and considered an intelligent, trustworthy friend, he told me what I needed was to have more children. Just one had not fulfilled my purpose. This, he said, was the root of my unhappiness. I got my divorce. Enough said about that.

You probably don't remember the trip we made to Zürich. But just as your grandmother had asked, I walked into the bank and withdrew enough money so that you and I could live comfortably for the rest of our lives. I told the young teller that my mother was Annaliese Hagen, founder of Hagen Pharmaceuticals. She was a chemist, I said, though he seemed to have no idea who I was talking about, or maybe he simply didn't care. The war had just ended. Everyone was focused on that.

When we returned, I purchased a home for us with a library large enough for hundreds of books, as you were already taking such a big interest in reading. I bought a yearly membership to the theater, and every weekend we attended plays or ballet or concerts, which included one female violinist, an instrument I myself had begun to play with surprising talent. My teacher encouraged me to join a local orchestra. Do you remember the small concerts I played in the outdoor theater in the park? It wasn't so long ago. You and I were so happy. Then came the letter from your father's lawyer suing me for what he claimed was rightfully his. He claimed that by law I had withheld property that would have belonged to him through marriage, and therefore he had a right to it, even after we'd been divorced for two years.

I wept in that courtroom. It made me appear weak, I knew this, but I could not help myself. It was beyond my comprehension that the law could be so cruel. By law, your father received half of what I brought back for us, plus a bonus thrown in by the judge because I had lied to my husband. He was still trying to figure out a way to gain half if not more of the remaining shares in Hagen Pharmaceuticals, but the tides had suddenly turned, and not long after the war had ended Hagen Pharmaceuticals became branded as Nazi sympathizers for providing the new anesthesia to the German military at below cost, as well as dispersing, free of charge, pain relievers. The value of the shares dropped significantly, and now, decades later, even though the company has been through many different incarnations, they have never quite recovered.

Your father died of a sudden heart attack not long after he took our money. He left everything to his brother, who left everything to his son, who now lives in an estate in Texas surrounded by oil wells paid for by Hagen Pharmaceuticals.

I've come to the end of my life far too soon and without much to show for it, aside from peace of mind, which is certainly nothing to scoff at. I would have liked to have done things differently, studied more, discovered the violin early on, understood more of what was in my own heart. But it is late, and I leave those reins to you. You must carry on where your grandmother and I have left off. You must pursue your love of reading, of the written word.

I lift my eyes from the page. How is it that I have never known of my mother's love for books? For the written word? Is this where I've gotten mine?

The shares that I bequeath you have spent years going up and down, but overall their value outside of containing our family history has remained quite low. Even so, in honor of my mother I stipulate that you do not let your husband or anyone else try to take them from you. Should there ever be a significant amount of funds that you wish to withdraw, you will do as I have done, as my mother wished it to be, and show yourself at the bank with your head held high for everyone to see. Feel free to mention you are the granddaughter of the chemist Annaliese Hagen, founder of Hagen Pharmaceuticals. They may not remember her, but I believe the

mention of her name within those walls is like a talisman, deliver-
ing us all a little something on the air.

My eternal love to you, dear daughter,
Sonja Hagen-Williams

I find myself on the balcony with no recollection of how I got there. The letter is no longer in my hands. It feels as if someone has come along and told me that my hair isn't dark and wavy. I don't have a dimple. My name isn't Celia. Oliver isn't my son. I'm not who I think I am. I never have been. I descended from a whole other group of people, from women of principle, women with backbone and talent. What am I? Who am I? Who was my own mother?

I look out across the water and squeeze the railing. Is it a coincidence that I took such an interest in German? I wonder now if my mother might have spoken it to me as a child. Did she read the German fairytales to me?

I've been to Switzerland, once, passing through a corner on my way to Italy with my host family during my exchange. Did I sense something about it then? I can't remember. There's so much I haven't paid attention to.

+ + +

Willow arrives with plates of chicken and beans and tortillas.

"You're early," I say as I close the door behind me. "My God, that smells delicious."

"I decided to close early."

"You didn't need to do that for me."

"I know. I did it for me. The curiosity is killing me. What'd you find?"

I hand her the letters. There aren't any words to describe what I feel. How does one deal with the contradiction of having a new past?

I sit back and stuff the food down my throat, moaning involuntarily with every bite.

"Oh my God," Willow says every other paragraph until she finishes. "You never knew any of this?"

"Not a thing."

"I love these women."

"Don't you though?"

"So, where's the next one?"

"What next one?"

"The one from your mother to you?"

It didn't even occur to me. "I didn't see anything." I set my empty plate aside and hand Willow half of the stack.

A minute later Willow hands me several sheets of paper. They're typed, easy to miss, blending in with everything else. My name at the top of the page has caught her eye.

I read out loud:

My sweet, sweet Celia,

I sit here before this piece of paper the way my mother once sat before hers and her mother once sat before hers so many, many years ago. It doesn't seem real. My time has come and gone too quickly. I'm not ready yet. I wonder if anyone ever is.

But yesterday I received the shock of my life. I am not expected to survive more than a few months, perhaps weeks. I am late in my writing of this, might have been too late if I'd waited much longer.

Included in the will are the letters from my mother and grandmother. I read them again for the first time in decades. I understand now that I failed by not letting you see these letters sooner. But I was of the generation that thought the past was supposed to remain in the past, especially for those of us whose families came from other countries. Everything was about being modern. Being new. These days everyone likes to brag that his family came from this place or that. But back then we had a kind of Old World shame. We were embarrassed by our pasts. They made us less American, and now it embarrasses me that I ever felt this way about my own mother and grandmother.

I regret letting it go so completely. I should have saved a bit of history for you.

But let me move into the present for a moment to tell you that I am so proud of the woman you have become. I was already married by the time I was your age and completely absorbed into domestic life, forgetting all about what I thought I might want to be when I was young, which is a good lesson in why we should not forget our pasts, even our most recent one. Did I ever tell you I wanted to be a journalist? I loved the idea of traveling and uncovering facts about people and places, and then sharing those facts with others so that they could discover them, too. But I met your father my second year in college, and since he had already graduated we decided to get married. Once I was married, going to school seemed silly. The idea of being a journalist felt even sillier, unrealistic at best. How would I have had time for marriage and motherhood if I were traipsing around the world all alone? This was how I understood things to be at the time. This was the way things were all around me. I didn't know a single woman who had a career back then. And I'm ashamed to say I pushed aside the legacy my grandmother left behind for my mother and me. It seemed so Old World, so insignificant to modern life, to my life. I didn't feel repressed. Was I? My friends and I knew such things were talked about in certain circles, but *they didn't seem to apply to us. We were happy. We loved our husbands and they loved us. We didn't feel as if we were being restrained. We didn't feel, necessarily, that something was missing.*

I admit I remained ashamed of my family history, especially where your father was concerned. I didn't want him to know I came from a long line of what appeared to be pushy, feminist types. My mother died before he had a chance to meet her. I never had to tell the truth. It simplified things. As you know, your father's father was a WWII veteran who had returned from the war a changed and damaged man. I could not bring myself to show your father the letters.

But after your father died I began to see things differently. I missed him terribly, but it was as if my eyes had suddenly opened and I could see all kinds of things that had been lost in my peripheral vision. Your father didn't like me getting involved in our finances. He said it was like having too many cooks in the kitchen. All right. I understood that. But I was actually interested in finances, and that seemed a very unladylike thing to be. I realize now how stupid I was. I realized too late.

You've seen me try to make up for lost time, even chided me over what you've called my "obsession" at times though I never took your teasing as anything but good-natured. At first I tried to invest money in things the way my mother and grandmother had, but frankly speaking, I didn't know what I was doing. Needless to say, I didn't have much luck. I suppose in the end I more or less came out even. I've always had enough to live off of, and that was good enough for me.

There is no way to get around the fact that I should have told you about your legacy before now. My face is flushed with shame and my heart with sorrow as I write this. But some things cannot be changed, and so with the remaining days I want to impress upon you that I think your grandmothers would be so proud of the independent woman you have become. You are the first woman in the family to ever graduate from college. And not only that, you did it with honors. I admit that at times I have envied you and your successes, but I never begrudged you them, I never stopped feeling an overwhelming excitement for you. I love you more than words allow me to express.

So in keeping with tradition, I am writing this letter to ask that you please abide by the same rules set by my grandmother. You will not relinquish the shares in Hagen Pharmaceuticals. Though its name has changed, you still own those shares, even if they have failed the family time and again, and as of this writing are worth next to nothing. Your grandmothers suffered beatings and worse over what those shares stood for. I insulted them both by hiding their memory in a drawer.

Perhaps I am going too far in my request. Perhaps I was too far one way and am swinging too far the other to make up for it. So be it. It is better than doing nothing to honor their memory and sacrifices, the way I have done for decades.

I have contacted all lawyers involved on both sides of the ocean. The dividends are to be distributed through the Bank of Switzerland, the same bank where the tellers enjoyed keeping my grandmother waiting. If there should come a day when these shares are worth something and you wish to withdraw from them, I insist you travel to the same bank in Zürich, as my mother and grandmother insisted of me, even though I never had the opportunity or the fortune to do so. But there is more. I have instructed my lawyer to liquidate all my assets and pour everything into shares at Hagen Pharmaceuticals in your name. It's a matter of principle. I pray something will come of it someday. I pray that in your lifetime these shares will finally see their potential.

Of course, it goes without saying that should you ever marry, your husband will not be entitled to these funds. Unlike the laws my mother and grandmother were subject to, there are now laws that will protect you from such things. These funds are for you and you alone until the day you die, in which case they will be left to your own daughter should you have one—or a son, of course, you cannot begrudge a son; but in the case where there are no children I instruct that your remaining shares be left to the Women's League of Zürich, an organization your great-grandmother helped to found.

I lower the paper from my face.

Willow picks it up and reads the final paragraph.

You are the legacy I leave behind, my sweet, bright Celia. I could not be more proud of you than I am, not just for your scholarly achievements but also for the beautiful human being you have become. I will be watching if at all possible. Loving you from wherever I go.

Your loving mother,

Gilion H. Williams

Silent tears spill down my face.

Willow rises and hands me a tissue. She sits with me and strokes my back in soft, wide circles.

I blow my nose and dry my eyes, repeatedly shaking my head.

30

I shuffle through the papers again and realize I've overlooked a line on Marc Jacobson's note. *I apologize for the oversight. My father passed away before this file was complete. Your address was never forwarded to the Swiss bank; therefore all of your statements were returned.*

It takes the entire evening for us to comb through everything and figure out that my mother's liquid assets after her death would have been around two hundred thousand dollars. All of that money went in to buying stocks at Hagen Pharmaceuticals, which, I discover on the Internet, has been renamed The Odin Health Institute (TOHI) since she passed away. We aren't able to find what the stocks were worth at the time of her death, but it isn't hard to guess that two hundred thousand dollars could buy a lot of cheap shares. Jonathon would have figured this out, too, when he requested these same copies weeks ago. He would have laughed at the coincidence of pharmaceuticals. He would have taken it as a sign. Something meant to be.

"Holy crap," Willow says after pecking away at the computer on the tiny kitchen table. "This company makes all kinds of weird stuff."

"Like what?"

"Like guns that shoot pepper spray."

"Great."

"And acne cream."

"Sold separately?"

"Oh." Willow's voice turns serious. "My God." She continues to read.

"What is it?" I linger through the letters on the bed.

"Um. You better sit down for this," she says.

I look up. "I am sitting down."

"Then maybe you better lie down."

"What?"

Willow sits next to me on the bed with the laptop. "It says here that Hagen Pharmaceuticals, better known as TOHI, was the first maker of a drug called Sildenafil Citrate. They patented it back in the nineties, right after your mother passed away. Right after she bought all those shares." She slaps the laptop shut and squeezes my arm. "Are you ready for this?"

I nod slowly.

"It's a drug known today by the name of *Viagra*."

My eyebrows shoot up. I blink, and blink again.

"Those shares must be worth a fortune," Willow says. "All the ones that were already there, plus the ones your mother bought?"

I'm too stunned to speak. The letters shake in my hand. Has my mother turned out to be a brilliant investor after all?

"Your husband knows those shares are worth a fortune," Willow says.

It takes a moment for this to sink in. Thoughts race around my head. I can barely get a grasp. "I don't understand. Why did he take me to Mexico?"

"Didn't you say that when you first called Oliver he told you your husband was in the garage getting another suitcase for a business trip?"

I nod.

"And then when you called back that afternoon, Oliver said your husband told him you were in Switzerland and they had to go get you."

I'm following the same trail.

"Right."

"Why would he say that?" Willow asks. "You obviously weren't in Switzerland."

"I don't know. That's the part I don't—"

The inside of my head feels as if it's caught fire. My forehead breaks out in a sweat.

"Are you all right?" Willow asks.

My pulse races. My vision sharpens. I jump off the bed and grab my hair by the roots.

"What is it?"

"I need a suitcase, a backpack, something." I scramble around the room gathering my things. "I need clothes. Warm clothes."

"Why?"

"I have to go."

"Where?"

"He needed to get me there. This whole time this is what he was trying to do. I threw it off when I escaped. I need to get it back on track."

Willow grabs me by the shoulders. "I don't understand."

I jerk loose and reach for the computer. I type as fast as my fingers will allow.

"Please tell me what you're doing."

"The thing is, it's like he's reading my mind. Do you think he knew I'd come to this conclusion? Is it just a coincidence that I had those copies faxed? That I found all of this out just like he did?"

"What conclusion?"

"I think Benicio is in on it, too. He never overheard them say anything about Switzerland. It was a setup."

"Wait! What are you saying?"

I stop in the center of the room and draw a deep breath. "Switzerland. I need to get the next flight out. Where is the closest international airport besides Puerto Vallarta? I don't want to be seen."

"Guadalajara. Are you sure you know what you're doing?"

"No. I can't be sure until I get there."

PART THREE

31

I stumble slightly when asked about the nature of my visit.

"Finances," I say.

"Finances?" The female customs agent in a crisp blue uniform scrutinizes my passport a moment longer. "You are here to do some banking," she says, half-question, half-correction of terminology. She types something on her keyboard.

"Yes. Banking." I like the sound of it. "Here to do some banking."

"And what is the reason for your one-way ticket?"

I rehearsed the answer to this question with Willow on the way to catch my flight. "I have various business deals to take care of afterward. I wasn't sure at the time of my departure which part of the United States I needed to return to first."

"What is your business?"

"The book business."

"You sell books?"

"No, not sell. I edit them. Make sure the English is correct."

"And you do not know which part of your country you need to go to in order to correct the English?"

"No, I, it's that…" Dear God. "Sometimes I have meetings in New York, and my son is currently out of town so it's possible I might need to pick him up at the same time I'm working…" and on I continue for what feels like a bloated minute before I finally stop myself and force a smile onto my face.

"What were you doing in Mexico?"

"Vacation." Still smiling.

"One moment please."

She leaves her station for one of a series of small rooms along the wall, each with a window whose blinds are mostly closed. She enters one and closes the door. The line of people behind me groan. My nerves burn like tiny candelabras beneath my skin. I have to stop my foot from bobbing on the floor, my fingernails from tapping the counter. I shove my hands into the pockets of Willow's pea coat so I won't have to feel them shake.

The door opens, and she walks back to her station without looking me in the eye. She punches something into the computer, briskly hands me my passport, and without a single word gestures me into Switzerland.

"Please be careful," Willow whispered as she hugged me good-bye in Guadalajara. Her words linger in my ear. I'm wearing her clothes and can smell her as I make my way out of customs, feeling a little less frightened in her pea coat, blue sweater, the soft leather shoes I insisted on paying for. Over my shoulder is her backpack stuffed with more of her warm clothes. I was given all of this in exchange for a promise that I'll return everything in person before the weather cools again in Victoria, British Columbia, where Willow is from and plans to spend two weeks in the fall.

I promised.

But as I hop on the S-Bahn in a country so far away, so vastly different from Mexico, those words feel as if they were spoken years ago by someone other than me.

The train doors close, and a sly, burning panic fills my chest. I take a seat and breathe deeply, the smell of newness and cigarettes and cold. People chatter in German. Finally a language I can understand. The weather is a popular topic of conversation, along with who just got back from where on holiday. I lower my nose to Willow's jacket and feel a flicker of something short of happiness.

The whistle startles me. There's no turning back. I'm on my way toward my past and future at once. The train shoots out of the dark to reveal half-timbered houses in the distance, church spires, rolling hills in ten shades of green. The Swiss Alps soar in the background, rugged and white, ancient grandparents standing watch over the hills. The houses, the land, the mountains would have looked like this for centuries. Annaliese and Sonja would have witnessed the very same scene.

I reread both of their letters. I study the city map, and read the letters yet again. By the time the train pulls into the Hauptbahnof, their voices and stories are woven inside me like braided strands of my own DNA. I've arrived in a place I've never been with a familiarity of home.

The doors slide open and I buzz with energy from so many sources as I wind my way through the streets of Zürich.

The digital sign in a USB bank window flashes fifteen degrees Celsius. I double it and add thirty to get sixty degrees Fahrenheit. The sun peeks in and out of clouds.

My leg has stiffened from so many hours sitting, and it aches as I cross the Bahnhofbrücke over the Limmat River to the east side. I stroll south along the water's edge. The Strassenbahn rumbles past every few minutes. According to my map, I'm staring at the financial district across the river. I wonder if Annaliese and Sonja lived on that side of the river or this. I picture Annaliese standing where I stand now, looking out onto the same medieval streets, her eyes lost in the ornate details of arches, shutters, buttresses, the weathered copper spire of the church. But Annaliese had been spit on. Annaliese had been raped. These beautiful medieval streets might have stood for something else. And what a horrible tragedy that is. To have such beauty represent something so heinous.

I glance around, jet-lagged and half-conscious of the fact that I'm searching for the Metzgerei Annaliese mentioned in her letter.

Bicycles line the sidewalks. The trees show only the first signs of spring, but the sidewalk cafés spill into the streets with people dressed in colorful scarves. Everyone strikes me as professional, as if whatever they do, no matter what it is, they do it well. Some hold cigarettes, most a coffee in one hand while gesturing with the other. Throngs of people browse shop windows, and I realize I don't see anyone going inside. A sign in the window of a women's boutique explains why. It's a holiday. Everything except restaurants and cafés is closed. That includes the banks.

The uneven cobbles throw my balance. A muscle on one side is overworked. I turn back for the sidewalk along the river until I come upon an Internet café.

White, spare, stainless steel, and honey wood, the café is exactly like something at home in Portland's Pearl District. I e-mail Oliver first, knowing he'll get it immediately on his phone. I keep it short. He'll have enough to deal with after having just arrived at the home of complete strangers. I apologize for not being there. Tell him I've been delayed but am safe. Has he heard from his father? I send all of my love.

Five minutes later—

Got here two hours ago. Seth seems pretty cool. His wife Julia made me a hamburger on the grill outside. Did you know Seth had a music room set up in his house? A drum set and everything. We were just getting ready to play. We even like some of the same bands. He says hi. When are you coming? Dad has been texting and calling NONSTOP. He says he called the police.

I can't shake the strangeness that Oliver is with Seth in Minneapolis. If someone told me that this was even a remote possibility I would have considered him insane.

He's bluffing, I write back. *Under no circumstances will he call the police. Ignore completely. Be there as soon as I can. A few more days. I'm sorry. Tell Seth I'm sorry, too. And, Oliver, thank you for trusting me. I love you more than you will ever know.*

A minute later comes, *I love you, too, Mom.*

I sit with that for a minute, soaking inside it like a warm bath, letting it coat me, solidify around me. Whatever happens from here on out I will carry this like armor into a fight.

I send an e-mail to Willow letting her know I've arrived on a bank holiday and won't be able to find out anything until tomorrow. I ask if there's anything new on her end.

Minutes later—

I'm so glad to hear you arrived in one piece! You won't believe it. Got news on your beau, Benicio. Big news. He showed up an hour ago. In fact, he's asleep right now in your old room! You weren't kidding when you said he was good looking. My God, even with the bruises you can still tell. Anyway, when I told him where you'd gone I thought he was going to faint. Seriously. He had to sit with his head between his knees, drink a glass of water, the whole deal. He was exhausted, though not nearly in as bad of shape as you were when you came crawling in. But more than that he was broken-hearted. You could see it in his eyes. I nearly cried just watching the fact dawn on him that he had missed you by just a few hours.

That's all I have. PLEASE keep me posted on EVERYTHING. I know we've only known each other a short while, but I swear you're like someone I've known my whole life. Corny, I know. But true.

xo,

Willow

I choke back the walnut-sized lump in my throat and wipe my eyes before anyone might see. I touch my runny nose to my sleeve.

I'm overcome with confusion and fatigue. I'm overcome with relief. It rushes in on a river so deep I'm sure that if I close my eyes I won't open them again for days. I'm certain Benicio has lied to me. Was the heartbreak Willow saw just another acting job?

I step out into the bustling street, into the smell of fresh-baked bread and coffee, wet stone, a trace of cigarettes. It's pleasant. Foreign. Inviting. Somewhere a half-timbered pension with a crisp white featherbed is waiting for me. An old woman is going to make me a boiled egg and fresh Brötchen with marmalade for breakfast. "*Herlizchen Willkommen,*" she's going to say. She's going to tell me all about the history of the place, going back for generations, all about the people who have lived there, all the people who have stayed.

32

A man in the tourist booth at the train station books me a room in a pension near Hagen Pharmaceuticals, or rather TOHI. He points me to the right train, smiles when the doors close, and waves when I pull away. I'm so weary, so lost in a fog of delirium that just before I step onto the train I turn and say to him in German, "Do you know who I am?" *Wissen Sie wer ich bin? Die Urenkelin von Annaliese Hagen.* The great-granddaughter of Annaliese Hagen.

I struggle against the rhythm of the train luring me into sleep. I picture Benicio in the bed I left only hours before. Blood rushes to my head and chest, keeping me awake. The longer I imagine him sprawled across the sheet, his head on my pillow, his hand reaching through my hair, the more the blood pools deep and heavy between my legs.

I didn't expect it to feel like that.

Like what?

I think you know.

A man in a blue uniform startles me by thrusting a hole puncher in my face.

The train ticket. Of course. I scramble for the ticket in the pocket of the pea coat. He punches it and moves on.

I push Benicio from my thoughts as the tidy, ornate, picture-perfect streets give way to green spaces and hills and then the glassy blue water of Zürichsee.

The cool, clean air is exactly what I need when I step off the train. The pension is a kilometer up the road from the stop. I raise the collar of the pea coat and walk, or rather limp along the river, passing quiet farms, sheep, vineyards, and long stretches of green until I spot the house atop a small hill lined with crops that slope away from the house on all sides. A lane splits through the squares of green to the front; another lane leads away in back. The house is white stone with double rows of a dozen windows along the side. Red shutters clap open beside each one. The roof is thatched. A smoke stack emits a wispy trail of smoke. In the distance the snowy peaks of the Alps. I can't help but be reminded of stark-lessoned fairy tales.

✦ ✦ ✦

I sleep like buried treasure. In the morning I'm delighted to find the boiled eggs and Brötchen with orange marmalade and fresh coffee waiting in the small dining room exactly as I imagined. The table is set for one. Apparently I'm the only guest.

"*Guten Morgen!*" someone booms from the kitchen. It's not Frau Freymann, the woman who checked me in the evening before, but a man, a large man, with a freshly shaven face, white cropped hair and pale blue eyes. He introduces himself as Frau Freymann's brother. The resemblance is striking.

"*Zwillinge,*" he says as I stare. Twins.

I nod. It's clear he's answered this stare a thousand times.

"*Bitte*," he says, gesturing to the chair behind the place setting.

I take a seat, and to my surprise, Herr Freymann takes a seat across from me. We begin the first real conversation I've had in German in nearly twenty years. Speaking comes slowly to me, but I understand most of what he says about the farm and lake, and when I don't, I ask him to repeat it. He seems to like this about me. The fact that I'm not afraid to ask. He tells me I have *Mut*. Courage. You have no idea, I want to say. "*Danke*," I say.

I finally ask about Hagen Pharmaceuticals.

He appears puzzled. Everyone knows of it, he says. They still call it by the Hagen name even though it's changed twice from the original.

He points up the road. "*Fünf Kilometers*," he says. It isn't far. He suggests I take one of the bikes they have for guests.

Then comes the question. "*Warum*?" Why? Why do I want to go there?

In that moment Frau Freymann comes through the kitchen and sits at the table across from her brother. She's overheard the question and wants to know, too.

I glance back and forth between their faces, the male version morphing into the female and back again. It's distracting. I'm trying to keep my story straight. Trying to tell it in English would be difficult enough, let alone German.

I'm a Hagen, I explain.

By the looks of their identically raised eyebrows I'm either not making any sense, or they don't believe me, or they understand me completely *and* they believe me but they're anxious to tell me something.

It's the latter. They ask if I know of the "Hagen Haus."

I shake my head.

A museum. The house Annaliese and Walter lived in is now a museum put together by the children's children of Annaliese's brothers and sisters. They're the only ones left. The closest in line with Annaliese. Or so they thought.

I have so many questions. Where do they live? What's the family name?

"Seifert," Frau Freymann says. Annaliese's maiden name. Annaliese's brothers had many children who in turn had plenty of their own. They're everywhere. They're her neighbors.

I want to run outside and knock on doors, introduce myself, and search their faces for my own. But the banks have already opened, and I need to catch the train back into town. There's a nine-hour time difference between Switzerland and the West Coast of the States. Not a very big window to work with.

I stand and shake Frau and Herr Freymann's hands. The twins even smell the same. Cherry soap and starched shirts, a trace of garden soil. Their faces are flushed and their grins large and loose, revealing the slight difference in their smiles with Herr Freymann's chipped front tooth.

They laugh and pat my back and appear to be nearly as delighted by the discovery as I am.

The cheer and lightheartedness stay with me on the train.

33

There are two e-mails from Willow. The first—

Where are you staying? Please send address.
xo,
Willow

I quickly fire off the address of Pension Freymann. If anything should happen to me someone needs to know where I am, or in the least, where I've been.

A peculiar feeling comes over me. Somehow I know that the second e-mail isn't from Willow before I even open it. It was sent from Willow's account last night, not long after I signed off.

Celia,
I can't tell you what these days have been like for me, not knowing if you were dead or alive, not knowing if I would ever see you again. The pain of missing you has been constant. It never stops. It never goes away. I can barely stand to be in this room knowing you were

just here. I can barely stand to NOT be in it, too. Knowing your body was right where mine is now brings a whole new torment.

But you're alive! This is enough to make it bearable. Willow explained some of what has happened, but she seems to be keeping the most important facts to herself. That's fine. She wants to protect you. I can't argue with that.

There is so much I need to tell you. Things I should have said before. Things I wasn't completely honest about. Just know this—if it's possible to fall in love with someone the second you lay eyes on them, then that is what happened to me with you. I fell harder than I ever knew was possible. If you don't believe me, just look at my damaged face.

B

My heart and mind splinter into a million pieces. I shut the computer down and wander out onto the sidewalk. *Things I wasn't completely honest about.*

I'm not paying attention to where I'm going and run straight into a teenage girl.

"*Entchuldigung*," I say. Excuse me.

"*Macht nichts*," the girl utters—it doesn't matter. She heads on her way. It doesn't matter. He lied to me. It doesn't matter. My feet chug against the cobbles. It. Does. Not. Matter.

There are too many things that need my attention for me to think about this now. I stuff Benicio down and vow to keep him there for as long as I can. I need to be strong. I think of Sonja weeping in the courtroom as she tries to fight for what's hers. *It made me look weak*, she said in her letter. I will not look weak.

I buy a scarf. Blue-sage, extra long, and surprisingly inexpensive for such soft wool. I wrap it twice around my neck. Looking like the Swiss woman I am, I set out across the Münsterbrücke where I drop down into the medieval streets in search of The Bank of Switzerland.

The Fraumünster church towers above me. The golden clock face on the spire reads shortly after ten. For a moment I stand mesmerized by the stained glass of the church, the blue so striking it feels like a living thing, reaching out, warming the skin on my face.

The lanes are narrow and the sun can't always reach through. People come and go in all directions. No one seems to take notice of me. And yet I can't shake the feeling that I'm being watched.

I stop for one small errand at the store Herr Freymann told me about. I stuff my purchases in the backpack and am on my way.

Grand double doors of ancient carved wood make up the entrance to the bank. Like stepping into the hall of an old castle, the ceiling towers several floors high. Glassy marble squeaks beneath my shoes. The acoustics are so tight it's as if everyone converses in whispers.

I'm standing on the same marble floor Annaliese and Sonja stood before me, surrounded by the same gray-blue walls of stone. I imagine Annaliese daydreaming past the tall, thin windows, devising chemical formulas above the teller's heads as she waits to get her money.

The longer I stand there, the more the place takes on the feel of a Protestant church. Simple and opulent, beautiful and plaintive. On closer examination I notice cracks in the grandeur, the frayed edge of a mural, an electrical outlet that's come loose, small chips in the marble floor where the sections meet at my feet.

A young man in a sharp blue suit cuts toward me and asks if I need help. He shows me to his desk in the open floor plan of the room.

The chair smells of fine leather, its back thick and stiff, and I feel too small for the size of it. The man—did he say his name?—looks and smells freshly scrubbed, dipped in cologne. His mahogany desk is obviously handmade, well made. An antique.

He writes down the information from my passport. He studies the paperwork from my mother and types something into his computer. After a moment a change comes over him. His shoulders seem to lift. His eyes, I'm sure, appear to concentrate harder on the screen.

"Did you find the account?" I ask in German.

"*Moment Bitte,*" he replies; the smile on his face from earlier has been replaced with a mouth that's all business.

And then the smile suddenly returns as he stands and asks me to wait, just a moment. He will be right back.

My heart begins to race. Has Jonathon done something? Is there still some missing piece I'm not getting? Or am I simply reliving Annaliese's nightmare? Are they going to make me wait just to amuse themselves? I squeeze my backpack to my chest, stare through the tall thin windows, and wait.

In the dense bubble of quiet, jet lag begins to unfold like a thick, heavy gel inside my brain, a weary burn in my eyes.

After what seems like ten minutes, the man returns with an elegant-looking woman wearing a creamy pantsuit over a silky blue blouse. Her makeup is tastefully done. Her blond hair is fastened neatly at the nape of her neck. She holds out her hand for me to shake.

"I apologize for the wait." She speaks English. "Erika Zubriggen. Nice to meet you, Mrs. Donnelly."

"Celia. Please. You can call me Celia."

"Would you like to come with me?" Erika asks.

"Is there a problem?" My tired brain struggles to make sense of what's happening. My hands are suddenly fists. I'm prepared to stand my ground.

"Not at all," Erika says. "It's just you've come to the wrong bank. Well. Not exactly the wrong bank. What I mean is you've come to the wrong, what is the word, branch, yes, I think that's it, the wrong branch of the bank."

Is it just my imagination, or is this woman behaving as strangely as the man? The man. Where is the man? He's somehow disappeared. I look down. The papers and my passport are still on his desk. I snatch them up and hold them to my chest.

"I don't understand," I say, stuffing everything into my backpack.

"Please. Come. I'll show you."

We walk out through the giant front doors, and I'm sure I'm going to find the Swiss version of the FBI waiting for me with handcuffs. My knees soften. The scab on my leg begins to burn.

Erika directs me with a hand to my shoulder down the sidewalk and around the corner. She's saying something about the yesterday's holiday, the sunshine, and a place not far with a Turkish bath, for women only, she adds. Lovely.

I look around at the cars, searching for the one they're going to toss me into. But there's nothing, and no one seems suspicious.

We come to stop in front of a sleek glass door. A gray stone building from the Middle Ages. It's been renovated, recently it seems, with the clean lines of tall modern windows, white, streamlined chandeliers, and the curvy pieces of art nouveau furniture I can see through the door. It doesn't look like a bank. It looks like a cross between Tiffany's and the house of Le Corbusier.

"Where are we?" I ask.

Erika swipes her key card against a plate near the door. "The bank. Your bank. The one with your account."

"Is this still The Bank of Switzerland?"

"Yes. We just split the bank in two. This is how we separate our retail clients from the premium clients."

"Premium clients?"

"The clients who carry a different kind of balance."

I don't ask.

The door opens with a satisfying click.

I've never been inside anything quite like this. It has the dreamy feel of a film director's home in a magazine. Someone who's married a European artist, both famous, both eccentric. Black chaise lounges with sheepskin throws to the right and left of a black, oversized fireplace that appears to get plenty of use. The floor is finely waxed parquet pulling the eye in all directions, demanding one take in the room.

Erika ushers me all the way in. We're approached by a young man who behaves like a waiter. He seems to be expecting us. He offers me the choice of champagne, wine, or espresso. Tea if I prefer.

Good God. No. I don't want anything. What I need, truly need in this moment, is to sit down.

Erika seems to be reading my mind. She directs me over to a black leather chair behind a cowhide rug. I settle into the plush seat. It's like a second skin. Erika sits across from me. An Eames coffee table fills the space between us.

"Annaliese Hagen was my great-grandmother," I blurt. By now my head no longer feels as if it fits quite right on my neck. I might have gone on babbling if not for the noticeable shift in the air when I spoke my great-grandmother's name. It seems to hover in the air above us.

"Yes. I know," Erika says. "I saw in the paperwork. I also saw that we've been trying for years to reach you. All of your statements were returned to the bank. Until recently when our research team dug deeper and discovered your married name and address."

"You mean you recently mailed them to my house?"

Erika nods.

So *that's* how Jonathon found out.

"I wasn't fully aware of the account," I say. "Apparently, the lawyer passed away before completing all the changes to the will."

"I see. Well, in any case, you must be very proud to be the great-granddaughter of Annaliese Hagen."

"I suppose I am. Are you familiar with her?"

Erika looks at me as if I've just grown another head. "Of course. She was one of the first to make the way for us. For women. Look at me."

"What do you do here?" I ask.

"I'm president of this bank."

"Oh. Well." I have to admit I wouldn't have guessed. In fact, I nearly blurt out that I myself am married to a president of a bank, but keep my mouth shut for too many reasons to count. "That's wonderful. Congratulations." I glance up at the wall clock. It's shortly after eleven. "I'm sorry. May I see my account now?"

"Of course."

Erika raises her hand and the man who appears to be a waiter crosses the room to her side. She whispers something in his ear and he nods and is off again.

"Jan is one of my assistants," Erika says. "He'll bring the file right over."

"Thank you."

"Not a problem. So what brings you to Zürich?"

How can I even begin to answer? I decide to stick with the simplest, and perhaps truest answer I can think of.

"My great-grandmother. I've only just learned about her."

"Really?"

"My mother died years ago. I never knew much about my family to begin with."

Erika leans back and shakes her head as if she finds the whole thing puzzling. How can a family not know such a thing about its own member? "You look like her," Erika says.

"Annaliese?"

"Yes. Strikingly so. Have you never a seen a photograph?"

"No."

Erika's eyebrows shoot up. I can just hear her thinking, *Americans, what an odd bunch they are.* "I'm sure you're planning to visit Hagen Haus. There are photos of her there."

"Just as soon as I finish up here. I'm staying at Pension Freymann not far from there, actually."

"Ah. The twins."

"You know them?"

"Of course. Switzerland is a small country. Zürich an even smaller town."

"Well, now you've got me intrigued. I'm looking forward to seeing those photographs."

"You will see. There's quite a resemblance. Now. Let's not keep you waiting."

Erika glances around, and Jan approaches her with a folder. She takes it and thanks him, and he walks away with a precision to his feet.

She hands me the folder. Her gold, embossed card is clipped to the front.

"I have a question for you," I say.

"Please."

"What is the law here in Switzerland if a will states that a spouse is not to be left the estate? Is there a way for them to take it anyway?"

Erika eyes me. "I'm not understanding exactly."

"What I mean is, can a husband take a wife's money even if her will specifically states he has no right to it?"

"I see. I'm not a lawyer, of course, but I do know cases of inheritance can be very complicated. I've seen incidences where a family member has proved through the courts that the person who made such a will wasn't in a clear mind at the time it was made and therefore the will became invalid."

"Is that the only way then?" I ask. "To claim someone is insane?"

"This is no easy task. It takes close observation and documentation for this to be considered. But I'm sure there are loopholes. There always are."

"Yes."

"Do you have some concerns about your estate, Mrs. Donnelly?"

"Celia."

"Excuse me. Celia."

"Yes. Yes. I do."

"We have plenty of financial advisors here on staff who would be more than happy to help you. If its legal assistance you need we can arrange that, too."

"Can I write up a will? I mean, just like that, and have it notarized and everything?"

"I assure you we can accommodate you in every way possible. Would you like a private room to go through the file?" Erika asks.

"A private room?"

"Yes. Of course."

"No, I don't think that will be necessary," I say. A private room? What do they think I'm going to do that I can't do right here?

Erika excuses herself, and I open the folder. No more than a minute goes by before I regret turning down the private room. Had I been tucked away somewhere, then all the posh people in the swankiest bank on earth wouldn't have heard me scream. They wouldn't have seen me bolt upright and then collapse on the floor at the sight of my husband being shown through the door.

34

Thirty million dollars in dividends alone.

I might be able to comprehend several million. It doesn't seem so outrageous when I think of what the average house is worth in my own neighborhood. Or college tuition for kids and grandkids. But thirty million? The number doesn't quite register. Not even after I'm fully conscious. Not even after I'm pretending relief upon seeing my husband there to help. Not even after walking out the door on his arm as he steadies me, and then continues to hold tight after it's clear I can walk on my own. What registers is that my backpack is on my back and I'm clutching the folder in my hand. No one has taken these things from me.

When we reach the corner I stop and feign weakness. Jonathon's car is against the curb, the door already open, a strange man at the wheel. Jonathon keeps a tight grip on my arm. He's close enough for me to smell his unwashed skin. It smells of our bed at home, a place that until this moment I've forgotten existed. We're husband and wife. We're complete strangers. We're enemies. Has he spoken to me yet? I can't remember hearing his words inside the bank. Perhaps I blocked them out. No, no, he's said something, I remember now. "She isn't well. She didn't bring her medication. I apologize."

A look exchanged between Jonathon and Erika. I saw it through the strings of my hair. Erika bore witness to how crazy I am. I flipped the hair from my face and exchanged my own look with Erika, one of concern, one that said I am a premium client and I will need your assistance, a look I'm sure holds much more weight.

Out on the sidewalk Jonathon speaks through clenched teeth. "Give me the folder, Cee."

I clutch it to my chest.

"I need you to get in the car."

"All right," I say.

The last thing I'm going to do is get into a car again with someone I don't know, even if that someone happens to be my husband.

I place my feet firmly apart, knees bent.

"Ready to go now?" he says.

"Yes. As a matter of fact I am."

I jab my elbow sharply into his gut, and he sinks forward with a groan.

I bolt across the street, narrowly missing the oncoming Strassenbahn, which blares its horn long and hard, drawing everyone's attention to Jonathon doubled over in his trench coat.

I stop and stuff the folder into the backpack. Beneath the bottom of the moving train I see the man from the car run to Jonathon's side. Jonathon remains hunched over with his hands on his knees as more and more legs gather around him. When the train passes I face him from across the street, my scarf tied neatly around my neck.

Jonathon and the man start after me.

I flee for what I know will be the very last time.

35

That night I barely sleep. I'm still unsure of my next move, still feeling that wherever I go, Jonathon is sure to find me. I can't just remove Oliver from the safety of Seth's home without a solid plan of what to do next. I'm rich beyond anything I could have wildly imagined, but it isn't as easy as paying my way back to Portland. For all I know there's a warrant out for my arrest.

I keep my backpack ready at my side. By morning there's no sign of Jonathon. I skip breakfast and catch the train to the nearest Internet café.

An e-mail from Willow—

I tried not to read what he sent but then curiosity got the best of me. Celia. You lucky girl. I look forward to the day when we can sit down over coffee and you can tell me what sort of witchcraft you're practicing so I can learn to cast the same kind of spells.

Anyway, what have you discovered? Btw, are you writing all of this down? You should. It would make a bestseller some day.

Nothing new here. I haven't seen Benicio all day. He didn't answer when I took him breakfast this morning. I assume he's as exhausted as you were when I first saw you. I'll go check on him later.

xo,
Willow

One from Oliver—

Dad finally stopped texting. Seth and I just got home a few hours ago. He had me stocking books all day at his store! Actually I didn't mind. His store is pretty awesome. It's an old house, kind of like ours, turned into a bookstore with a little coffee shop and a small selection of vinyl records. The place is super busy all day. He's paying me minimum wage so I guess I just started my first job. Anyway, what am I supposed to do about school? WHEN ARE YOU COMING? Seth wants to know, too, but he told me to tell you it's not because there's a problem, just because he wants to know if you're OK. Gotta go. We're jamming again. Did you know Seth has two daughters? They're like nine and ten and they already play bass and guitar.

All these ordinary words, both his and Willow's, are poetry to my heart. There's something so astoundingly beautiful in the unexceptional moments of their lives.

Oliver,
I'm so happy things are going well at Seth's. He's a good man. I've never met his wife, but I'm sure she must be extraordinary if he chose her.

It won't be long now before I see you, though from the sound of things you might not want me interfering with the good time you're having. We will figure something out about school. Don't worry. Please give my love to Seth and take a big hug for yourself.

Always,

Mom

And then—

Willow,

So much to tell, so little time. Everything under control. Details to come soon as they are ever changing.

xo,

Celia

Ps. thank you so much for letting me know about Benicio. But I think you got it backward. He's the one who casts the spells, not me.

✚ ✚ ✚

I'm looking for inspiration. For someone to tell me what to do next. I pedal uphill on a borrowed bicycle from the pension. It isn't easy, especially after running through town on my bad leg. What gets me up the hill is the boost of adrenaline coursing though my veins.

A large, boxy white building pops into view on the hillside above me. Until then it's been obscured through the trees and hills. Hagen Pharmaceuticals. I'm close enough now to see Hagen Haus, too, and the trail that once led my great-grandfather to his work. A trail that must have burned every time Annaliese laid eyes on it.

I park the bike outside Hagen Haus, a quintessential Swiss chalet with red begonias exploding from window boxes. I check behind me, as I've done all the way up the hill. The single lane slopes down toward Zürichsee. I haven't seen another soul, but the feeling of being followed weighs heavily on the air.

I step inside my great-grandparents' home and am smacked with a strange sense of bewilderment. I become disoriented, as if experiencing the ill effects of time travel. The laws of nature have been set adrift and it takes a moment to get my bearings.

A blonde woman close to my own age helps stabilize things by crossing the room to greet me. She speaks little English. I set several euros on the counter for the entrance fee. I don't have a lot of time. I tell her straight away that I'm Annaliese's great-granddaughter. I tell her of my mother and grandmother, of the letters that revealed all that's been hidden from me until now.

The woman cocks her head. And then her eyes grow large and round.

"*Mein Gott*," she says. "*Wir sind verwandt!*" We're related!

She steps around the counter and embraces me inside an incredible hug. "Petra Seifert," she introduces herself while searching my face and hair, my hands, which she holds inside her own. She says there are other cousins who look more like Annaliese than she herself does, though none so remarkably as me. "*Schau mal.*" She gestures to the photographs all over the walls and tells me to see for myself.

The sepia images are haunting. It's as if someone has taken images of my face and superimposed them onto the bodies of women dressed in long petticoats and gowns, portraits taken at a fair.

"I must call my sister," Petra tries in English. She picks up the phone and speaks quickly in a dialect I have trouble understanding. I get the gist of it. A granddaughter has come out of nowhere. Looking like the Geist of Annaliese.

Before long Petra and I have locked arms for my personal tour through the house. Upstairs is the desk, microscope, and chair Annaliese sat in while she worked on chemical compositions no one would ever see or use. "At least not in her lifetime," Petra adds.

I take in the room. The simple white linens and glass doors leading onto a balcony with a view of Zürichsee and the Swiss Alps beyond. Annaliese would have begun her day rising from this bed to such magnificence. But I'm more interested in what Petra meant by *not in her lifetime*.

"Oh my dear, there is so much you don't know," she says in German. Several decades ago a chemist who was researching Annaliese's papers came across something that the others thought insignificant. Some combination of properties, the purpose of which Annaliese had strangely never written down. This wasn't like her. She was an excellent record keeper. For years historians wondered if the pages might have belonged to one of Walter's assistants, but they were found with Annaliese's and the handwriting was unmistakable. But what this particular researcher found when he matched Annaliese's diaries to the time in which the papers seemed to have been written was that there was something troubling going on in her personal life, an issue with her husband, that they were trying to resolve in the bedroom.

My eyebrows shoot up.

"*Ja? Versteht's du?*"

I nod that yes, I do indeed understand.

Not long after Annaliese worked on this, Petra explains, it was discovered that arsenic was included in their cold remedy, and not long after that, Annaliese left Walter for America.

"Are you saying that all these years later Annaliese's formula was used to make Viagra?"

Petra laughs. "*Genau*." Exactly. "A woman before her time," she says in English. And then she switches back to explain that Annaliese's diaries clearly indicate that she was trying to help Walter as much as she was trying to help herself.

I can't believe what I'm hearing.

"*Ja*," Petra explains. She later wrote that she believed her husband's inability to perform stemmed from his inability to tell the truth.

36

Herr Freymann meets me at the door.

"A visitor for you," he says in German. A man waiting in the front room. He arrived not long after I peddled away.

I unbutton the pea coat, feeling as if I've just stuck my head inside a furnace. I unzip the top of my backpack and hold it down at my side.

Move, move, I tell my feet. The Freymanns are in the house. I'm safe. I can handle whatever he has to give.

I round the corner to find my visitor sitting in the winged back chair directly facing me, his arms lining the rests, his ankles crossed on the floor. He's dressed like a European, leather shoes and jeans, his jacket open, exposing the crisp white dress shirt against his lean torso.

His face comes alive when he sees me.

I don't trust my legs to hold me. I can't keep my bottom lip from trembling. "You clean up nicely," I say, oddly, my voice unsteady, my eyes quickly filling with tears.

He stands, and the sunlight catches his amber eyes.

✦ ✦ ✦

I lock the door to my room and brace my back against it.

"I took the first flight I could get out of Guadalajara just like you," he says.

"How did you find me?"

"An e-mail from Willow when I got in."

I slip off my jacket and toss it to a chair.

He takes my hand, and a ribbon of heat travels across my skin.

For a moment it seems all we can do is stare until we're sure the other isn't some kind of apparition born of all the yearning.

His hand shakes as he unwinds my scarf.

"Jonathon is here," I say. "He tried to make me get in a car with him at the bank yesterday. He could turn up any second."

"It's quite possible."

I grab his hand. "Why? What exactly is he planning?"

"I'll tell you everything I know."

"You lied to me." I let go his hand.

He returns to my scarf, unwinding. "There were things I should have told you." He drops my scarf to the floor. "I will tell you everything right here, right now if you want."

He caresses my lip with his thumb. His eyes search my mouth. The bruises are nearly gone from his face. Only the small bump on his nose remains.

He slides his jacket from his shoulders and tosses it on the bed. "Do you want to sit down?"

"No."

So many mistakes have been made. I've wanted to be so many things. Benicio, too. But we've failed, over and over. I've been lost in a fog of apathy and grief. He's been trapped beneath the weight of decisions he can't change.

What we need is a second chance.

I reach for him and he pulls me close. The days we've been deprived of one another have been like going without food or water. I'm starved for everything he has to give.

We devour one another on the bed, greedy and loud, our clothes snatched from our bodies as if by storm. I clutch his skin. I dig into the blanket when he slides down and spreads my legs and touches me with his tongue. I become aware of everything in the room, my senses heightened to the pulse of every living thing. I squeeze his hair as if through a dream.

When it's over I lay my head on his chest, but every part of me is still making love to him, my breathing not yet calm. I gaze through the window as Freymanns' sheep graze on the hillside like fluffs of white clouds floating against the green. Behind them mountains, the color of my eyes, tower like hulking guards.

"It was his plan for me to come here from the beginning, wasn't it?" I say.

"Yes."

"This is why you planted the seeds of Switzerland in my head."

"Yes, but that was before…"

"Is anyone helping him?"

"Yes."

"How many?"

"Two."

"Please tell me it's not the Freymanns."

He laughs. "No. One is a doctor."

I press my lips into his smooth chest, tasting the salt of his sweat.

"I'm sorry," he says.

My eyes swell with tears.

He holds his lips to my hair and breathes deeply.

"Has he been watching me this whole time?" I ask. "Does he know where I am?"

"How did you find this place?" Benicio asks.

"The tourism counter in the train station."

"All he'd have to do is show the guy your photograph. There's no doubt he'd remember your face."

"Easier than that. I told the guy who I was."

37

I want to feel Benicio in all the ways I never felt Jonathon. It's as if I've spent eighteen years in a box, a coffin, and now I want out. I want daylight on my skin, rich food in my mouth, ice-cold water down my throat. Benicio is all of these. I want to bite him, devour him, absorb him through my skin. I want to hear the sound of his voice, his breath, his moan, his cries inside my own head. I want to give him everything he gives me. I want to give him more.

No one comes for us. We make love until we can no longer speak, our hearts and bodies raw, seized so thoroughly that I wonder if there'll be anything left of me in the morning. I could die doing this. It feels this way, as if I'm disappearing with every touch, becoming the feeling itself, ethereal as smoke.

I lie back on the bed to catch my breath, watching him as he watches me, our bodies soaked in sweat, throats pulling for air. Within moments I feel a struggle inside me, the wanting, the need to touch while thinking it impossible, even as one or the other slides a finger across a collarbone, a hand on a belly, a cheek, the pull begins all over again.

By evening Frau Freymann gives a double knock. When we don't answer she says she'll leave our *Abendessen* on the table in the hall near the door. Peppermint tea begins to waft beneath the door. I rise naked from the bed and open the door. The long waves of my hair twist and hoist around my head. I tame them back and collect the tray with red and white napkins, fresh *Brötchen* and cheese, prosciutto and melon, and of course the peppermint tea. I lock the door and carry the tray to the bed.

"Most of our lives together have been spent locked away eating bread and cheese from a tray," Benicio finally says.

I watch as he chews, the small bump on his nose interrupting the elegance of his face. I search his features for some other imperfection, or perhaps the combination of what makes him so attractive nonetheless. I find him even more interesting to look at now. Flawed. Complete.

"We graduated to prosciutto and melon and tea," I say.

"True."

He kisses the line of sweat on my forehead. And then he peels a string of hair from the sweaty crease of my lid and places it where it belongs.

I turn my face and press my lips into his hand. He smells of sex and sweat and melon. "Do you know how much money I have?" I say into his palm.

"I have a good idea."

"Am I supposed to believe that you're here for me, not the money?"

"Money can't buy this."

"Sure it can."

"No, not like this." He kisses my neck.

I tilt my head back, feeling him between my legs before he even touches me. I feel his warm breath in my ear. I close my eyes. My mouth falls open and I feel the stretch of my lips, now raw. I feel drunk. Woozy and content. My tongue flushes with its own juices, readying for his mouth, his sex. He races through my veins. He's inside me, his breath, his sturdy beating heart.

38

Every hour together feels as if it's been stolen from some alternative life where the two of us never see each other again. But what now? We run through scenarios of where to go and what to do next, but nothing holds any weight. We're citizens of two different countries, and neither is a place we can call home.

"Do you like dogs?" I ask.

We're punchy, having spent the morning much the same way as the day before, only now we find the whole situation ridiculous in our delirium. We're sleep deprived, terrified, traumatized by our own good fortune lasting into another day. We can't stop laughing.

"Yes. But only brunette dogs with long ears."

"What the hell is a brunette dog?"

"The color."

"I know what brunette *means*, just not on a dog."

"Does it mean something different on a woman?"

"Yes."

"What?"

"I don't know."

"Well," he says.

"So, any dog with long ears?"

"Yes."

"All right." I shake my head in quick, little bursts. "What's your favorite color?"

"Orange."

"Orange? Orange is not an option."

"What's wrong with orange?"

"I don't know. It's not right."

"You expected me to choose red, didn't you? Mexican guy, Latino, red."

"Hot Mexican guy."

"Don't try to woo me away from orange. It won't work. She is mine. I love her."

"I love the smell of puppy paws."

Benicio raises himself onto an elbow. "Santa Maria. What does a puppy paw smell like?"

"Puppy paws. They smell like puppy paws. That's it."

"They must smell like something."

"Why? You wouldn't ask what a lemon smells like. Or what color orange looks like. It is what it is."

He lies back onto the pillow with his hands behind his head, staring at the ceiling as if thinking this through.

"When this is all over," I finally say, "I want to get a dog."

"What kind of dog?"

"A brunette dog. You know the kind."

"Yes. Yes I do."

By noon we've kissed our way into the shower and then finally outside. I bring my backpack just in case. The open air seems to contain Jonathon, his little angry eyes piercing the trees. I feel them on my neck as Benicio and I stroll toward Hagen Haus.

On the way, I tell him how eerie the resemblance to Annaliese is. I tell him about Petra and the diaries, the Viagra Annaliese invented a century ago, the feeling it gives me to sit at my great-grandmother's desk. And then I watch the look on Benicio's face as he studies the pictures of my family. He squeezes my hand, and I can see his heart fill with my own happiness.

By the time we return, the weather has cooled and the pension smells of firewood and cooked meat.

We share our wine and stew with the Freymanns, though everything seems to take place backstage, behind my anticipation that Jonathon is only hours, if not seconds, from walking through the door. I translate the Freymanns' story for Benicio, about how they came to live alone again, just the two of them. They married another set of twins and the four of them lived in this house for decades, fifty years, in fact, running the place, keeping one another company during the low seasons. Several years ago Herr Freymann's wife passed away from heart disease. Less than a year after that, her brother, Frau Freymann's husband of fifty years, died of the very same.

They must see the sad expressions on our faces.

"*Wir sind nicht hoffnungsloss*," Herr Freymann tells me. We aren't hopeless. He goes on to say they're grateful to have had such wonderful friends and spouses for so many years. Not many can say such a thing. Grateful that they still have one another.

"*Das Leben geht Wieder*," Frau Freymann says with a smile. Life goes on.

+ + +

I wake to the sound of a thud, as if something large and soft, a pile of blankets, has fallen from the top of a closet and hit the floor somewhere in the house. I reach for Benicio. He's already sitting, and then off the bed, pulling on his clothes.

"What was that?" I whisper.

"Get dressed."

I slip into my clothes and peer out the window. A half moon dims the cloudy sky. From where I stand there's no clear view to the drive in front of the house. It's impossible to see if a car pulled in.

The closest house is acres away. We're on the second floor. I'm sure to break an ankle if I jump from a window.

"What time is it?" I ask.

Benicio lifts the clock from the dresser. "Five thirty in the morning."

I feel the exhaustion of our lovemaking, the residue of jet lag still behind my eyes. Like a drug, a sedative, shortly before it knocks you out. "You don't suppose one of the Freymanns got up to use the bathroom and then dropped something, do you?" I whisper.

"No."

"Me neither."

I fumble for my backpack in the dark.

"What are you doing?"

I retrieve a black pistol with an orange tip.

"What is that?"

Footsteps lead down the hall toward us. Heeled shoes not even trying to be quiet. The knob jiggles. Someone bangs on the door.

A woman cries in a distant room.

Someone bangs again.

Benicio's head snaps toward me.

Whoever is out there is still standing on the other side of the door.

"What do you want?" I suddenly call into the dark.

Benicio shoots me a glance. He shakes his head no.

"What kind of coward waits outside a door, saying nothing?" I yell.

The steps stomp away down the hall. They quickly return with a set of others, though the second sound barefoot. The woman's cries are now muffled right outside the door.

"*Bitte*," Frau Freymann says. "*Mein Bruder. Die haben Ihn geschlagen.*"

"What?" Benicio asks.

"They hit Herr Freymann," I whisper.

Frau Freymann continues to weep. "*Er hat ein Messer.*"

Benicio looks to me for an explanation.

"He has a knife."

"*Wer*, Frau Freymann?" I call out. Who?

"*Der Mann. Ihr Mann. Er sagte, dass er Ihr Ehemann ist.*"

"Jonathon," I whisper. "He's here and he has a knife."

"We're coming out!" Benicio yells.

If Jonathon didn't know before that Benicio's here, he certainly knows now.

He reaches for me. I lean into his ear and tell him I love him.

He pulls me close and tells me the same.

Steps flee from the door. Frau Freymann cries for someone to please let go.

I open the door into the dark silence.

I flip the hall switch but nothing happens.

We slowly make our way into the hall, the old pine planks groaning beneath our bare feet.

At the end of the hall near the top of the stairs a dark shape lies on the floor.

Benicio puts his hand up to stop me but I creep closer, already sure of what I'll find.

A light from the kitchen sends a dull beam up the stairs. Herr Freymann lies on the floor at my feet, blood coming from the side of his head.

I fill with rage. "Get me a towel." Benicio grabs one from the bathroom.

I wipe the side of Herr Freymann's head. It's difficult to see, but the wound doesn't appear quite as deep as it might seem with so much blood.

He moans. He's alive. "Help me get him to the bedroom."

Someone is rifling through the kitchen. Furniture shifts; drawers open and close.

"They're going to come back," Benicio says.

"Help me," I say, and together we pull Herr Freymann into the bedroom across the hall.

I grab a pillow off the bed and place it under his head. "He needs a doctor right away."

"If I'm not mistaken there's one in the house."

My head shoots up. "Stay with him."

"Celia!"

I take off running down the stairs.

Frau Freymann sits at the kitchen table, her soft body shaking everywhere. Jonathon stands at the sink with a blond, bold-faced man, a business type in a jacket similar to Jonathon's.

"Hello, Cee," Jonathon says with clear, honest anger in his tone.

"I'll sign whatever you want," I say. "Just let them go."

"If only it were that simple."

I pull the pistol out from behind me and point it at Jonathon's acquaintance. "I understand you're a doctor," I say. "I want you to go upstairs and take care of Herr Freymann's head."

Jonathon laughs. I point the pistol at him.

"I wouldn't point that toy at me if I were you," he says.

"You're not me."

"True." He nods to the man beside him, gesturing to the pantry door.

The man makes a move to open it.

"Don't," I say.

"I have something for you," Jonathon says. "Something that I think is going to simplify everything." He gestures to the man again. "Go ahead. Open it."

I take a step back as the pantry door swings open.

My eyes are playing tricks. What I see can't be there. I gape into the dim pantry, but it won't go away. It won't turn into something that makes sense. There's no trick of light, no optical illusion. It's there. He's there.

Oliver.

My son is tied to a chair, his mouth gagged with duct tape, his eyes sluggish and red. He doesn't seem to see me. He doesn't seem to see anything at all. Behind him stands the man who drove Jonathon to the bank. He has a kitchen knife in his hand. It rests on Oliver's shoulder.

My mind struggles to take this in, but my heart refuses to accept it.

Jonathon's acquaintance lets go and the door swings shut.

"Oliver!" I jab the pistol in the air at Jonathon. "He was in Minneapolis! He was with Seth!"

"You remember Maggie? Couldn't wait to tell me everything so I could bring her boyfriend home."

I blink in slow motion. The mother in me seizes my mind, seizes Oliver's neck. *This is what you get for not listening to me!*

"All I had to do was e-mail him a few shots of you wandering around Zürich. He was on a plane within hours. Worried sick about you."

"Let him go."

Jonathon shakes his head. "Not yet."

The man inside with Oliver steps out and stands near Jonathon, the knife still in his hand.

"Kevin," Jonathon says with a nod.

The pistol is still pointed at Jonathon's face. Where's Benicio? He must have heard me scream Oliver's name.

"If you shoot me with your little BB gun it'll be the last thing you ever do," Jonathon says.

"What did I do to deserve this? What in God's name did Oliver do?"

"I am sick to death of this whole thing. You have no idea. You can't even begin to imagine the trouble I've gone through. You came this close to ruining everything, causing me to run all over kingdom come to pick up the pieces. It's over, Cee. It stops right here."

"Yes, Jonathon. Yes, it does."

"This is not some game. This is serious beyond anything your little mind can comprehend."

"You mean the little mind that's caused you to run all over kingdom come?"

He smiles his menacing smile. "You try anything, anything at all, and you won't live to regret it."

I steady the pistol on his face.

"Here's what's going to happen. You and I are going down to the bank. You're going to withdraw nearly all of what you have in that account. I'm allowing you to keep a bit for yourself and Oliver. I don't have to do that, you know."

He's snapped. I have no idea who or what I'm dealing with.

"We're going to bring the money back here, and once we've had a chance to look it over, we'll be on our way."

A muffled moan comes from the pantry. I lower the pistol. "Let him out of there."

"Not yet."

"He's your son, for Christ's sake!"

Jonathon's face reddens. He jabs his finger at me and clenches his teeth. "You have no idea how long I've tried to keep him out of this! This is *your* doing. If you hadn't been so uncooperative in Mexico, this would have been over by now."

I nearly laugh. "You mean if I'd let your girlfriend shoot me in the face everything would be fine?"

Kevin laughs.

Jonathon clenches his jaw.

"If you'd just remained traumatized like a normal person under the circumstances, I could've brought you here, easily persuaded you to do what needed to be done. I would've been gone before you even knew what hit you."

"Let Oliver go, Jonathon."

"You didn't even know about the money. It's not like you're going to miss it."

"It doesn't belong to you. It's mine. And Oliver's."

"You have no idea what kind of mess we're in. You have no comprehension of these things. I can't tell you the pressure I've been living under for years. I did everything I could to keep our house, our savings, Oliver's college fund. I invested in some very sound ideas. I'm president of a bank. I know what to do with money."

"You stole from your own bank."

He looks as if he's about to hit me. "It was a simple, stupid mistake. The market fell. I lost a lot of money. I was sure I could put it back."

"Why didn't you just tell me? You could have told me you knew about the money. I would have come to get it. It would have been ours to do with whatever you pleased."

"Right!" He laughs maniacally into his hand, shaking his face. I can no longer tell if he's laughing or crying. He drops his hand and I see that it's both. "You've been so kind these past years," he whines. "Of course. Why didn't I think of that? Of course you would have understood everything. Oh, here you go, sweetheart. No more worries. Please!" He gets in my face and I see how unkempt he is. His sour teeth, his face oily, bristly. "You would have left before I even finished the first sentence."

"Let him go, Jonathon."

"It wasn't my fault. You need to understand that."

"He's just a boy."

"I'll let him go when I have what I came for."

Frau Freymann weeps quietly at the table behind me.

With every passing minute, with every word I speak, I know I'm winding the thread of his insanity tighter, and yet I can't stop. I need to stall him.

Oliver moans behind the door.

"I will not go to jail for this," Jonathon says. "Do you understand me? I would rather die and take every one of you with me than spend the rest of my life in prison."

I set the pistol on the table. "What exactly do you want?"

Kevin immediately snatches up pistol. "What is it?" he asks.

"*Die Pistole von meinem Enkel*," Frau Freymann answers.

"What'd she say? Kevin asks.

"A toy pistol from her grandson," the man I take to be the doctor says.

Kevin points it at the sink and pulls the trigger. Nothing but the sound of plastic clicking.

He has no way of knowing it needs three empty shots pumped out the first time it's used for it to engage. Kevin tosses it on the counter after one.

"I'll do what you want," I say. "But please," I turn to the other man, "I'm begging you. Go upstairs and help Herr Freymann."

39

The doctor carries a small leather satchel and an ice pack. I follow him into the bedroom where Herr Freymann is still lying on the floor.

Benicio turns the bedside lamp on. He sits beside this tender lump of a man and presses the bloodied towel into the wound. Herr Freymann is awake now, mumbling.

I read the sorrow in Benicio's face. It's my very own sorrow, burning inside of him.

"Oliver is here?" he asks.

I barely nod, picturing him in the chair, the knife at his shoulder. I bite my lip. Tears spill down my cheeks.

Benicio stands and holds me to his chest. I feel the bulk of something beneath his shirt at his back.

The doctor kneels down and looks over Herr Freymann's head. He pulls tiny strips of adhesive from his satchel and tapes the wound. Then he helps Herr Freymann to sit. He tells him to stay awake and keep the ice on his head. The white of Herr Freymann's eye is bloodshot, the bone out around it already blackening. He can't, or possibly isn't willing, to look at me.

By eight thirty I'm on the train headed to the bank with Jonathon at my side. "Amazing how they really do run on time," he says of the trains. "This place is impressive," he says, looking out the window as we roll into the Hauptbahnhof.

By nine o'clock Jan is offering us champagne and espresso. Jonathon holds up his hand to say no thank you. I say I'd love some tea.

We're given a private room to wait in. Erika greets us accompanied by a gentleman named Franz whom she says will assist us in matters of high security.

Erika appears only slightly concerned. "You mentioned yesterday that your wife wasn't feeling well," she says to Jonathon as if I'm not there. "Something about her medication. Are you sure, Mrs. Donnelly, sorry, Celia, that you want to make such a large cash withdrawal?"

"Yes. It was just a misunderstanding," I say.

"If there is something you would like to purchase here in Zürich, jewelry, real estate, anything at all, we can safely wire the money into another account. We don't recommend carrying this amount of cash on the street." She looks from me to Jonathon and back again. "Zürich is safe, but nowhere in the world is so safe that one should be walking around with that amount of cash."

"We understand," Jonathon says. "I happen to be president of a bank myself, Ms. Zubriggen. I understand the circumstances are unusual. But they're not illegal. Am I right?"

"I'm sorry. Am I mistaken? Or is your name not included on this account? I only ask in case we missed something somewhere."

Jonathon slips his hand into the pocket with his phone. He threatened to call Kevin if anything goes wrong. The ones I love will pay the price. His eyes meet mine.

"No. That's correct," I say. "He's just here as a financial advisor to me. It's perfectly fine."

"Then you're aware that he has contacted the bank several times trying to gain access to your account?"

"Yes. Well. I asked him to. He knows everything about banking, obviously, and he's just come along to give me a little guidance. I plan to do some wonderful things with Hagen Haus."

"Ah, so you've seen it then? What did I tell you?"

"Yes. You were right. I look exactly like my great-grandfather, Walter. The resemblance is striking."

If Erika catches what I said she doesn't show it. She gives us the money now, no more questions. "Well, then," Erika says. "No need to keep you waiting. Franz will help you with everything you need, and if there is anything else I can help you with in the future please don't hesitate to let me know."

I try to pass her a look of desperation. But Erika turns on her heels, all business. "Give my regards to the twins," she says, and then she's gone.

An hour and a half after entering the bank we're being shown out the door with three large satchels.

"Let's take a cab, shall we?" Jonathon says. "It's too much to carry."

We slide into the back of a cab, and for a moment I worry that the man behind the wheel is just pretending to be a cab driver. That he's actually someone paid to drive out into the woods and shoot me.

Jonathon gives the man the address of the pension. Why will he let me go? It doesn't make sense. He runs his finger aimlessly around the window like a child drawing pictures, spelling his name in the steam. "That was easy," he says. "Effortless. Didn't you think?" The closer we get to Pension Freymann, the more I'm sure he plans to kill me.

Everyone is gathered in the kitchen. Benicio, Herr Freymann, even Oliver, still tied to the chair, though his feet are free and the tape has been removed from his mouth. Thick pink welts rim his lips. He groans and quiets in turn. I can feel his mind struggling to come to. I pray this won't happen before everything is over.

I cross the room and lift his face into my hands. He's cold. His eyes are closed, but when I touch him he makes a deep rumbling in his throat. My heart crumbles. I kiss his forehead and draw in the smell of him. I hold his wobbly head against my shoulder, see the bruises on his cheek and arms, and fight back my rage, my tears.

Jonathon sets the first satchel on the large kitchen table and begins pulling out the cash. The doctor and Kevin tear the bundles open and hold several bills to the light, apparently searching for watermarks.

"Genuine," the doctor says.

I feel a raw excitement coming off Jonathon's skin. Beyond greed or desperation, he seems to have entered a fugue state, having lost all awareness of who he is, who everyone is.

Benicio watches from his chair in the corner near Herr Freymann. I can practically see the wheels spinning inside his head.

Oliver jerks his shoulder as if from a dream.

After another ten minutes of examination, Jonathon begins bundling the stacks together again. "Well then," he says to the doctor, who's opening his own satchel and pulling out a needle and syringe.

"What's going on?" I ask.

"He's an old friend. Henri, this is my wife. Celia, Henri."

The doctor nods politely as if there's nothing unusual about meeting under such circumstances.

Benicio shifts in his chair.

"That's right," Jonathon says, addressing Benicio. "She's still my wife, no matter what the two of you have been doing upstairs. Just remember, I was there first. Remember that, you lying son of a bitch."

Benicio gives nothing away. He isn't afraid of Jonathon. That's clear to everyone in the room. Including Jonathon.

"You think I'm a terrible person," Jonathon says to me. "I betrayed you. Yes, I betrayed you. I lied. But I was trying—" He gazes at the floor and pokes the air above his head as if gouging a hole. He looks at me. "This is what you never understood about me. I was trying to hold everything together. Trying to fix all the things that were bringing us down. Whether it was you and your affair or our finances or Oliver's shitty attitude. I was trying to do the right thing. You want to look at me with such disgust, but what did you do? You hopped in bed with a man who betrayed *his* whole family. He lied, too. To them, to you, to me. And look at the way you're leering at him!"

He grabs my hair and squeezes, pulling my face toward him.

Benicio makes a move to stand. I lift my hand to stop him.

"Not once in eighteen years have you ever looked at me like that," Jonathon says.

"I'm sorry," I say, my throat giving way to tears.

Jonathon lets go of my hair and sneers.

Kevin takes a stance with his legs apart, like a football player ready to rumble. He's a caricature of man, a night watchman brute Jonathon must have borrowed from the bank.

I glance at Benicio, see the slight turn in his lip.

"What are you planning on doing with us?" I say.

"Well, I can't very well have you running around here wreaking all kinds of havoc the minute I walk out this door."

Henri opens his satchel and begins drawing a clear liquid from a small bottle into a needle.

"Just a little something to help you rest," Jonathon says. "But obviously you're not going to let Henri inject you without some kind of incentive to sit still."

"What do you mean?" I'm terrified that whatever is in that needle is meant to kill us all.

"Kevin here is going to hold his knife to your neck while Henri injects your boyfriend. He makes a wrong move and that will be that." He laughs. "I guess you're about to find out just how much he really cares about you, Cee."

Kevin takes his stance again, the kitchen knife tightly in his fist.

Benicio is ready and waiting for Henri to make a move toward him. Do the rest of them not see this? Can they not feel what he's about to do?

Frau Freymann gets up and sits by her brother. Her face is fixed with defiance. No one says a word.

Henri finishes filling his needle. He sighs as if the whole thing bores him.

"Did you ever love me, Jonathon?" I ask. I have to. I can't help it.

This seems to take him by surprise. He lets out a small, tired laugh. "Yes," he says, and then, as if he's too tired to speak, "I suppose I did." He takes a deep breath.

I step toward him.

Kevin reaches out to make me stop.

"It's all right," Jonathon says.

I'm close enough to see the pores of his dirty, oily skin, the black and gray whiskers poking through, the small red lines of eyes that appear to have been open for days. He's lost weight. His cheeks are drawn, the fullness of them eaten away. He's a stranger to me. No one I've ever loved the way I should have. It was all wrong from the beginning. And yet here's Oliver, my boy, my love. A miracle born out of a hideous blunder.

"We need to get started," Henri says, clearly growing impatient. "The ship leaves in an hour."

"What ship?" I ask.

Oliver stirs. He lifts his head and groans. His eyes slowly peel back before closing again.

I step around the table and hold his head. "Oliver," I whisper in his ear. "It's all right, sweetheart."

I glance up and see a flash of something in Jonathon's face. I want to believe he's having second thoughts. For a second I convince myself he's incapable of harming his own child.

"We have to go," he says, and just as quickly the look disappears.

"What ship?" I ask.

Jonathon nods to Henri. "We're wasting time."

"Wait." I come around the table and gently place my hand on Jonathon's heart. It hammers so hard, so fast I think his chest will split open from sheer force, his heart lash out like a ball into the mitt of my hand. I can feel his loneliness, the vacancy inside him like fumes released into the air. He's been forgotten for so many years. By me. By everyone. Who has ever really cared for this man? Who has ever been allowed that far in? His love is nothing more than a vacant ditch, a place where others' feelings went to rot.

"Mom?" Oliver murmurs.

Jonathon takes hold of my hand. He kisses it.

"Are you OK?" Oliver mumbles.

"Yes, Ollie," I say. "I'm fine. Go back to sleep."

It seems all I need is to hear my son's voice. I now know exactly what to do.

I rear my head back and with the single pop smash my forehead into Jonathon's chest.

There's screaming, whose exactly I can't tell. Bodies leap everywhere. The Freymanns fly out the door behind me. Cool air sweeps into the kitchen. Only Oliver struggles to move at the center.

Jonathon collides with Kevin on his way to the floor. The knife in Kevin's hand carves a long, clean incision into Jonathon's cheek. The flesh hangs open, spilling blood down his face.

Benicio punts a foot into Henri's groin. He pulls a pair of scissors from his waist and slices through Oliver's bindings. Then he brings the scissors down into Henri's shoulder as the man collapses with a sickening groan onto the floor. But not before his needle sticks Benicio's leg.

Kevin shoves Jonathon out of the way and dives toward me.

I jump back and grab the pistol from the counter. I jerk the collar of my shirt over my nose and shoot three times at Kevin's face. The third shot releases the ball of pepper spray and knocks him backward. He claws his eyes. The kitchen is a maelstrom of poison.

Benicio pulls Oliver to the floor and drags him outside just as Jonathon grabs one of the satchels and runs past them.

My eyes are ablaze, cut through by molten steel. I know not to touch, even as they slam shut and won't open. I've never felt such scalding. I don't know where I am, where anyone is. I feel my way along the counter and out the door where I hear Oliver wrenching for air.

Grass beneath my feet. So many people choking, my eyes and nose a fountain of tears, my throat scorched with pain. I blink repeatedly until the blurry outline of Oliver in the grass finally appears. He calls out to me, gasping for air.

I stumble past him. Past Benicio on the ground next to him.

Jonathon is a blotch on the horizon, a ghost stumbling down the field into the shallow ravine along the road.

I run blindly after him, every breath an inferno of pain. Nausea grips my middle, and there's nothing I can do but stop and vomit a blowtorch from my lungs.

Jonathon is headed toward the lake. But he's no quicker than me. Every other step his balance is lost.

I catch him by the back of his hair. He swings the satchel, and it lands hard against my head, right where I slammed him in the chest.

I'm on the ground, sobbing with rage. I kick his ankles, and he falls next to me; blood from the cut in his cheek is everywhere, face, clothes, hands. I roll onto his chest and flail my fists at whatever I can hit.

Then another kind of heat slices through my body. I can barely make out the Swiss Army knife in his hand, even as it slides between my ribs.

A small, vacuumed suck. I tumble into the cold grass. Shock absorbs me, wraps me in its trance.

Jonathon leaps to his hands and knees. He lunges and knocks me flat on my back where he straddles my chest and pins my hands with his knees. He tosses the knife to the side. He laughs in my face. He wraps his hands around my neck and squeezes.

His face hangs above me. Bloated and bleeding. A Halloween mask. Blood dripping into my face. I can't move. My mind shuts off. My senses go cold. I begin to drift into a painless trance when Oliver's voice from the kitchen—*Mom, are you OK?*—slings me back to life.

My hand wrenches from beneath Jonathon's knee. I hook my fingers inside the piece of open flesh in his cheek as if it's nothing more than old wallpaper. I yank and a chunk comes loose.

Jonathon releases my throat with a cry world has never known. He scrambles over my head for the knife. He snatches it up, but I'm already stumbling above him, slamming my heel between his legs.

He rolls to the side, clenching the knife, his bloodied mouth like the opening in a slab of raw bloody meat.

My foot comes down across his nose. He swings the knife, slicing my ankles and calves, slicing me everywhere in tiny strips, my hands now dripping red.

Red lights flash over the hill. The staccato blare of sirens. Voices rise from a place I can't see.

All I see is the shape of my foot stomping, crushing the hand with the knife. I trample flesh wherever I feel it, wrist bones snap beneath my heel.

His hand lies limp in the grass, his eyes closed, the bloodied knife in the grass beside him. My foot continues to stomp.

Mom.

I grind him into the earth, grind him like a powdery black ash.

Mom!

"I can pinpoint what's wrong now, Jonathon," I try to mouth. "Are you going to fix it?"

"Mom!"

Oliver spins me around to face him. He shakes my shoulders. "Stop!" His voice a shrill alarm in my face. He touches my ribs, my hands. "You're bleeding everywhere!"

"Why didn't you listen to me?" I say, my words croaking past a singed larynx.

It's only then that I remember the knife went into my side. I remember Benicio sprawled across the grass as if blown by a giant wind.

Oliver stands before me, untouched. My mother's dimple. Annaliese's eyes. My beautiful, beautiful boy.

40

Katerina comes with her husband Simon and their ten-year-old daughter Frida. They bring yellow tulips tied with thick blue ribbon and a family photo album I get to keep. Detlef and his brother Lukas bring pink roses. There's Anseln, his wife, Dagmar, with their newborn baby, Maximillian. They bring chocolate and white daisies. Sophie, who's the exact same age as Oliver—and could be his sister for all the likeness—comes with her father, Emil, and his girlfriend, Klarissa. They speak perfect English, having lived for a time in New York City. They bring red Gerbera daisies and a copy of the *New York Times*. They bring Oliver, too, having offered to keep him however long is needed. Sophie and Oliver immediately take off for a Coke in the café downstairs, instant friends, a united teenage front against so many adults. There's Lena and Tillie and Ulrike and Magda, all sisters, all great-aunts. There's Rolf and Astrid and Karl and Rainer. I can't remember how we're related. My own nurse, Vanessa Seifert, turns out to be my second cousin.

They give me advice on what to eat and drink to speed up the healing of my wounds. How to tame unruly frizz when the damp summer heat moves in. They give me advice on parenting, baking, where to buy a home, where to buy furniture, even whether or not to ever marry again.

And if that isn't enough, Willow is arriving at two that afternoon with plenty advice of her own.

Benicio rests quietly in the hospital bed next to me. The doctors finally moved him into my room this morning. He spent three days in intensive care. The cocktail in Henri's needle was designed to paralyze, and then stop a beating heart.

If it hadn't been for Oliver's arm accidentally flopping in the way of Henri's hand, the needle would have plunged deeper into Benicio's leg. He could have died within minutes. I'm lucky, too. Jonathon's knife came within a quarter of a centimeter from puncturing my spleen.

It's noon and the bustle of doors and carts and voices rouses Benicio. He opens his eyes.

"Hey, you," I say.

"Hey," he answers groggily.

I wave the giant bundle of my bandaged hand like a puppet. "Welcome back."

He smiles. So beautiful. So sleepy, and I know so warm beneath his blanket. It takes everything I have not to crawl in beside him. I'm stitched up everywhere. The pain in my ribs upon standing is unbearable. It hurts to breathe.

A nurse's assistant slides Benicio's IV to the side and helps him to sit. I can see how weak he is. He moves carefully, slowly, as if everything is bruised. His eyes seem to be adjusting to the room.

"Lunch," he says. The first word out of his mouth.

The young woman wheels the convertible table to the side of his bed, turning the top so the brothy soup and mashed potatoes are on a tray suspended over his lap.

The young woman hands me mine and hurries to the next room.

I watch as little by little he comes back to me.

I try the soup, feeling his eyes on me. I know what he's going to say.

"Don't you dare," I say, holding up my puppet hand. "Not a word. My insides are literally going to split open if I laugh."

"I was going to say, *Guten Appetit*."

"Sure you were. You don't even know what that means."

"Of course I do. It means enjoy your meal. Stuck in this room. Eating off a tray."

PART FOUR

41

It's been four years, but I never tire of the view. The tiled rooftops, especially when covered in snow, the twisty river splitting the city in two, the spires and domes and trees, and beyond that, the Alps, *my* Alps as I've come to think of them, all there when I open my eyes.

I sit up in bed, quietly, my pillow raised at my back. Any moment the sun will crest over Fraumünster Church, reflect off the spire, shine through the towering bedroom windows, and settle across Benicio's face on the pillow next to me. He'll scratch the bump on his nose as if the golden light itches. He won't remember when he wakes. I watch him without touching. Not an easy thing to do.

Soon Benny will wander in and slip under the covers with what's left of his floppy yellow bear, its fur worn to a net so thin it scarcely contains what is left of the cotton stuffing. Benny is an early riser like me. Some days the two of us make chocolate chip pancakes alone in the kitchen while everyone sleeps. Benny likes to explain to Pinto, our long-eared brunette mutt, when to put the chips in and how to wait for the top to bubble before flipping it to the other side.

Today is special. I'm thinking waffles with summer berries. Benny loves to try new things in the kitchen. He has opinions about salt and leeks, dense bread and peppered salami. He is a chef in the making. He'll get a kick out of whipping the cream.

When Benny scrunches his face just right, Jonathon appears in his eyes. The first time this happened I had to look away. But that was years ago. These days what I see in Benny's face, in the shape of his hands and mouth, in the sound of his little voice, is Oliver fused with a fairer version of Benicio. When Benicio walked off the plane carrying sleepy-eyed Benny on his hip, my love for the boy was undeniable. It was immediate. Instinctive. He was Oliver's brother. Benicio's nephew. I wanted to bite his chubby arms and feet. I wanted to swallow his entire body whole.

Benny turns five today. Waffles with summer berries and whipped cream. After that a short sail around the lake. Sometime in between will come the phone call. Benny understands, as well as can be understood at his age, that he has a birth mother named Isabel. But he has always called me Mutti, and I have always referred to him as my son. Deep inside this is who he is, who we are, together. In the end Isabel got what she wanted, at least for her son. Benny will have a better life. I see to it every day.

Benicio scratches his nose and sighs.

I smile but continue thinking of Isabel. Her call to wish Benny happy birthday like last year and the year before that leaves him confused, distracted from the joy of his day. Isabel's cards and letters have grown more frequent in recent months. A red flag Benicio tries to lower, but the facts are the facts. Isabel's six-year sentence will be up in the middle of next year. I've never quite trusted Benicio's custody arrangement through Family Services in Mexico. I've never quite trusted that everyone who is supposed to be is sitting behind bars.

Isabel's cards and letters feel like a way of preparing Benny for her return. The thought of this makes me want to pull the blanket over my head and go back to sleep. My mind tunnels back to the very first time I held Benny in my arms, the time I lifted him from his crib and then turned to Isabel and said, "You don't call the shots anymore, *chica.*"

All of this is causing me to begin the day off balance. I shake it from my mind, yet the joy I've come to know these past four years feels threatened, and I find myself falling into a hole.

What did Benicio know? How did he know it? When did he know it?

Every now and then shades of doubt tiptoe in unexpectedly. Benicio and I might be setting the long family table, or riding the Strassenbahn, or sweating in the sauna, or reading a book by the fire, and suddenly I have to ask—*Tell me again how you felt in that moment when you changed your mind. Tell me again what made you change.*

You're what made me change my mind. You, in the car next to me, so close I could have touched you.

Such conversations get inserted, strangely, between chasing one another around the table, dishcloths snapping, Pinto barking at our heels.

Benicio opens one eye and snaps it shut against the sun. He smiles with eyes closed and caresses my thigh with a lazy finger. He was up late working on his most recent script. I ought to slip out of bed, close the drapes, and let him sleep. But I know he'd rather be in the kitchen with me and the boys, running his finger through whipped cream. Celebrating.

It's summer now, which means picnics in Zürichhorn Park watching Oliver play soccer with his cousins. There are enough of them to fill two teams. Oliver is on break from his second year at NYU, a double major in journalism and music. He knows exactly what he wants to do with his life. Write album reviews, interview bands, keep people up on the latest in the music industry. He has an internship at *Pitchfork* magazine in the fall. He's a grown man, hugging me in the mornings and at night before I go to bed. He tells me he loves me, and not just before he hangs up the phone. He squeezes me when I cry at the airport. Tells me it's all right, that he'll be back in just a few months' time. I wipe my tears and call him Ollie. "Don't call me that," he says with a smile.

It's when Oliver's away, when the feelings of loss swirl through rooms empty of him, that so many questions reappear in my mind.

When did you first know the couple in the jungle were there to help us? I might ask in the middle of brushing Pinto's matted ears.

When I woke up alive and everyone had a smile.

Do you still think of Emily? Of the life you wanted so badly to return to? I might whisper in the phone late at night when Benicio is away in Los Angeles, meeting with producers.

I didn't know you existed when I wanted those things. I didn't know I could have the life I have with you.

I didn't know either. Sometimes I feel guilty for having more than anyone could hope for, while Jonathon remains locked in a cell, bearing my scars, living forever in a place he claimed would be worse than death. I've heard the cells are spacious with televisions and books, a soft rug at the center of a clean tiled floor. Jonathon spends his days sitting in a modern chair writing his appeals behind a wooden desk. There are worse things than a Swiss prison.

The FDIC seized Pacific Savings and Trust. It most likely would have collapsed anyway, but it was certainly kicked down the road by Jonathon. For years his focus had been on digging himself out of a hole rather than actually doing his job. In the end customers lost hundreds of thousands of dollars. I felt partially to blame. If I'd been honest with myself, I would've left Jonathon years ago, and all that followed might have gone differently. I made up for this by offering to return money that went beyond what the FDIC could insure. I paid off mortgages and set up college funds. I reinstalled home care nurses to the elderly, returned charities to their work at hand. The number of Christmas cards I receive every year is staggering.

This is what I need to focus on. My life today. Here, with all of my boys. My family. So much family I had to order a custom-made dining room table to fit everyone around it. And Willow visits so often I have given her her very own room.

I need to focus on the future. Benicio and I have plans to collaborate on one of his screenplays. Most of his films feature a female similar in character, if not looks, to me. At least this is what he tells me. "If only," I say with a wave of my hand, while secretly aspiring to their beauty, cleverness, and wit. Right now I'm too busy with my own work. The screenplay will have to wait.

My office down the hall overlooks the old town and the Limmat River. Some days it's all I can do not to stare at the winding streets, the wet cobblestones walking me back through time, back to where my story began. But most days I look out, and then I look right back at my computer screen, my own way of looking ahead. Sometimes words feel like tiny jewels between my fingers, so precious I'm afraid to set them down. Other times they drop heavily to the page, boulders thrown from the roof. But most days they gush like sweat from my pores. I forget to breathe. Remember with a gasp. These are the moments I live for.

I never did see Seth again, though it's only a matter of time. He and his family have accepted my invitation to visit. I've become friendly with his wife Julia, our lives intersected when my career took off over a year ago. We love the same authors, send excited e-mails back and forth over the same books. My own book, *Illume* has been on several best-seller lists for ten weeks now. Critics compare me to Joella Lundstrum as *Illume* inches closer to Lundstrum's number one. Julia removed Seth's display of Roth and Vonnegut and put my book front and center in the store with a bright yellow sign that reads, *If you're a fan of Lundstrum's, then Celia Hagen is your only man.*

Benny slowly opens the bedroom door and peeks in. His eyes are big with sleep and anticipation. By this evening twenty people will be seated around the long table celebrating his life, toasting him to many more. Oliver will play guitar, and everyone will crack up trying to remember lyrics to old pop songs in English. There'll be more food and cake than we can eat. More laughter than our stomach muscles can stand. Children will fly in and out of the room with Pinto trailing behind. The phone call will be behind us then. Pushed away until the next.

I smile at the big eyes in the crack of the door. I cannot wait to see his face when he opens his very own popcorn popper. Parmesan, he's told me. He likes it best with butter and Parmesan cheese.

Benicio stirs and sits up as if sensing the start of the day.

I open my arms and wave Benny in.

ACKNOWLEDGMENTS

I owe thanks to the following people for their sharp and generous insights, as well as years of unwavering support:

David Ciminello, Kathleen Concannon, Jonathan Eaton, Rachel Hoffman, Patricia Kullberg, Monica Spoelstra Metz, and Linda Sladek. I especially want to thank Rachel and Linda for working overtime on the manuscript and pushing me in all the places I needed to go.

I would also like to thank Rima Karami, Stefin McCargar, Jessica Donnell, Stephanie Sutherland, and again, Monica Spoelstra Metz for their friendship, encouragement, and for being such shining examples of kick-ass women we can all aspire to.

I'm grateful to my sister Melissa for her good humor, eleventh-hour eye, and infectious enthusiasm for getting the book out into the world.

And lastly, there are no words to convey the depth of gratitude I feel toward my husband, Andrew, for his love and kindness. Without him there'd be nothing but a blank page.

ABOUT THE AUTHOR

Photograph by Andrew Reed, 2011

Audrey Braun has lived all over the United States and Europe. She currently resides in the Pacific Northwest with her family. *A Small Fortune* is her first novel.